SERVING THE MAESTRO

SERVING HIM SERIES

M. S. PARKER

BELMONTE PUBLISHING, LLC

This book is a work of fiction. The names, characters, places and incidents are products of the writer's imagination or have been used fictitiously and are not to be construed as real. Any resemblance to persons, living or dead, actual events, locales or organizations is entirely coincidental.

Copyright © 2022 Belmonte Publishing LLC

Published by Belmonte Publishing LLC

PROLOGUE

TRENT

Ten years ago.

"Please tell me you didn't bring me to a strip club for my birthday."

My best friend met my gaze from where he sat across from me. The luxury of the stretch limo muffled the outside noise, most of it coming from the line queued in front of the sleek building.

Stephen McVey looked at me, bemusement in his eyes. "Just what about this place makes you think it's a strip joint?"

"Well, you said it'd be a magical night." Looking at the marquee-style sign over the black glass doors, I shrugged. "Sure, I guess the typical strip clubs don't look this high dollar. But I know you, and the only thing you find magical is big tits and red lipstick."

"I've broadened my worldview." His lips quirked. "Although tits and red lipstick are delicious, especially when paired together."

The driver opened the door. After one last look at my friend, I climbed out and took another look around. Something caught my attention. "Huh. Stephen?"

"Yes?" He moved to join me, smoothing down his deep red shirt.

"Why are half the people in line checking us out?" I was a good-looking guy and used to female attention. But this was something else entirely, and I couldn't quite put my finger on it.

"Only half?" He whistled under his breath. "Damn. I thought we'd do better."

"Well, I wasn't counting the guys since I don't swing that way." Smirking at my friend, I hitched up my shoulder. "So, what's with the club?"

"Wait and see." Stephen's smug grin usually annoyed me.

Right now, though, I was amused—and curious. "Okay, show me what you have in mind."

"Excellent." Stephen clapped me on the back. "Let's go."

We didn't move toward the line. Stephen led me to double doors with a velvet rope, each side guarded by security personnel in sleek suits. They both nodded as we approached, one moving to unclip the royal blue velvet rope. The other said, "Mr. McVey. How are you tonight?"

"Doing great, Jenkins. This is my friend, Trent. Bringing him in for a—"

"A drink," I said, cutting in and shooting a sharp look at Stephen. I had no idea why some people felt the need to announce your birthday to strangers.

"Enjoy your evening." Jenkins gave me a bland smile.

"He will." Stephen's smug grin widened.

I should have figured it out by the people in the line—the dresses made of little more than straps of fabric and leather, men wearing leather short-shorts and collars. But it took me several moments, walking through the club, to figure out what sort of establishment this was.

Subtle lights placed strategically around the main floor lit up the stage. Several elevated platforms were also cleverly lit, clearly showing the cages.

Cages. And the dancers inside.

"Here's your table, Mr. McVey."

I heard the hostess, but the words didn't connect. My attention was locked on a woman on the stage. She was in a sleek black leather catsuit. In front of her, a man knelt, and at first glance, he looked naked.

"Okay, so not a strip club," I said softly. It was the whip that cinched it. The sight of it rising in the air sent blood roaring to my head, pulsing in time with my heartbeat, which had jacked up as the curled whip came down and struck taut, tanned flesh.

Air trapped in my lungs, making the roaring in my head grow even louder, drowning out the sound of music, even Stephen's voice.

He nudged my shoulder.

I forced myself to breathe as I met his eyes.

"Yeah, I knew you'd get into this."

"You ever think that *I know it all* attitude gets annoying, buddy?" I broke the eye contact and looked back at the stage, watching as the woman lifted her arm, the whip's lash swaying behind beguilingly until she snapped her wrist.

"It's not as annoying as the fact that I'm usually right, though."

Ignoring the smug response, I looked at the table, then at the tall, slim brunette still standing with one hand on the seat closest to me. With a nod, I sat and murmured, "Thanks."

"Of course, Mr. Dixson." She circled around to the end of the table, where an unopened bottle of scotch awaited. Once Stephen had settled into his chair, she lifted the bottle. "You'd requested the Thirty-Year Laphroaig Single Malt Scotch, Mr. McVey. Shall I pour?"

Stephen gave her a distracted nod, his attention focused on me.

I was glad when the hostess put two crystal highball glasses in front of us, the peaty aroma of the expensive scotch rising to tease me. I lifted the glass and swirled it, then took a sip as I looked back to the stage.

My body temperature skyrocketed at the display.

The woman tied the nearly nude man to a wooden bar lowered from the ceiling on sturdy chains.

"What's going on?" I asked, my voice gritty.

Stephen looked toward the stage, a glance that turned into a slower look, his lips curving in a wolfish smile as his lids drooped.

"The second act." Picking up his glass of scotch, he settled more comfortably into his chair. "Relax a little, Trent. Watch the show. Enjoy. You earned it. Hell, we both earned a little fun. All the hard work you did on the musical score and the haggling I did to get you an audition for the spot." He finally looked at me, eyes gleaming with satisfaction. "We're celebrating, man. You're twenty-three, and you've already picked up your first nomination for an Academy Award."

Before I could formulate a response, a shadow fell over the table. Stephen's eyes flicked up, then he smiled and gestured to the single open seat. "Avery, you're looking lovely as always."

"Thank you," she said, her voice husky, almost too soft to be heard in the din. She took the seat and slanted a quick look at me.

Stephen cleared his throat, amusement gleaming in his eyes. "Avery, this is a friend of mine, Trent. We're here celebrating his birthday."

"How lovely." She slid me a second look, a longer one, interest in her eyes. "Is this your first time at our club?"

"Yes."

She licked her lips, then leaned over to murmur something to Stephen, voice too low for me to hear.

Whatever she said, Stephen's smug grin returned, and he nodded as she pulled away.

She didn't get up, though. She turned to me, then, to my surprise, she slid from her chair onto her knees...right next to me. Placing one hand on my knee, she tilted her face up.

"Would you like to join me in one of the club's private rooms, sir?" she asked the velvety warmth of her voice an aural caress.

The tempting promise in her eyes had my body temperature spiking again. But I had no idea what the fuck she was asking for.

Stephen, the damn know-it-all, apparently read my thoughts loud and clear.

"Avery is a submissive, Trent. If you're interested,

take her up on the invite." From across the table, Stephen lifted his glass to me in salute.

Judging by his amused smile, he wasn't surprised when I stood and offered a hand to Avery.

Asshole. I meant it in an affectionate way.

I met the woman's pretty eyes and said, "Shall we?"

ONE
TRENT
PRESENT DAY

"You know, if you're really hurting for money, you could ask your dad."

Narrowing my eyes at Stephen, my manager, I bit back a pithy retort as the server put our drinks in front of us. "I prefer to work for my money, not ask for a handout from the asshole who knocked up my mom—and half a dozen other women."

"Ouch." Stephen winced at my sharp tone. "You're in a shitty mood, aren't you?"

"I wonder why." Taking the glass of Kentucky rye bourbon, I sipped and stared off into nothing while I brooded over the way the past year had unfolded.

My last big project tanked. Usually, something like that wasn't a huge blow, but not only had I written all the music, I'd also been an investor in the film.

But my bad luck hadn't ended there.

I'd been in a car wreck—nothing major—but I was the one at fault. Which just fucked up things more because my license and registration were expired. I'd been so engrossed in writing the musical score for the last project I'd forgotten annoying stuff like *paying bills*.

The insurance company refused to pay, and I'd had to cough up money to pay for the car repairs for the other driver. They'd been steep, too. Steep enough that I still hadn't bought a new car to replace the one I'd totaled.

I needed another project. Soon. Eying Stephen across the table, I swirled my bourbon and wished he didn't have such a good poker face.

"So, are we here to chat, or do you have a line on a project for me?"

"You're no fun when you're broke, my friend," Stephen smirked. "There's no catching up. No asking how I've been. Just jump right to business."

"I talk to you almost every damn day," I pointed out. "What do we need to catch up on? Unless you met the love of your life while picking up your dry cleaning or parking that ugly-ass car of yours, I already know what's going on with you. And you know what's going on with me."

"Yeah, yeah." He sipped the bourbon and grimaced. "Why'd I let you talk me into this? I hate this rye shit. Anyway, you're being a bitch because you're broke, and you can't get a new car until you pick up a new project." He cocked a brow. "I told you not to back that Steinert deal. Didn't I tell you?"

"Contrary to what you think, *I told you so* isn't a good look for you. Or anybody." I grinned as he took another sip of the rye, mouth tightening in distaste. He had no appreciation for the finer things in life. Served him right, too, for being an asshole.

"Wipe that smug look off your face, pal, or I won't tell

you about the possible gig I've got for you." He put the nearly empty glass on the table and flagged our server. After ordering a Jameson whiskey, he pulled out his phone, tapped on the screen, and studied it for a few seconds.

"What gig?" I demanded, glaring at his lowered head.

"Gimme a minute." He kept reading another ten seconds, then put the phone away. As he leaned back in his chair, he said, "You aren't going to like it, man, but it pays well, and there are some sweet side perks. I almost wish I could bang out a song myself."

Too used to him by now, I ignored the comment about *banging out songs* and focused on the critical part —*pays well*.

"Tell me."

When he explained the initial specifics, I almost said no, right off the bat—I bit my tongue because I couldn't afford to say no if it paid anything decent.

But then he started detailing the perks.

"They'll set you up in a corporate apartment near Central Park, with two-thousand dollars weekly for meals, entertainment, expenses, whatever you want. It gets direct deposited into your account, and you can do whatever the hell you want with it." Stephen grinned as my brows shot up. "Yeah, man. Room and board and I haven't even discussed the fee yet."

"So get to it." Even with a corporate apartment near Central Park and the weekly funds, I wasn't sold on the idea. Transcribing a recent Broadway musical into a piano score? I wasn't sure about this.

Before the epic failure, the last project I'd done had

received Oscar nominations. One bad turn of events, and I was doomed to transcribe someone else's songs?

Well...beggars couldn't be choosers and all the shit.

"What's the transcription fee?" I asked, cutting Stephen off as he started waxing on about the musical's director and the composer of the original score—the composer was a fan of my music. They both wanted to be involved in the process if I took the job. That was another reason to say no.

"Thirty grand." Stephen gave me a smug smile. "And because I'm just that good, that's *your* cut. I talked them up a little." He named a slightly larger figure. "That's the total offer, but I get my usual percentage, leaving you with thirty large. And I'm not expecting a cut from the weekly living expenses."

"How considerate." I flipped him off while mentally running some figures in my head. Two grand a week—I could live pretty well in New York City on that and still save money, especially since I didn't have to pay rent. "Where would I be working?"

"That's up for discussion." Stephen smiled. "Did I mention the composer's a fan? They really want you for this job. They've also promised to fly you to NYC first-class and when the job is done, give you the same treatment on the return flight."

I'd grown up with a single mom who'd barely scraped by above the poverty line. I had more than a little disgust for the sperm donor who helped conceive me—a rich son of a bitch with more money than sense—more children, too. I shouldn't so easily be swayed by the nice, but unnecessary perks Stephen detailed.

But I was.

"Alright." Nodding, I said, "Set it up."

"Excellent." Stephen grinned and clapped his hands together, his eyes sharp and bright, a look I often saw when he was about to close a deal. "I knew you'd see the light on this one."

TWO
JAZZ

"To Cam, the best friend and business partner a girl can have!"

Numerous other voices rose in chorus as I lifted my drink and let it clink against the salted rim of my best friend's virgin Margarita.

She leaned back, her face glowing. The glow had nothing to do with the drink, or even the surprise birthday party she'd somehow put together at our office.

Cam Hollander, my best friend, was five months pregnant, and she had the stereotypical 'glow.'

She was sailing through pregnancy, her happiness practically contagious.

I was glad we'd been able to upgrade our office to a larger space a few years ago. The sound of somebody puking was usually enough to make me do the same, but in the new location each of us had a bathroom.

That made me sound awful. But Cam had laughed when I told her. *It's okay, honey. I wouldn't sit around and listen to me puke either, but I don't have much choice.*

Then she hugged me. *But when you get hitched and end up in my condition, I'll be there and hold your hand or your hair while you're puking. I've got a stronger stomach than you.*

She would, too. I hated that I couldn't look at her without hurting.

I loved Cam dearly. She was the best friend I had, my only "family" since my mom had died a couple of years earlier. Before the accident that killed my mom, I'd been even closer to Cam.

That only made me feel worse about the envy I felt looking at her. Today was my thirty-fifth birthday, and the clock was running out fast for me. But maybe a baby wasn't in the cards for me. A relationship certainly wasn't on the horizon, which was okay. I actually enjoyed being single and independent.

Forcing a light note into my voice, I said, "There's nobody pounding down the door to be Mr. Moors, Cam." Giving her fiancé a teasing look, I winked. "I think you grabbed the last good man in New York City."

Danny Padua, her fiancé, said. "Hey, I do have a younger brother, Jazz."

He delivered that remark while I took a sip of wine, and I almost choked.

Once I managed to clear the tears from my eyes and the wine from my windpipe, I shot him a dark look. "That's not funny."

"Hey, he's a good kid! And in five years, he'll be done with medical school."

"Ha, ha." I knew Danny's brother. He was a nice kid —emphasis on the *kid*. Definitely not what I was looking for. I wasn't going to discuss that I didn't know what I was looking for—or even if I *wanted* to look for anything.

The whole relationship thing was a mystery to me.

Rubbing my still tight chest, I accepted a glass of water from the server. When the conversation around us picked up, I was grateful for it. Cam got up from her place by Danny and came to my side of the table. After moving several gift bags, cards, and boxes out of the way, she took the empty seat and perched next to me.

With big, bright green eyes, she studied me.

"You're never going to find it if you refuse to look, honey. You know that."

Resisting the urge to squirm, I caught Cam's hand and squeezed. Being honest, I said, "I don't know if I even *want* to look for *it*, Cam. Really."

It was the whole kit and caboodle—what Cam had managed to find, the guy, the happy ending...the baby. But Cam knew me too well not to recognize what she saw in my gaze from time to time.

"So, you're not feeling that baby fever every time you see me rubbing my belly or hear me talk about how to decorate the nursery?" she asked with wide-eyed innocence.

"I might be having baby fever, but that's about it." Giving Danny a rueful smile, I added, "As cute as your soon-to-be brother-in-law is, Cam, I'm not interested in dating a guy more than a decade my junior and lately..." I struggled to articulate my lack of interest in any of the guys I'd dated over the past few years. "There's just nobody catching my interest."

I was either hooking up with jerks, jokers, or jackasses, and that'd been the case non-stop since things had ended with my last semi-serious boyfriend.

That had been shortly after my thirtieth birthday.

I was thirty-five now, and if it weren't for the fact that I had baby fever, I'd be pretty content with my life.

"Maybe that's because you're not willing to trust a guy." Cam took my hand and squeezed. "Honey, not everybody is like your dad. And you're stronger than your mom ever was."

"That's not what this is about." I didn't want to think about my parents. For all intents and purposes, I was effectively an orphan. My dad had hooked up with a younger, bustier version of the country club blonde years ago. He'd signed over custody of me, his only child, without a blink, faithfully paying child support until I was eighteen but never bothering with a birthday card. I hadn't seen him since the day he came to pack the rest of his clothes.

"Yes, it is." Cam sighed at the expression on my face. "But I'll let it go...for now. It's your birthday, right?"

"Exactly." I tipped my wine glass in her direction before tossing back the rest of it. "I still have presents to open, wine to drink, and cake to eat. Right?"

"You said the magic word. *Cake.*" Cam stood up and returned to her seat at Danny's side after returning the bags and boxes to the chair she'd emptied. "Just don't shut down the possibility of finding somebody, Jazz. There are still other decent guys in the world who aren't a decade younger."

She stuck her tongue out at Danny as he playfully tried to convince me of the virtues of younger men.

Their light-hearted attitude cheered me up, and soon I forgot my melancholy.

For a while.

"YOU KNOW, Danny's got this friend..."

I groaned in the middle of tucking away a couple of gift cards. "Cam, no. Just, no."

"Come on, Jazz." Her voice slid to a wheedle as she finished repacking several gift bags, so we didn't have as many to carry. We were taking a taxi to my place before they jumped on the subway to finish their ride home, and the fewer bags we had to carry, the better. "He's cute. He's quiet but funny, too. He's not boring. I think you two would be great together. Don't you think so, Danny?"

Catching the deer in the headlights look from Danny, I sighed. "Cam, I'm *fine* as I am. I don't need help being set up on blind dates. They never work out."

"Seriously..." She gave me a pitiful, pleading look. "It's not like I'm the one who set you up with that investment banker."

"You mean the con artist pretending to be an investment banker?" Rolling my eyes at the memory, I said, "That's the best recommendation you can give yourself? You didn't hook me up with a con artist?"

"Well, it's better than being the one who suggested him, isn't it?"

When I laughed, she beamed and continued pressing her advantage.

"Just do it, Jazz...one date. Tell you what...I've got tickets for a Broadway show coming up—four tickets. We can all go. Think about it. A double date with your best friend, that takes the pressure off, doesn't it? If he's boring and you don't click, at least you've got Danny and me around, right?"

"You're relentless." Gathering up a couple of the bags, I rose. They did the same, then followed me through the crowded restaurant. Tavern on the Green was a New York City landmark, and when Cam had told me she'd made reservations for my birthday, I'd expected it would only be for me and her—maybe Danny, too. I hadn't expected most of our employees to show or have several friends outside of work.

Except for Cam and Danny, everyone else had already left. I was grateful they were both on hand to help with the gifts as we made our way out of the restaurant.

Either gratitude or the two glasses of wine made me give in when Cam pushed again.

"Fine. *Fine!*" I said, laughing at the mock pout while Danny flagged a taxi. "But we're arriving separately, leaving separately. Make sure he knows that, okay?"

"Yay!" Cam was enthusiastic even while being pregnant and laden with several gift bags. She threw her arms around my neck and squeezed, bouncing with glee. "This is going to be *fun*. It's been forever since we've done a double date, Jazz.

"CAN YOU BELIEVE THIS SNOW? It's the middle of April!"

Glancing at the chatty cab driver, I smiled politely.

"It's something else. I'm glad I check the weather every morning."

"Yeah, me, too." He snorted, then laid on the horn as somebody in the next lane tried to nose over when a truck eased forward all of six inches in front of us. "Stay in your lane, dumbass! Or use your signal!"

I couldn't help but smile.

"Pardon my French," he said, glancing at me in the rearview mirror, eyes crinkling at the corners. "You going to a play tonight or just hanging out at the Square?"

"A play." I wasn't always chatting with strangers, but I was nervous about the blind date, and this talkative cabbie made it a lot easier to focus on something else. Looking at my watch noticing the time, I heaved out a sigh. "Honestly, though, I'm beginning to think the whole thing is cursed. Maybe this weather is a bad omen."

"Ahhh...you're going on a date, aren't ya?" He waved at the person in the Mini Cooper, letting them merge into our lane. "See, this guy has his signal on. You be nice...other drivers are nice to you. So, are you?"

Frowning, I thought back through his rambling. "Oh, a date? Yes." With a huffy sigh, I added, "My best friend set it up. I hate blind dates."

"Why didn't you tell her that?"

"She knows." The cars on either side were moving easier now. Damn it. So much for the weather holding us up. Guess there's no excuse now for canceling.

We chatted easily for another ten minutes, although the tension in my neck and shoulder muscles grew ever tighter as we got closer to Times Square and the theater district.

"Look at that," my driver said, sounding pleased with

himself as he pulled to a stop at the corner. "Practically right at the door."

"Yes." I swiped my card and added a tip. As I climbed out, my phone chirped with a message alert. A cold wind sliced through my coat like it was made of thin paper, and I hurried inside. The message could wait that long.

The coat check line was heinous, so I skipped it, found a quiet spot in the lobby area, and checked my phone.

We're running behind, Jazz! This crazy weather has everybody driving like idiots. Burton's already there. He's in the bar. He's good-looking, wearing a red scarf. You'll find him. XXOO

"Well, that's helpful," I muttered. Good-looking and a red scarf?

Resigned, I shoved my phone into my pocket and began my search. Navigating the clusters of people, I made it to the bar, where I found even *more* people. Man, I hoped she meant he was sitting at the actual bar. Otherwise, I would still be walking around looking for this guy at intermission.

It was a relief when I made it to the long stretch of polished wood and saw a couple of open seats—including one that held a coat and a long, fire-engine red scarf draped over it, sitting right next to a guy with broad shoulders that nicely stretched the fit of his shirt.

I approached after a quick look to make sure there weren't any other bearers of red scarves.

"Hi."

He turned his head and looked at me.

I was too logical to believe in romantic ideas like love

at first sight. But *lust* at first sight? That could totally be a thing, even if I'd never experienced it.

His pale green eyes met mine, and it was like falling into a pool of sweet, delicious sin.

He blinked, thick lashes briefly hiding those lovely eyes while a warm smile curved his lips. "Hello."

The smile was just as beautiful as his eyes. Closing my hands over the back of the chair that held the red scarf, I decided maybe this wouldn't be so bad.

"Lame conversation starter, but this weather sucks, doesn't it? Especially for April." This was the part of dating I *really* hated, that "getting to know a person" part. Cam should be here, so this would be a little less awkward.

"I'm used to warmer weather." He paused, then added, "I'm from California." He grimaced and glanced toward the windows that marched down the front façade of the building. "I'm not much for cold weather, so yeah, I'm not loving the April snowstorm."

He shifted on the barstool, facing me fully, and giving me a better view at him.

It was a *nice* view, too.

Those pale green eyes made me think of spring. His hair was a rich, warm brown that looked overdue for a cut, but it suited him anyway. The glint in his pale eyes made warmth curl in my belly, and that heat only intensified as I recognized that spark for the interest it was.

As far as my personal life went, it had been a long time since I'd felt a kind of reaction to a guy other than annoyance.

Maybe this date wouldn't turn out to be so bad.

Too many years of horrible experiences with men

kept me from settling in the seat next to him, but I did ease closer. Resting a hand on the chair holding his coat and scarf, I returned his smile. "What's California like?"

"Warm. In some places, it's beautiful. Watching the sun go down over the Pacific." His lips curved, a far-off look entering his eyes. "There's nothing else like it."

"I guess it's pretty different here in New York."

"Yeah."

The intensity in his gaze sent a shiver rushing down my spine, and I was glad I had my coat on. I burrowed into it as if still chilled from the snow.

"But I'm definitely finding plenty here that appeals to me."

He didn't clarify, but the eye contact spoke louder than words.

"New York has its perks." I eased closer, wondering how long he'd be in the city. "I take it you enjoy the theater?"

He smiled. "Sometimes more than others, but in general, yes. Have you seen the musical before?"

I had to think before I answered. "No. I was planned to see it when it first opened, but got busy with my work, and I forgot." Shrugging, I added, "That happens a lot."

"Getting busy with work? Or forgetting about plays?"

"Both?" I smiled and hitched up my shoulder. "I tend to hyper-focus, especially when I'm on a big project."

"If I'm enjoying the work, I do the same." He picked up his glass and sipped. "Can I buy you a drink?"

"Sure." After he flagged the server, I asked for a Manhattan. "I hear the play's good, though. A couple of songs from it are pretty popular—I hear them on streaming sometimes."

"Yes." He swirled the amber liquid in his glass and lifted it to his lips. "There's a...sensuality to the score. Powerful."

I found myself hypnotized by his mouth, lips and how they moved as he formed those words. My skin felt tight and thanks to the blood rushing through my veins, I wished I *had* taken my coat off. Tightening my hand around the glass, I took a sip of my Manhattan, loving the burn of the icy liquor and the burn of sexual heat even more.

Maybe Cam was right. Perhaps I needed to loosen up and have fun and try the dating thing again. Even the intimacy thing—especially if the night continued to go so well.

THREE
TRENT

So far, my stay in New York City has been uneventful—except for the April snowstorm that had blown in and whited out the city. It started earlier in the day and still hadn't let up.

New Yorker's never let a pesky thing like snow interfere, though, so I didn't see any reason to let it stop me. My hotel was only one stop away via the subway. With that convenience, it was easy to hit the theater and see the play.

Arriving at the theater, I confirmed my theory about New Yorker's never letting the weather interfere with their plans, because the lobby bar was jumping.

The guy next to me had spent the past twenty minutes flirting with any female who came close enough. So far, the reactions he'd received elevated my opinion of New Yorker females. Every single one had shot him down.

After the third put-down, he started grumbling into his martini about the problems with uptight bitches.

I considered pointing out he was the problem, but he was the type who'd try to pick a fight. Getting thrown out of a Broadway theater didn't seem like the ideal way to spend a Friday night, and it would piss off Stephen.

Luckily, the asshole got up and left. He forgot his coat and a bright red scarf on the barstool, but I didn't feel the desire to chase him down.

The noise of the lobby bar faded down to background noise, and after checking the time on my phone, I pulled up the search engine.

If I was going to be here for a couple of months, I needed to figure out what private clubs were in the area.

New York City might be the most populous city in the US, but that didn't mean it would be easy to find a decent BDSM club.

Shit, the way my head was, maybe I should have a sex sabbatical.

Spying a familiar forum in one of the links, I went to log in but stopped. I really didn't have that much interest in finding a club. It involved getting a membership and finding a sub—a temporary one.

Honestly, the whole idea made me tired.

"Hi."

A polite brush-off already forming on my tongue, I glanced over, then put my phone face down.

The second I saw her, I forgot all about the brush-off, the phone, the search, and the asshole who'd left his coat and scarf behind.

She had the most beautiful eyes I'd ever seen.

Rich and deep, a shade caught between blue and purple, almost like the twilight sky as it yielded to the night.

Her mouth was unpainted but wide and lush, soft lips I already wanted to feel against mine.

Those lips parted on a soft intake of breath, and there was a faintly stunned look in her eyes, almost like she felt the same erotic, instant attraction.

I blinked away the erotic image of stealing a kiss and made myself respond to her greeting. "Hello."

She gripped the back of the chair next to me, her hands buried in the soft material of the asshole's scarf. Still smiling at me, she said, "Lame conversation starter, but this weather sucks, doesn't it? Especially for April."

The weather wasn't my favorite topic, but if it made her linger, I wouldn't argue.

"I'm used to warmer weather. I'm from California." Absently, I looked out the windows and saw the same steady snowfall. Damn glad the subway system wasn't affected by snow. "I'm not much for cold weather, so yeah, I'm not loving the April snowstorm."

Turning my back on the windows, I focused on the woman. She was a much more appealing subject. Those eyes alone were stunning.

"What's California like?" she asked, her body angled toward me.

"Warm. In some places, it's beautiful. Watching the sun go down over the Pacific...?" Thinking about the home I'd left under Stephen's watchful eye and the balcony where I'd enjoyed a hundred sunsets had me wishing I was back there instead of here, in New York City, where people bundled up like it was the North Pole. "There's nothing else like it."

"I guess it's pretty different here."

"Yeah." Maybe different was what I needed. Back in

California, I'd been losing interest in just about everything—even my club, the balcony where I'd watched sunsets and written a dozen songs. I'd been all but drowning in the apathy.

Now, talking to this woman, interest stirred something inside I hadn't felt in a while.

"But I'm definitely finding plenty here that appeals to me."

Awareness bloomed in her eyes, and her cheeks flushed a soft pink. She swayed a little closer, only a few inches away now. "New York has its perks."

I offered her a drink and debated asking her to sit in the seat still empty next to me. The asshole had been gone for a good ten minutes. He probably wasn't coming back for his coat. But there was still something skittish about the pretty brunette. I didn't want to rush her.

The soft flush on her cheeks intensified as our gazes connected. The pulse in her neck fluttered, and her eyes darkened. Yeah, she might be skittish, but she was definitely turned on.

I sure as hell was. The idea of a sex sabbatical no longer interested me a bit.

"You know, I don't think we—"

"Hello. Excuse me, but that's my chair."

She straightened and turned.

Recognizing the man as the asshole who'd left his scarf and coat behind, I sighed.

"Oh." The woman gave me a quick, embarrassed look as she stepped back, letting the asshole claim his belongings. He didn't spare me a look.

I wasn't concerned about that.

But now, the cute brunette with gorgeous eyes looked uncomfortable.

That did concern me. I'd been about two steps away from asking her name—and number.

"Jazz!"

She turned, giving me an excellent look at her profile, her long, slim neck bared by her upswept hair.

Jazz. I couldn't help but smile.

"I'm so sorry we're late—oh, you and Burton found each other!"

The asshole glanced toward Jazz while she darted another quick look at me.

"Sorry," she said with a grimace. "I thought you were somebody I was meeting here. The scarf."

She gestured to the scarf the asshole had draped around his neck.

"Blind date, huh?" It wasn't so easy to smile this time.

The light in her eyes was markedly dimmer as she nodded. "My friends invited me. Sorry to have interrupted you."

"You didn't." I nodded at the tall, pretty blonde next to her, then at her. "It was nice talking to you...Jazz."

As they walked away, I tossed back the rest of my whiskey.

"Don't brood over it," I muttered even as my thoughts drifted back to the woman. I looked in the mirror over the bar again without any conscious decision, searching for her.

I found her just as the bell signaling it was almost curtain time sounded.

She was walking between the asshole and the cute

blond who must have facilitated the blind date. Either the friend didn't know the asshole well, or he was good at hiding his asshole tendencies.

Either way, none of it was my concern.

I was here for a job, after all.

FOUR

JAZZ

"I'M SORRY WE WERE LATE," CAM SAID, GIVING ME A quick look as we settled into our seats on the private balcony. She'd scored excellent seats from a company we were thinking of merging with. Greg Means, the owner, knew Cam was into the theater and wasn't above using tickets to woo us.

As I sat next to her, I shrugged. "It's alright."

I shouldn't be feeling this, but part of me wished I was still in the bar, talking to the hot guy with the killer smile. That smile made things in me warm up and tingle in unfamiliar ways. Unfamiliar and in very *nice* ways.

Even now, thinking about the slow curve of his lips made my belly tighten.

"Cam didn't tell me you were so gorgeous."

The words were practically growled into my ear as Burton leaned into my personal space.

His breath, hot on my neck, made me want to recoil, but the seats weren't designed for that.

"This color is beautiful on you."

I felt his fingers on my shirt sleeve, rubbing the soft chenille. I grabbed the playbill that had fallen to the floor and moved over to stand in front of Cam and Danny. "So this is the third time Greg has let you use this box. Seriously nice seats, Cam. Is he flirting with you? Should Danny be worried?"

Both Danny and Cam broke into laughter.

I saw Burton stretching out his legs from the corner of my eye, and I breathed a little easier. Maybe he'd gotten the point.

"If anybody should be worried, it's Danny." Cam grinned at me, mirth in her eyes and completely unaware of my discomfort. "Greg's gay."

"Oh." Shooting a look at Danny, I caught sight of the blush on his cheeks and the echo of laughter in his eyes. "Danny does have a nice ass," I pointed out.

Cam pretended to smack me with her playbill. "Mine. Go flirt with your date."

"Yes," Burton said, angling in his seat to face me better. "Come flirt with me. I promise I'll be as easy as you want."

The comment made Danny laugh, but Cam's glance at me looked uncomfortable. Having her fuss over me wouldn't make the play go by any quicker, so I just smiled and shrugged.

The lights dimmed as an announcement came over the speaker. I returned to my seat, and as I settled in, Burton leaned closer. "Speaking of nice asses..."

I bit back the retort on the tip of my tongue.

Instead, I gave him a blank look. "Hmm? Oh, look. It's starting."

I had practice when it came to rebuffing assholes.

Any woman with a job in the gaming industry dealt with shit. Many still assumed tech and gaming were careers for guys, like having a dick was some imaginary joystick that made them more qualified.

Cam tended to be more in your face about brushing off jerks—or calling them out, while I kept altercations low-key, avoiding them altogether if possible.

Being stuck in a private booth with a groper on my left and my pregnant best friend on the right made it hard to avoid the douchebag gracefully.

Halfway through the first act, I had to smack away the hand he put on my knee, wishing that Cam hadn't found me in the bar. I could have spent the evening flirting with the hot guy I'd mistaken for my blind date.

Why couldn't I get hooked up with somebody like *that* guy instead of...Burton?

I was attractive. Successful, too. I wasn't hung up on my age or the fact that I'd noticed tiny lines fanning out from the corner of my eyes earlier this year. Smile lines, right?

But no matter what happened, I always found the assholes. I knew good guys existed. Cam had one—Danny was devoted to her. She made more money than he did, which didn't bother him.

He had already made arrangements to take some time off the first month after the baby was born, so Cam wasn't going it alone.

I'd never been one for anything long-term, true. But there were times when it would be...nice to spend some time with a guy who wasn't constantly looking for excuses to paw me and was entirely focused on what *he* wanted. Most were ignorant of whether or not I was interested. Then if we ever made it to bed, they were clueless if I was even *aroused*.

Again, the gorgeous guy from earlier came to mind, a frisson of heat shivering through my veins. The look in his eyes had been one of interest, and for the first time in forever, I'd actually felt a tug of heat in return.

I'd pretty much given up on sex a while back.

My last encounter had...sucked. The guy and I had both been attracted, and after a couple of dates, we had sex.

It ended three minutes later, three minutes of him lurching inside me, fingers digging into my hips, and then he'd climaxed, climbed off me, and grabbed his clothes, barely pausing long enough to throw away the rubber.

That was when I decided I was done trying to make the relationship thing happen.

I should have stood by that decision and refused this bullshit blind date.

As the curtain descended for intermission, I deliberately turned my back on Burton and smiled at Cam. "Ladies room?"

"HE'S OBNOXIOUS, ISN'T HE?" Cam said.

This was our fourth trip to the Ladies room so far—we'd gone once more during the second act of the play, again after it ended, and here we were now, in the restroom of my favorite restaurant, all to get a break for Burton McGrabbyHands.

"Obnoxious is one word to describe him." Since Cam

had already picked up on the problem, I saw no reason to dance around the subject.

I wished I'd stuck to my decision to go home after the play, but I thought surely, Burton wouldn't continue to be such a twat once we were seated at a table and talking.

Plus, I was starving.

"You wanna bail?" Cam finished washing her hands before dropping her purse on the counter and digging inside.

"Yes." Just the thought of spending another thirty minutes with him was enough to kill my appetite. "If I didn't know and love Danny, I'd seriously be questioning your taste in men right about now."

"*I* am seriously questioning my taste right now." She made a face at her reflection as she leaned forward over the sink, only to stop and cover her rounded belly. "You are making it hard to keep up with the daily beauty routine, babydoll."

"Leave my godchild alone." I stuck out my tongue.

She laughed and checked her makeup despite the baby bump. Her laughter faded as her gaze came to mine. "Seriously, Jazz. I'm sorry. I've met Burton several times, and I've never seen him act like a sleaze until today."

"Danny's presence probably helped some there." Lifting a shoulder in a shrug, I dropped my makeup mirror back into my small bag and turned to her. "It's all good. And now I have something to hang over you the next time you try to hook me up with somebody."

Her cheeks colored. "So, if you want to bail, we'll grab the server on our way back, tell him to box up your food."

"You don't mind?" I hesitated, not liking the idea of leaving her in the lurch.

"Nope." With a thin smile, she said, "I'm fine with it—and I'm going to tell Danny *why* you bailed, so if he wants to knock some sense into Burton, later on, he can."

"Geez." I rolled my eyes. "No need to have him get physical about anything."

"But he's so much fun when he gets...physical." She batted her lashes at me.

"No." Turning away, I covered my ears with my hands. "I can't hear you."

She laughed and came up from behind and hugged me. "Love you, Jazz."

I squeezed her hands. "Love you, too. Now, let's go hunt down that server."

Burton was done with his first drink and possibly into his *third* by the time we got back to the table. He gave me a look, eyes bleary but smiled.

He said, loudly, "You two sure do have to piss a lot. Or are you doing something else in there?"

"Burton." Danny's voice came out hard.

Burton swiveled his head around and blinked. "Aw, fuck, man...issa fuckin' joke, dude," he said, laughing and smacking the table. "Unless you think your wegnant pife—your *pregnant wife*—is getting her rocks off in the shitter."

Cam's face went a hot shade of pink, her eyes flashing with anger.

"Ma'am."

I saw the server, my food already boxed up and tucked into a bag stamped with the restaurant's logo. "Thank you."

"Tell the kitchen to cancel the dessert orders," Cam said, catching the server's attention. "And hold on...here."

The server frowned but glanced past us to Burton, his mouth going tight. "Should I get the manager?"

"Up to you," Cam said. "He's not leaving with us. Don't cancel his food, by the way—the cash should cover my friend's meal, our drinks, and your tip." She shoved it into the man's hand. "He's paying for his. Danny?"

Danny had been sitting close enough to follow the conversation and was already on his feet. He stroked a hand down Cam's back and looked from her to me. "Everything okay?"

"Since I'm going home now," I said with a bright smile. "Yes."

"Hey!" Burton called out as I turned and started for the door.

I didn't look back, and soon, I was outside in the cold night air, the snow still gently falling.

The weather wasn't enough to slow New York City traffic, though, and damn, was I glad. Waving down a taxi, I told myself to put the night out of my head. I would enjoy what was left of the evening, have a glass of wine, my meal, and pretend I'd never met a sexist ass named Burton.

"THIS SNOW IS SOMETHING, ain't it?"

"Yes." I gave the cabbie a vague smile as I swiped my card and added a tip. "I'm ready for the cold snap to end so we can start bitching about the heat and humidity."

The man, somewhere in his forties, burst into loud

laughter, creases fanning out from eyes the color of dark chocolate. His teeth flashed white against skin only a few shades lighter than his eyes as he smiled. "Spoken like a true New Yorker."

I winked at him. "Born and bred. But the truth is we'd find people like that everywhere. We're always going to complain about the weather."

"True, true." He nodded at my building. "Get your nice self on inside now, ma'am. Stay warm."

He waited until I was almost to the door before easing away, and I couldn't help but smile at the courtesy. From the corner of my eye, I saw somebody approaching the doors, and I hurried through, not wanting to block anybody but equally determined to follow my driver's advice—*stay warm*.

As we passed through the lobby, I caught a glimpse of the man behind me. I took in the red scarf, and a dark coat out of habit. I thought of Burton for a split second, but immediately brushed it off.

Cam would have texted or called if he'd left about the same time I had, right?

My phone vibrated in my coat pocket, and I scowled as I pulled it out. I reached the elevator bank as I glanced at the name on the screen.

Cam.

Punching the number for my floor, I unlocked my phone. The hair on the back of my neck prickled. As I passed by an accent mirror, I caught a flash of the same man again, collar up, scarf wrapped around his neck.

Was it Burton?

The doors slid open. I darted into the car and hit the button to close the doors the second I cleared them.

A shadow fell across the tiles just outside the elevator, but the doors didn't stop, and I breathed easier.

While my heart slowed to a normal rate, I checked the message from Cam.

Sorry, he was such an asshole, sweetie! Lunch tomorrow is on me!

I texted her back with a wry grin, and a simple heart emoji. Now that the date from hell was over, I could relax and hopefully convince my best friend to let this shit go.

The elevator stopped on the Mezz level. Retreating to the corner, I tucked my phone away. Two teens spilled into the car, giggling as they huddled together against the far wall. When the elevator stopped again, and they exited, I watched with some melancholy.

Had I ever been that young and carefree?

No. Not ever.

I hadn't had the chance.

My mood was grim by the time I reached my floor.

The last thing I needed to see was the scarf guy when I exited.

But there he was.

He'd beaten me to my floor.

Was he stalking me?

His eyes flicked toward me, and nerves danced down my spine, my heart clenching.

I stopped and shoved my hand into my purse without any conscious thought.

The pepper spray fit neatly in my hand, and I pulled it out, holding it close to my leg.

"Are you following me?" I demanded.

My heart knocked against my ribs as he reached up

and tugged his scarf loose, revealing his face—his *familiar* face. It wasn't Burton.

No. It was the hot guy I'd been flirting with at the bar.

"No," he said, his voice as warm and smooth as I remembered. "Although I can't say I'm sorry to see you."

I backed up a step.

His lips twitched in a cynical smile as he reached into a pocket.

My chest hurt. I sucked in air and realized that I'd stopped breathing at some point. As I gasped in another breath, he pulled out a keyring and gestured at a door—the one right next to mine. Apartment 1410.

"I just moved in," he said, his expression neutral. "I thought I'd mentioned earlier that I'm in town for business for the next few months."

My face burned hot with embarrassment as he unlocked the door. "Oh."

I couldn't seem to manage anything else, even a lame apology.

"Good night." He stepped inside and closed the door, not once looking my way.

Feeling like an idiot, I moved to apartment 1412 and unlocked it.

I hurried inside and bolted the door. My mind was racing. Could all this be a coincidence or was this...hot guy stalking me?

FIVE
TRENT

Although I was still adjusting to the eastern time zone, I woke feeling refreshed.

It probably had something to do with the hot and highly sexual dreams centered around my neighbor—dreams of her naked, except for the scarf I'd been wearing. Draped around her neck, hiding her tits as she sucked my cock, but then, I used the scarf to bind her arms as she bent over in front of me.

Once I'd had her bound, I'd fucked her until she begged me to stop—then begged me not to.

As a result, I'd woken up with a raging hard-on and enjoyed some self-satisfaction.

The music score whispered in the back of my mind by the time I finished showering.

Maybe this change of scenery was all the inspiration I'd needed.

It could be New York in general or the sexy woman next door who'd looked at me last night with slight terror in her eyes mingled with lingering hesitation.

I should probably be more worried by the terror I'd glimpsed in her eyes. I wasn't, though. I didn't get off on terror or anything. It was understandable—she was a single woman, and it was kind of weird how we'd been at the theater and was staying in the same building where she lived.

The fear faded pretty fast, and I forced myself to leave before I ended up lost in her big, blue—purple eyes.

One thought had dominated my brain—she hadn't brought the asshole home or gone with him. Somehow that made me feel good.

I needed to know more about her.

What she liked. What did she do for a living?

And maybe her name.

"YOU MEAN MS. MOORS?"

The doorman glanced around before accepting the hand I offered—and the fifty-dollar bill.

"She's a nice lady." He smoothly accepted the bill and tucked it away as he went to open the door.

I waited for the woman who'd walked inside to be out of earshot and the door was shut before pushing for more.

"Is she married? Dating?"

"No. I mean, at least, not that I know of. I worked the evening shift until about two weeks ago, and I don't think she's ever brought a guy home." He shrugged. "I guess she could be involved with somebody here in the building, but I've never seen her with him if she was."

I asked a few more questions, but beyond her name—

Jasmine Moors—and the fact that she gave all the lobby staff and housekeeping nice tips on the holidays and never treated the employees poorly, I didn't learn much.

It was a decent start, though.

I had her full name.

LATER IN THE DAY, coming out of the building elevator, I heard her voice.

Slowing my steps, I looked around and caught sight of her pacing by the bank of windows with her phone in hand. My heart pounded faster when I saw her all decked out.

After getting her full name earlier, I had looked her up online, and found an interesting interview from the New Entrepreneur magazine's website.

Jasmine Moors—Jazz—was single, thirty-five years old. Along with her best friend, Cam, she ran a gaming company that was considered one of the best up-and-coming platforms in the world.

I'd read half a dozen more interviews, listened to a couple of podcasts, and now wanted to spend time with her.

Everything I'd found was all business related, though. My attempts to learn anything personally beyond her single status and a long-standing friendship with her business partner, had come up empty.

That was fine. I'd prefer to find out about her the old-fashioned way—a few dates, hopefully culminating with her in my bed. Bound or in handcuffs, maybe.

Her gaze bounced off my face as she swung around.

I slowed, her frustration obvious even though she wasn't speaking at present, as she listened to the person on the other end of the line.

Her eyes came back to mine, and her cheeks flushed a pretty shade of pink, but she offered a faint half-smile in greeting before focusing back on her call.

"Of course, Saul. I just want you to understand I'm not going to be able to get another afternoon free for several weeks."

She came to a stop in front of the large window, and stared out at the bustling New York City traffic, her shoulders rigid, spine unbending.

"Of course. I'll see about having my PA reach out in a few weeks."

She lowered the phone but didn't turn, the air around her charged with tension.

I hesitated, not sure if I should approach.

In the end, I moved to stand at her side, keeping a good two feet of distance between us.

"Everything alright?" I asked.

She sighed. "More or less. I'm just supremely annoyed about giving in for an interview I didn't want to do in the first place, and now it's been canceled on me—thirty minutes before I'm supposed to be there. I was just about to catch a cab, and they called and canceled."

"They canceled on you with only a half-hour notice?" I scowled. "Well, that's unprofessional. Did they have the decency to be in a car accident or something?"

She laughed, the sound bright and open. I couldn't *not* look at her. Facing her, I caught her eyes just as she went to look away.

Her breath caught as our gazes connected, and I could all but hear a little *click*, as something in me recognized something in her.

She cleared her throat and looked away, tucking a golden-brown hair behind her ear. "No." She scowled at her vague reflection in the window. "There was a last-minute chance for him to interview with a competitor—one who tried to buy us out last year—and he made sure to point that out."

"Ah, he's an asshole, then."

She laughed again, and I wanted to say something else, so that she'd keep laughing.

It was music, that sound.

Just hearing it made me itch for a piano so I could try to capture the essence in a melody.

Maybe that was why I asked, "Well, since you don't have an interview for the afternoon, why don't you join me? I'm heading over to the Theater District—watching the rehearsals of the play we saw last night."

She tipped her head back, studying me with those brilliant purple-blue eyes. "The rehearsals?"

"Yes." I smiled, careful not to push but not holding back on the attraction I felt. "It's actually a work assignment for me. But if you enjoy theater, you'd probably have fun seeing what's involved before the curtain goes up."

"I would." She pursed her lips, her thoughts racing across her features. "You know, I don't think we ever bothered to introduce ourselves."

"That's a problem easily solved." I offered a hand. "Trent Dixson."

"Jazz Moors." A smile tugged at one corner of her

mouth. "Trent Dixson...did you say you work in the theater industry?"

"Not theater per se. Entertainment."

"Oh...*oh!*"

Her lips parted. Even as she started to talk, I wanted to lean in and kiss her, taste her full lower lip, bite it, then suck it into my mouth. I forced myself to focus on her words rather than her mouth and my dirty fantasies.

Completely lost in the visuals, I barely caught the tail end of her question.

"... writer...that was you, wasn't it?"

What had she asked? I had no fucking clue. With a sheepish smile, I admitted as much. "Sorry. I didn't catch all of that. Can I plead jetlag?"

Her cheeks flushed, and I'd bet she knew it wasn't jetlag so much as the pure male interest, but she repeated the question.

"Yes," I said. "That's mine—one of my best if you want my personal opinion."

"I have to agree. So why are you going to watch a dress rehearsal?" Curiosity brightened her lovely eyes.

"Work." I let it go at that. "My contract limits me to how much I can discuss. But nothing says I can't take a guest. Are you interested?" I asked, forcing my thoughts to move before I made *another* offer—one that would have us up in my apartment, both of us naked and preferably her on her knees as she sucked my cock. My oh my, that mouth was made for it.

Her lips bowed in a slow smile. "Well, I do have the afternoon unexpectedly open. It sounds like it could be fun."

"Then say yes." Moving closer now, I lowered my voice and nodded toward the window. "I've got a car waiting outside right now. Say yes, please."

SIX
JAZZ

My Saturday had gone straight to shit until three minutes ago, when Trent asked me to accompany him for a dress rehearsal. If I were smart, I'd go to my apartment, change into my pajamas, and binge on a TV series and ice cream.

But an afternoon with Trent Dixson sounded more enticing than wallowing in sorrow on pistachio gelato.

"Okay." The word came out before I'd made the conscious decision, but as a smile brightened his face, I wasn't about to take it back.

"Excellent." He nodded to the window—or rather, the sleek black sedan waiting at the curb. "Are you ready now, or do you want to change?"

I debated, as I looked at the long skirt I'd paired with a form-fitting blouse and knee boots. The outfit was dressier than what I'd typically wear on a Saturday, but because of my interview, I'd put more effort into my appearance than usual.

"As long as I'm not overdressed, I'm fine with what I'm wearing."

The appreciation in Trent's eyes brought a flush to my cheeks. Good thing I'd made the extra effort.

"You look lovely." He offered his arm.

My heart did a crazy tap-dance as I accepted and let him lead me to the waiting sedan outside.

My phone vibrated in my hand as he opened the car door for me. Once I was seated, I checked the message. Unsurprised to see Royce's name, I huffed out a sigh.

There were a lot of great people in the gaming industry. But the guy who ran the gaming podcast behind my now-canceled interview? He wasn't one of them.

Honey, look, if you're willing to wait until tonight, I might be able to fit you in.

Snorting, I muttered, "It figures."

I fired back a quick response as Trent circled the car to the other side.

I've already made other plans for the day, Royce. If you want to reschedule, you can contact my PA on Monday.

"What's with that shark's smile?"

Startled, I looked up to see Trent eying me with a great deal of interest—and heat.

"Ah, my interview." I flushed and shrugged as I slid the phone away. "The guy behind it texted to let me know that he could try to work me in tonight if I'd be willing to wait a while."

Trent made a derisive tone. "Tell me you told him to take a hike."

"No." Crossing my legs, I smoothed my skirt down and folded my hands on my knee. "I told him I'd already made plans, and he could contact my PA on Monday if he wanted to try to reschedule our interview."

"And is your PA going to be able to find an opening for him?"

Pursing my lips, I considered the question. "I haven't really decided yet."

Trent chuckled. "Bust his balls, Jazz."

"Oh, I'm going to. Happily. A company run by two women doesn't make it to the top in the gaming industry by being meek and mild." I picked a tiny piece of lint from my skirt and slanted a look at him. "You have to be willing to bust a guy in the balls when needed."

"SO YOU FLEW OUT HERE for the next couple of months to...what, watch dress rehearsals?" I asked Trent after we arrived at the theater.

He had made a few comments that gave me a vague idea of why he was here, but he hadn't confirmed or denied anything. All I really knew was that he lived in California but was staying in New York City for the next two months as he finished a project. Since he wrote musical scores, I could only assume it involved music tied into the Broadway production.

"It's a living," he said. "Can I be honest here and say that I think Leo's understudy does a better job in this part than the regular actor?"

"Hmmm." Nodding, I voiced agreement. "He has more heart for it, that's for certain. Especially in this scene."

The scene was an intimate one. Just sitting there with

my eyes on the two actors, standing in a pool of light and the rest of the stage dark, added to the sexual tension.

Trent leaned closer, his body heat warming me. "Watch...see how they barely touch, but they manage to convey all their need, all their yearning..."

The words *need,* and *yearning* sounded more erotic when spoken in that warm, sexy timbre of his. "Yes. I noticed last night, too. The music...it changes everything, especially in this scene."

He curved a hand around my nape. "Yes. I'm glad you can appreciate that. Not everybody realizes how important the musical score is to a production—be it on a stage, in a TV show, or a movie. Or maybe I shouldn't be surprised. A number of games have excellent musical scores."

"Yes." I was having a hard time breathing. And when in the hell had it gotten so hot in here? "It's hard to see how anybody could discount the value of music, especially when it's as evocative as this."

Wow.

Was that thready rasp my voice?

When had I stopped watching the actors on the stage and focused on the man next to me?

His pale green eyes all but glowed with intensity as he stroked his fingers along my neck, then up to trace the line of my jaw.

"You're not watching the play," he murmured.

"That's because you're distracting me."

With a wicked, playful glint in his eyes, he asked, "Am I? How?"

"You're..." *Staring at me like you want to eat me up.* "Talking."

"Ah, I see." His eyes made it clear he didn't buy that excuse. But he eased away and settled more comfortably in the seat, the two of us all but alone in the sprawling, nearly empty theater. "I'll behave so you can enjoy the show."

I wanted to tell him no, but for my sanity's sake, he needed to behave.

My heart raced, and my skin was flushed. I wanted to look at him, tell him I wasn't interested in the play right now.

Maybe if I'd known him better, maybe if I'd had more confidence in sexual hunger like this, I could have.

Instead, I settled more comfortably into the seat and gave the rehearsing cast more attention.

"WHAT DID YOU THINK?"

On the ride up to the fourteenth floor, I considered the question. "It was fun. I can't believe the lines they have to memorize. Then there are the dance moves. And how they rush off the stage from scene to scene, change and get back to their places..."

Trent cocked a brow, waiting.

"I like the finished version. Watching a play is kind of magical. Today was fun. But I think if I worked in the theater and had to see behind the curtain a lot, it would take all the magic away."

Trent's face softened, and he stroked my cheek. "You're one of those who'd never wanted to know how a magician performed an illusion, aren't you?"

"Yep." I shrugged. "Why take the wonder away from it?"

"Some people think the wonder is knowing *how* the illusion was done."

"Nope." I shook my head, eyes on the numbers speeding by. I dreaded seeing my floor. This had been a great...time. I couldn't call it a date, could I?

As the doors slid open, I felt his eyes on me.

Stepping into the hallway, I looked over at him.

I had fun.

Thank you.

I enjoyed myself.

Good night.

A half dozen other suggestions circled through my head. But as our gazes connected, my thoughts went blank, and the only coherent thought was...*please*.

He stepped closer, the toes of his boots nudging mine. I had to tip my head back so I could hold his gaze, and then because my head was spinning, I fell back against the wall behind me, my hands splayed wide on the cool, flat surface.

He followed me, hands coming up to delve into my hair.

"I'm going to kiss you," he said in a gruff voice. "I've wanted to since last night. If you don't want the same, tell me now."

Heart racing, I reached up and curled my fingers into the soft, fine wool of his forest green sweater. "I want the same."

Rising on my toes, I met him just as he lowered his head.

Our mouths touched, and a blistering inferno exploded within.

Oh.

Oh, my.

This is what friends meant when they talked about a guy who kissed so well, that their minds just went blank.

Trent tangled the fingers of one hand in my hair and tugged my head back, changing the angle until he had me where he wanted me. The other hand went to my hip, holding me steady as he moved closer, his body pressing mine into the wall with sensual force.

His tongue stroked over my lower lip, then dipped into my mouth, a groan vibrating out of him as the kiss deepened.

More.

That was the only clear thought now.

I wanted *more*.

Rising on my toes to press closer to him, I curled one arm around his neck and tugged. He reacted by gripping my hip and pulling me in against him, his cock a hard, pulsing length.

My knees went weak, legs threatening to give out under me.

Shoving one hand under the hem of his sweater, I touched hot, silken skin. He groaned against my mouth and then nipped my lower lip.

I whimpered, the sound totally foreign, full of wanton, raw need.

He broke the kiss, and I tried to follow, take his mouth again.

Trent caught my chin, holding firm. The feel of his

fingers against my skin, slightly rough, strong, and thoroughly masculine, sent a shiver running down my spine.

"Come inside with me," he said, voice rough.

I was torn. Getting involved with your neighbor was so cliché, and almost always ended badly. But Trent's only in New York for a couple of months so he's not *really* a neighbor. More like a visitor.

SEVEN

TRENT

Her almost instant agreement surprised me as much as my spontaneous invitation.

But I didn't waste energy analyzing why I'd invited her in. It was clear. I hadn't felt such a hot pull toward a woman in a long time.

What made it even crazier was that Jazz wasn't into the lifestyle. I could tell. I doubted she'd had more than a handful of lovers, and if even one of them had managed to give her a mind-blowing orgasm, I'd sell my Steinway.

I rarely got involved with a woman who wasn't into BDSM. I just didn't get my needs met otherwise.

But I was already craving feeling her hands in my hair as I went down on her, craving the feel of her mouth on my cock as I taught her to suck dick the way I liked.

And yeah, I was getting ahead of myself.

Taking her hand, I led her to my apartment, just a few feet from the elevator.

Her fingers tightened on mine, her skin hot. Her

breaths were ragged and her expression spoke only of blind need and lust.

Unlocking the door, I dropped my keys on the small table beyond the threshold, then stripped out of my sport coat, eyes already on Jazz.

Her hands trembled as she went to unbutton her bright pink jacket, but I caught her hands, and nudged them down.

"Let me." Lowering my head, I took her mouth as I unbuttoned her jacket, then stripped it away.

I'd meant to slow things down. Take off her jacket, seduce her with kisses and caresses, control the pace now that I had her in my place, confident I would quickly have her naked under me.

But she rose onto her toes and pressed a kiss to the side of my neck, hands coming up to grip my waist.

Darker urges pushed aside thoughts of seduction. I dropped her jacket, all but tore mine off before grabbing her hips and boosting her up. Placing her against the door, I went to nudge her legs apart, but her straight skirt stopped me.

Holding her eyes, I reached down, and fisted one hand in the fabric. She sucked in a breath, barely breathing as I tugged it upward. "Can I?"

"Yes." She licked her lips and nodded. "Yes, please, fuck, yes."

I used both hands, desperate to feel the silken softness, and once I had her skirt out of the way, I moved between her thighs, the heat there threatening to destroy the little control I had left.

It was insane.

I never lost control.

I broke the kiss and eased back.

The hot glitter of frustrated lust in her eyes almost brought me back to her. Before putting more distance between us, I stroked my hands down her arms, and eased her skirt down.

"I'm rushing this, and I've lost my manners? Would you like some wine?"

She hesitated more than a second. "Yes."

Despite my overwhelming desire to continue, I turned away and scooped up our discarded jackets. After a brief pause to hang them on the coat tree, I led her to the kitchen.

The *tap-tap-tap* of her heeled boots marked her progress through the apartment. I breathed a sigh of relief that she hadn't bolted.

"Red or white?"

"Ah...white, please."

After pouring each of us a glass, I led her to the grand piano in front of the floor-to-ceiling windows, the setting sun over Manhattan as a backdrop.

I didn't turn on the lights.

Sitting at the piano, I put the glass of wine down and met her gaze. She leaned against the gleaming black Steinway, a smile on her lips.

"Are you going to play for me?" she asked.

In answer, I put my hands on the keys. The feel was familiar, welcome. For months, I'd been fighting to find a way to spark the creative drive that fired my songwriting.

All afternoon there had been a melody dancing in my head. I let it flow, the music winding around us.

The piece was short, less than two minutes.

When it ended, I flowed into another, looking up to see a rapt expression on Jazz's face.

"What was that one, the one you just played?"

"I'm not sure yet." I gave a half shrug. "I'm still playing with it." I thought about telling her that our afternoon had played some part in it and decided against it.

I had every intention of getting her into my bed, but I didn't want to use flattery or anything else to get her naked.

She edged closer, her lashes shielding her eyes, lips curved in a half-smile.

Fuck, she was gorgeous.

Tearing my gaze away, I focused on the keys, on the music.

One song gave way to another, Jazz moved closer until she perched on the chair next to me, the scent of her filling my head, the heat of her a whisper away.

After bringing the song to a close, I took a sip of wine.

"It's amazing," Jazz said softly. "Listening to you play...I...well, I've heard music before. A lot. But..."

She stammered on, voice husky, breaths unsteady.

I took her wine glass, put it down, and placed mine next to it.

While she was still talking, I pushed away from the piano, the bench's feet scraping loudly in protest. Jazz stopped talking at the strident sound.

I caught her staring at me, purple-blue eyes wide, filled with want and nerves in a mix that left me hungrier than I already was.

"Come here."

The second she moved toward me, I captured her waist and pulled her onto my lap, pushing her slim-fitting skirt up to her hips and cupping her round, firm ass in my hands.

She moaned and pressed closer, her mouth seeking mine.

"Jazz." I groaned into her mouth, sealing our lips together as hunger burned inside.

She rocked against me, and the heat between her thighs had my cock jerking in savage demand. Sliding my hand down her ass, then delving lower to touch her intimately from behind, I found her swollen and hot, already wet.

"You're wet," I muttered, breaking the kiss to pull back and look into her eyes as I spoke.

Her cheeks went pink, but she didn't break eye contact. "I have been since the moment you kissed me."

"I want to fuck you. Right now. Do I stop?"

Her lips parted, and she blinked rapidly, the rosy hue in her cheeks deepening. "No."

"Good." Still holding her gaze, I pulled aside her panties, stroked one fingertip through her wet heat, and then dipped inside her honied pussy. "Because I've been thinking about having you hot and wet and wrapped around my cock since the moment you first spoke to me."

She clenched around my fingertip with a soft, surprised cry.

Note to self. She likes it when you talk dirty.

Withdrawing my finger slowly, I dipped my head and bit her full lower lip. "The night we met, I spent hours wishing I'd asked for your number, kicking my ass because I hadn't done it. You walked away, and there went my chance to know how you sounded when I touched you like...this." I pushed two fingers inside this time, my thumb spreading the cheeks of her ass apart.

Jazz arched her spine, a broken moan tearing out of her.

I held firm, not moving.

She rocked against me, whimpering. "More..."

"Take your shirt off." I pressed a kiss to her neck. "My hands are...otherwise engaged."

Her cheeks were pink, but her eyes lit up, something that might have been sensual amusement. She had to let go of me and brace her weight on her knees, which changed her center of gravity and drove her more fully down on the two fingers penetrating her. A throaty *hmmm* of pleasure escaped her. Her lashes drooped as she unbuttoned her sweater, baring one pale inch of flesh at a time.

She shrugged out of it, then, without waiting, freed her breasts from the bra, the front clasp decorated with a small bow.

Jazz hesitated as the bra fell away, some of her confidence fading.

"Mmm. Pretty." I rubbed my lips over hers, then kissed a line down her neck, along her collarbone, then down the delicate slope of one breast, my goal, the pink tip of her nipple.

She gasped and arched up as I took the hard bud into my mouth, scoring it with my teeth.

The sudden, harsh movement threatened our balance on the piano bench, the seat only built for one. I steadied us, gripping the bench with one hand, the top of the piano with the other.

"We should move this away from the piano," I murmured.

"Ummm."

Urging her off my lap, I stood. My cock protested painfully, and I shoved my palm against it with a grimace.

Jazz drew in a slow, uneasy breath.

I looked up to see her gaze on my groin—specifically, on my hand as I tried to adjust the uncomfortable fit of my jeans, my dick trying to punch a hole through the denim.

"Blue jeans weren't made to accommodate an erection," I said, stroking the flat of my palm down the front of my pants, watching her pupils dilate.

Her breasts trembled on the unsteady breath she hitched in, her eyes all but black now, the thin rim of purple-blue barely visible as the pupil swelled even larger.

Tempted as I was to take her hand and invite her to touch me right there, I knew if I did, I'd end up fucking her bent over the Steinway bench.

So I took her hand and led her to the bedroom down the hall.

Jazz went to the bed, her slim back to me as I stripped off my shirt, the elegant line of her spine tapering down to the waistband of her skirt.

"What's on under the skirt, Jazz?"

She glanced over her shoulder at me, a sexy yet oddly sweet smile on her lips. "Panties. My boots. A pair of boot socks."

"Boot socks?"

She arched a brow. "Know how uncomfortable knee-high boots can get without them?"

"I can't say I've ever worn knee-high boots." I approached, pleased when she didn't turn to face me. Putting my hands on her waist, I stroked up, and cupped her breasts. "Maybe you should show me the boots, and the socks, give me an idea."

Her breath came out on a raspy sigh.

Over her shoulder, I met her gaze in the mirror over the dresser, and smiled.

But I didn't say anything about the mirror, or how she stared at my hands on her beautiful tits. "Can I see your boots?"

She nodded jerkily, but when she went to unzip the skirt, I caught her hands and nudged her forward until she was bent over the bed, her hands supporting her upper body. Taking a step back, I caught the hem of her skirt and worked it upward, still holding her gaze.

Once I had the skirt to her waist, I palmed her ass, the silken fabric of her panties no barrier.

"Stay right like that while I look at your boots."

She shivered but said, "Okay."

I could easily imagine that soft, throaty voice whispering, *Yes, master.*

But I didn't need it, and that was a fucking shock. I was harder than I'd ever been, about ready to come, and she hadn't even touched me.

Stepping back, I let my eyes take a leisurely tour of her body, the long lines of her back, the skirt rucked up around full hips, thighs clenched together and trembling, the boot socks reaching to just over her knees, a soft, blue with pink that matched her sweater while the shiny black boots provided a stark contrast.

"Nice socks," I told her. "You're right. I think you do need them. Even for this."

I rubbed against her wet heat and felt her shudder. "You don't need these, though." I tugged on her panties and saw her slow nod.

I slid them down to just below her hips, let them linger where they gathered at her hips because I wanted to touch her, feel the soft silken wet heat that was her pussy.

Pushing two fingers into her, I bit back a curse, concentrating on how her hips lifted, how she fisted her hands in the blanket, the sharp, single cry that escaped before she buried her face against the bed.

Lust tore at me, sharp and demanding, and I held onto control with desperation. Working her closer to the edge, I cataloged each moan, each sigh, noting what made her voice break and hips shudder and twitch as if the coming orgasm might send her flying into a thousand pieces.

Then she was there—*right* there on the verge.

I stopped.

She cried out in frustration.

"Shhh," I murmured, stroking my hand down the soft curve of her ass.

With my other hand, I pulled out my wallet, and found the condom I'd stashed earlier. I'd had some random thought of trying to hit up one of the private clubs and see if I could get in as someone's *plus one* for the night. The idea hadn't been all that enticing, but now I was glad I'd thought ahead because it meant I didn't have to go far to find a rubber.

In seconds, I had it on, and I looked up, and saw Jazz

pushing onto one elbow, reaching back with her other hand as if searching for me.

I caught her wrist in one hand, held it tight for a second, then released her.

She gasped, her spine bowing up as I pressed the head of my cock to her cunt. "Trent!"

I gripped her hip and held her still as I thrust.

She bounced up onto her toes as the sudden, deep penetration.

I tangled my hand in her hair, keeping my grip tight so she couldn't go back down to the bed. The soft, surprised whimper of female pleasure was like music. I leaned in and pressed my lips to her ear. "Open your eyes, Jazz."

She did, but it was slow, her lashes fluttering until she finally looked at our reflection with a passion-drugged gaze.

Still gripping her silken hair in my fist, I withdrew. She whimpered, tightening the muscles in her pussy as if that could hold me inside.

The milking sensations were an erotic caress bordering on the sublime, but I didn't give in to the urge to stay locked inside her.

She twisted and moaned, trying to move back on me, and I rewarded her with a deeper, harder thrust that brought another moan to her lips.

"More," she pleaded, her eyes seeking mine in the mirror again.

"More..." I bent closer again and pressed my mouth to her ear. "Harder? Faster?"

"Yes!"

I let go of her hair and gripped both hips.

As she went lax and fell forward onto the bed, I slammed into her. The keening cry and the way she called out my name were almost as delicious as how she yielded her body to me.

The orgasm slammed into her, her entire body flushing a soft pink.

As she shuddered from it, I gave in and dropped the reins of control, my climax powerful enough to leave me shaking, to make me forget everything but the woman quivering against me.

"THAT WAS...WOW."

Jazz snuggled against me, her head tucked under my chin, her body soft and warm.

I'd never been one for cuddling, but I wasn't feeling any urge to hurry along. All I wanted at that moment was to catch my breath and let her do the same—all so I could fuck her again.

Preferably with her on her knees, hands behind her back. Or maybe spread-eagle, bound, open and vulnerable to me.

"What would you say if I told you I was into bondage?"

She went quiet and still, her erratic breaths stopping for several seconds. Then she pushed up onto one elbow and met my gaze.

I breathed a little easier when all I saw in her lovely eyes was a bit of surprise mixed with a healthy dose of curiosity.

"Bondage," she said softly. "As in you like tying up your sexual partners?"

Stroking a hand down her arm until I could manacle one soft wrist, I squeezed lightly.

"Tying my sexual partner up is one thing I enjoy. There are other pleasures." With a faint smile, I added, "I notice you went straight to assuming I'm the dominant in the situation."

Her cheeks colored, but she shrugged. "I learned to read people at a pretty young age. Since you took the lead there, I'm guessing my assumption was right."

"It is." Squeezing her bound wrist, I felt her pulse under my thumb speed up. "Have you ever given the idea of BDSM any thought?"

She blinked, then shook her head. "No. I can't say it's a turn-off, but I've just...never thought of it. What kind of..." The words trailed off.

I could see her trying to formulate what she wanted to ask. "Are you curious about just what I'm into? What I like?"

She nodded, looking both nervous and intrigued.

"I like having a woman submit—having her turn over her trust and her pleasure to me. Trust and pleasure—those are key because why would a sub give control of her body over to somebody she didn't trust to care for her? Somebody she didn't think would give her pleasure?"

Circling my thumb over her pulse, I smiled. "It's a heady feeling, having somebody trust you to do that. It's arousing as fuck to have that person trust you enough to let you tie them up, bend them over, or stretch them out and touch, taste, explore every inch of their body while they lay there...vulnerable."

Her lips parted with a ragged sigh.

"I'm not very good at trusting...or being vulnerable," she said quietly.

"It's a learning process." Nuzzling her neck, I added, "Taking a woman like you as a sub, teaching you all about the lifestyle is something I would very much enjoy."

A tiny noise left her as I pressed a kiss to the sensitive spot behind her ear.

Then I stretched back out next to her and pulled her closer. "Just maybe an idea for you to consider."

She nodded jerkily before settling back against me, one hand resting on my chest.

She hadn't jumped up and left.

She'd actually looked curious, if somewhat anxious.

I just might have found a sub to play with for my short stay here in New York.

I considered the idea, and decided I very much liked it.

But when I went to kiss her, I found her eyes closed and her breaths soft and steady.

She'd fallen asleep.

EIGHT
JAZZ

I woke up almost instantly.

It was pretty normal for me, a holdover from a childhood where I'd never know if I'd wake up to find my mother still half-drunk and crying into a bottle about my dad, or in a foul mood because she was hungover and late for work.

What wasn't so typical was waking up to the smell of breakfast cooking...bacon? My mouth watered, and I had a temporary fight with my nerves while debating whether to slip out and go next door to my apartment or act normal and go out there to face him.

This was only the second one-night stand I'd ever had.

Unlike the first, this one I had a desire in repeating, but that could be awkward because Trent was a neighbor, and I already saw myself liking him.

However, he was only a temporary neighbor. No need to panic.

Romance, marriage, love, all that jazz, pun intended,

was nothing I believed in, not after seeing what love could do to a woman.

My dad had fallen in love with my babysitter when I was a kid and abandoned my mother and me. He'd signed over rights and agreed to pay child support but had no interest in seeing me ever again. Eventually, I'd gotten over it; my mom never had. She'd died still broken inside. Why would I want to risk that kind of pain?

Temporary neighbors and short-lived sexual flings were the ideal relationships for me.

If only...

I sat up in bed, an idea taking root and exploding to life in seconds.

Why the hell not?

Hearing movement in the apartment beyond the bedroom, I lurched out of bed and darted for the nearby open door, hoping it was a bathroom.

It was.

Closing the door, I locked it and leaned against it, my heart racing and my mind whirling.

It could work.

Why the hell wouldn't it work?

He was smart, funny, and decent. He played piano and looked healthy.

A giddy laugh threatened to bubble up out of me, and I clapped a hand over my mouth before it could.

After a few seconds, I thought I could behave relatively maturely, and I lowered my hand.

Pushing away from the door, I walked over to the mirror and faced my reflection. "It could work."

SERVING THE MAESTRO

OUTSIDE OF MY few experiences with men, confidence had never been my issue. I knew how to talk business, strike deals, and get what I wanted.

Trent struck me as somebody who'd appreciate that in a woman, both on a personal level and a professional one.

I took a few extra minutes to dry my hair, and when I left the bathroom wearing only a towel, I was pleasantly surprised to find my sweater, skirt, and bra waiting on the end of the bed. Glad I wouldn't have to dart into the living room on a semi-naked clothes-hunting expedition, I got dressed.

I had no idea where my panties were but decided not to worry about it when a quick look around the bedroom didn't yield anything.

Blowing out a breath, I put on a pleasant mask and left the bedroom.

The scent of coffee and bacon seduced me, making my belly rumble in demand.

Trent was leaning against the counter in the kitchen, shirtless as he sipped his coffee and read something on his cell phone. When he looked up at me, it was with a warm smile.

Some of the nervous knots in my belly eased.

That wasn't the look of a man ready to kick a woman out after a night tangling up the sheets.

"Sleep well?" he asked.

"Very." My cheeks warmed, but I didn't look away.

"Same here." His lashes lowered, the sleepy-eyed look incredibly sexy. Nodding at a cup on the counter, he said, "I didn't know if you drank coffee, but I saved you a cup just in case."

"You might want to brew another pot." With a wry smile, I picked up the cup. "I love coffee."

Taking a sip, I shivered in appreciation. If Trent agreed, I might be switching to decaf. Anticipation rose and spread through me, champagne bubbles in my veins. "Are you going to share the bacon I smell, or do things have to get ugly?"

"I suppose I could spare a couple of slices. Eggs?"

"If you don't mind. Is it okay if I sit?" Angling my head toward the island with high-backed chairs, I curled both hands around the cup to keep from fidgeting.

"Please. Scrambled? Over-easy?"

"However you're eating them is fine." I hoped he was eating with me. I'd never be able to eat and keep a casual conversation up otherwise. I had a killer poker face, but I wasn't usually playing with such high stakes.

"Sounds good. Give me a couple of minutes."

Soon, he was sliding a plate in front of me, and I breathed a small sigh of relief when he settled at the far end of the island, taking the chair opposite mine instead of a closer one.

I ate a couple of bites to fill the silence that had started to grow tense. Before it could become too awkward, I put my fork down and cleared my throat.

"I have a rather...personal question," I said, deciding it was best to jump right in.

He lifted a brow. "Okay."

"When was the last time you were tested?"

Now both brows went up. The fork he'd been lifting

lowered back to the plate, and he leaned back into the chair.

"That's really personal," he said, voice taking on a slight edge. "Any reason why you're asking?"

Face hot, I told myself to push on. In for a penny, in for a pound, right?

"Yes. I'm probably going to sound crazy, but...anyway. Just hear me out." I cleared my throat, putting my hands in my lap so he couldn't see how they were shaking. "I want a baby. And...well, I want you to be the father."

Now he really looked surprised.

Before he could speak, I rushed on. "I'm just asking for the biological aspect. Your sperm." Man, that sounded so...clinical. "I don't need or want anything beyond that...um, donation. If you agree, we'll draw up papers. You won't be responsible for the child in any way. Ever."

"You barely know me," he said in a gruff voice, a muscle ticking in his cheek.

"I realize that." He hadn't kicked me out, hadn't lost his temper—he seemed to be listening. Maybe he would agree. I placed both hands on the table with the embarrassed flush starting to ease. "Look, I'm thirty-five. I'm not interested in marriage or even a long-term relationship with anybody."

"Why?" His eyes narrowed thoughtfully as he studied me.

"My parents. Their marriage...well, it sucked," I told him bluntly. "After my dad left my mother, I watched her spiral downward until she was little more than a zombie. I have no interest in a relationship. But I *do* want a child."

"There's adoption. Sperm banks."

"I've considered adoption. Sperm banks..." I shook my head. "I don't want to pick out some guy blindly. I want to...well, I prefer to know the man who will...ah, donate."

"Hmmm." Crossing his arms over his distractingly bare chest, he studied me. "Are you planning to get pregnant the traditional way?"

"I'd prefer it. We could always use a clinic, I suppose. But...well, we seem compatible enough in bed." I picked up my coffee. There. I'd made my pitch without choking up or dying of embarrassment. And he hadn't laughed or told me to leave.

But would he just give a hint already?

"Okay."

Coffee splashed out of my cup. Putting it down, I looked for something to clean up the mess, but Trent was already on his feet. He handed me a paper towel while he wiped up the coffee with a damp sponge.

"You clearly weren't expecting an answer—or at least not so soon."

Looking up into his pale green eyes, I swallowed. "I'm not sure what I expected."

"I'm clean." He shrugged. "We should both get tested just so we're comfortable going forward." He took a sip of coffee, a pensive look on his face. "I should tell you—I have a...minor issue, health-wise."

My gut tightened. "Oh?"

"Relax." He smiled, the sardonic twist to his lips telling me I hadn't quite succeeded in sounding casual. "It's nothing major, but seeing what you want from me, it's only fair to tell you. I was born with just one kidney."

"Ah..." Frowning, I shook my head. "What?"

"One kidney," he said again. "It's called renal agenesis. Up until I ended up sick for a few weeks when I was twenty-five, I've never had problems—and it was my own fault I ended up sick—those energy drinks can be hell on the kidneys—or in my case, kidney."

"Probably all the caffeine," I said absently, considering what he told me. "You're healthy now?"

"Yes. As long as I don't binge on energy drinks. I don't drink much alcohol, either—less stress on my one kidney. It's just a fluke—nothing I inherited or anything." He looked down into his mug then, but not soon enough—the expression on his face had darkened, grown heavier. "But you might want to research it yourself or reconsider altogether."

"Ah...well, I'll do some research," I said. "But I don't need to reconsider."

His head came up slowly, the intensity of his gaze knocking the breath out of me. "So you're still interested?"

"Yes." My heart was doing double-time, beating so hard I was light-headed. He was going to say yes. "Does this mean you'll...consider the idea?"

"Yes." A slow smile curled his lips as he crossed to stand before me. "But I do have two conditions of my own."

"Oh?"

He bent down and deliberately bit my lower lip, sucking it into his mouth before releasing it and straightening to his full height. "I'll try to get you pregnant on two conditions, Jazz. The first—we have two months. If nothing happens, then it's done."

"Okay. That's fair." Two months. That would be two cycles, right?

"The second condition..." His gaze dipped to my mouth before returning to hold mine. "I want you to be my sub."

"I...what?"

"My sub. I told you I'm a Dom, and I'm only here temporarily. I don't want to spend time trying to find a private club I like, then trying to find a sub I like in such limited time...especially when all I can think about is you on your knees in front of me, hands bound as I fuck your mouth."

A soft whimper filled the air, and I realized it was me.

"Are the terms acceptable, Jazz?"

His voice was cool, almost remote.

But his eyes burned as if there was a fire inside them.

"What..." I cleared my throat. "What if I don't like this...sub thing? I'm not really big on submitting to men."

"Outside of sex, you don't need to submit to me. And I don't give a damn how you handle other men." He dipped his head, and nuzzled my neck before murmuring into my ear, "But Jazz...I can already tell you that you will love submitting to me."

Something told me he was right.

"Okay. We can try...once." As he straightened, I scrambled to put on my game face. It wasn't much of a success, but I didn't feel like melting into a puddle at his feet.

"Once?" He cocked a brow.

"For now." My cheeks burned so hot, that I thought I'd burst into flame. "I'm...okay, well, to be blunt, last night was the first time in..." well, *forever* "...that I enjoyed sex. I've never done anything remotely kinky, so I don't know if I'll like anything...intense. But we can try. If I don't like it after one try, we go back to regular, vanilla sex for the rest of the two months."

"Deal."

But the calm assurance in his eyes told me he wasn't concerned.

Oh, man. What had I gotten myself into?

NINE
TRENT

I'd been playing piano for nearly thirty years and writing music for the last twenty.

Falling into a world of music and sound was effortless, welcomed, even. My life didn't suck. To me, music was life.

So it was a pain in the ass when I found myself struggling to concentrate.

For the third time in under ten minutes, I restarted the song I'd been listening to. Not twenty seconds in, my mind drifted back to the conversations with Jazz days earlier.

To our agreement.

She'd delivered a contract a few hours ago, blushing as she handed it over. Her gaze had been level, holding mine steadily as she mentioned the appointment she'd had the day before for bloodwork.

She'd even spoken with a friend of hers who was a doctor about the kidney situation.

She'd hurriedly assured me that she'd been discreet

and hadn't shared any names, the earnestness on her face oddly...endearing.

A discordant note jerked my attention back to the music, and I sighed, then rose from the couch. Pacing over to the floor-to-ceiling windows that ran the length of the room, I stared out. It was finally getting warmer. The snow from several days ago had mostly melted, except for the graying, dirty clumps where it had been shoveled to clear a sidewalk or road.

"Go for a walk," I told myself. Clearing my head might help me focus on getting some work done, but I doubted it. My thoughts were trained on two things—Jazz...and the night I had planned.

Pulling my phone from my pocket, I opened the messages. All day, I'd resisted calling or texting, and it hadn't done any good.

Are we still on for tonight?

Three little dots popped up almost immediately, indicating she was typing a response.

Yes.

I smiled. She was quick with a reply.

I didn't respond. I tucked the phone back into my pocket, then braced my hands on the treated glass in front of me, arm spread wide. Anticipation pulsed inside. Having Jazz in my bed again was already reason enough for distraction.

But tonight, I was going to take the first few steps into showing her how to be a sub. *My* sub.

In exchange for some biological fluids that would hopefully impregnate her—not *too* fast, I hoped, Jazz had consented to letting me introduce her to BDSM.

A whisper of music slid through the back of my mind, a soundtrack for the excitement building in my veins. Turning from the window, I went to the piano and started to play, letting the new melody filter into my consciousness.

JAZZ WAS RIGHT ON TIME. I was still at the piano, refining the melody that had come to me a few hours earlier. I'd paused briefly to text her, telling her to come in, the doors were unlocked.

She'd responded with a thumbs-up emoji and asked if I liked Chinese.

I'd responded in kind and resisted the impulse to offer to buy.

We weren't dating.

But I figured it wouldn't hurt to keep in mind what was going on between us had an expiration date.

Although I couldn't hear her over the rising swell of the music, I knew when she came in. Bringing the song to a close, I continued to lightly stroke the keys. "Hello, Jazz."

"Hi." The husky sound came from behind me.

I didn't turn to face her.

"You make music sound so...alive," she murmured, moving into my line of sight.

"For me, it is." I looked at her, anticipation humming in my veins. Skimming a look over her, I took in the simple black wrap-style dress and knee boots, in a murderous red. "I'm going to have a serious boot fetish by the time I leave New York."

Her cheeks colored. "Blame the weird weather. I'm ready for sandals and sundresses."

"Then I'll have a thing for sandals and sundresses." Meeting her gaze, I smiled. "Take your panties off."

She tensed, her lashes flickering in surprise while color flooded her cheeks. "I guess we're starting our lessons right away."

"Yes. Take them off."

"Here?" She licked her lips. Holding up a bag, she said, "I've...uh...the food?"

"Go put it in the kitchen. Then come back out here and let me watch as you take off your panties."

Instead of replying, she turned and walked into the kitchen. I played to keep my hands busy more than anything else. The second they weren't occupied, I'd have them on her, and I wanted to draw out everything about this night.

Curious, I waited until she returned to the living room. "The other night, you said it was the first time you'd enjoyed sex in a while. Why is that?"

She smoothed her hands down her skirt—but made no move to pull it up or remove her panties.

"Ah...bad luck? I haven't clicked well with guys lately," she said. She made an attempt at a casual shrug, but it fell flat, the movement stiff and awkward.

"We clicked." Sliding my gaze down and appreciating the curves under the sexy dress, I said, "Panties."

She huffed a small breath and then reached under the dress.

"Slowly," I said, my hands settling into a slow ballad, one of the first I'd written. "Good sex starts with the build-up...the anticipation."

"The teasing, you mean." Her voice hitched, but she did as ordered, her movements slowing. She swayed forward fluidly, so fucking female and sexy, as she pushed the panties down, the skirt demurely hiding her hands while providing a teasing view of her cleavage.

"You call it teasing. I call it build-up. Some might consider it foreplay. Are your nipples hard?"

She sucked in a breath and froze, her impossibly gorgeous eyes locked on my face. Her voice was a tight whisper as she answered, "Yes."

"Good. Drop the panties, Jazz, and come sit next to me."

The lacy blue scrap lay on the floor a few seconds later, and I moved over a couple of inches to allow her more room on the bench. "How wet are you?"

A sound caught between a squeak and a laugh escaped her. "Trent..."

"Answer the question." I studied her, taking in the heat-hazed expression on her face, her eyes glassy. "It's part of the deal, pet."

Her lips parted. She licked them, then haltingly whispered, "Very."

"Good. I'm going to tell you what I plan to do tonight. I'm not into giving my subs pain, so you don't have to worry about that. But as this progresses, I will push you to your limits, maybe beyond them. If you're not comfortable, or if you've had enough, you say the word, and I'll stop."

"Is this the safe word thing?"

"Yes." Over the past few years, BDSM had been talked about some. I wasn't surprised she knew about safe words. "You should choose a word you'll remember."

"Piano," she blurted out, gaze tracking to the baby grand in front of us before returning to mine. "I won't forget that one."

"Neither will I. One thing I do enjoy—a lot—is binding my subs. Another? Blindfolds."

"Okay." She cleared her throat. "I think I can handle all of that."

"I also want to spank your perfect ass while I fuck you."

Another one of those soft sounds fell from her lips, but it was closer to a whimper this time.

"What idea made you excited, Jazz?"

At first, I wasn't sure she'd answer. Then she did, and I wanted to bend her over and come into her right there. "All of it. I can't believe I'm saying this, but I like all of it. A lot."

Control always came easily for me. But right now, it was slipping through my grasp.

"Here's another idea I hope you'll like—I want to spread the cheeks of your ass and push inside you there—with my cock. Has anybody ever fucked your ass, pet?"

"No." It was a bare rasp of sound.

"Good. I can't wait to be the first." Rising, I held out a hand to her. "Let's go eat."

THE CHINESE TAKE-OUT WAS GREAT, and I'd hoped a meal would give me some time to cool down and breathe, but no such luck. I couldn't think of anything except Jazz naked under her pretty black dress, of the soft, aroused moan she made as I told her I wanted to tie her up, spank her, then fuck her ass.

I wanted to do all three things—now—*right* now, but I knew better. She was interested enough that I wouldn't have to be gentle through every step. Still, I couldn't go straight from vanilla sex to tying her up so I could turn her ass pink before stretching her wide and teaching her how to take a man's cock up the hot, snug tightness of her anus.

The sexual tension stretched between us was taut, the air heavy.

When I rose from my chair, she jumped.

"Any second thoughts?" I asked softly. As much as I loved breaking in a new sub, I wanted somebody truly willing.

"No." Her cheeks were still flushed as she watched me circle the table, her intense blue-violet eyes darkened to the color of the eastern sky as twilight settled. "I'm nervous, but I'm not backing out."

"Because you want a baby."

She pushed aside her empty plate and drew in a deep breath, then released it slowly. "I want you to uphold your end of the bargain, but I'm also...curious. Very curious."

"Good." I offered my hand, and she accepted, rising from the chair with fluid grace despite her nerves. She licked her lips, her gaze drifting to my mouth.

"Do you want to kiss me?"

"Yes." Her breaths shuddered, making her breasts rise and fall erratically.

"Take off your dress, and your bra. Then ask me."

Her eyes widened slightly, and then she pulled up

the dress. This time I didn't have to tell her to go slowly. She went with such seductive leisure I was tempted to push her hands aside and do it myself. By the time she was naked in front of me, wearing only her vivid red boots. I was rock hard and ready to fuck.

She stepped closer. "Can I kiss you now?"

"Yes." But when she went to lean in, I pushed my hand into her hair and fisted it, holding her just a breath away. 'You can kiss my cock, Jazz."

"I...oh. Okay."

"But not until after I've tied you up."

IT HAD BEEN a long time since I'd taken this much pleasure with a sub. Some of it could have been because everything was so new to Jazz, and each gasp, each small whimper that escaped her when I paused to pinch her nipple or slide a hand between her thighs, was like throwing napalm on a blazing inferno.

But not all of it.

Some of it was from *her*. Despite her nerves, she had this way of watching me, that told me she knew how much this aroused me.

It was hot as fucking hell.

Now, bound and kneeling in front of me, she looked like a woman straight out of my most erotic fantasies.

Her dark hair spilled around her shoulders in loose, tousled waves, the ends barely long enough to flirt with her nipples.

Those nipples were tight, hard buds, intensely pink against the pale softness of her breasts. Her tits were

SERVING THE MAESTRO

driving me to distraction, too. My hands ached to touch and stroke, my mouth watered to taste.

I held back, keeping my hands in my pockets as I circled her, touching her only to test the bonds restraining her wrists.

There was another set of restraints within reach, this set designed for her ankles. Once her ankles were bound, I could hogtie her using a connecting bar or a chain.

I hadn't ruled the idea out, but it would come later.

After.

In front of her once more, I pulled a black scarf from my pocket.

"One last thing."

Her mouth parted as I used the silky length of material as a blindfold, erratic breaths coming hard and fast.

When I undid the zipper of my jeans, she stopped breathing altogether for several long moments.

"Breathe, pet," I told her. "I can't have you hyperventilating."

She gave a jerky nod. "Yeah, ok."

"Say yes, sir." I pressed my hand against my election, then shoved my clothing down and out of the way, freeing my aching cock. "Yes, sir, or yes, master."

She hesitated.

You're rushing it. I knew that but couldn't seem to stop.

"If I call you sir, do I get to kiss your cock?"

The punch of sexual need hit me hard, almost laying me out flat. Pushing my hand back into her hair, I fisted it and tugged gently, urging her to lift her face to mine.

"Call me sir, and suck my cock, Jazz...do it well, and I'll spank that gorgeous ass of yours as a reward."

Her lips bowed up. "It almost sounds like you get all the rewards...*sir*."

"You're going to be a brat," I murmured, easing my hold on her hair. I gripped my erection with my free hand and guided it to her mouth. "Open."

As she did so, my brain imploded. The way she slid her tongue out, licked the head of my cock before taking it in, the way she sucked on me before moving to take more of me into her mouth.

She pulled back—too soon—then started forward again.

At first, she moved tentatively, despite her boldness, and I suspected she hadn't done this all that much, either. Did that mean she hadn't had many guys go down on her? I'd have to remedy that, too.

Maybe next time. Hogtied.

That mental image had me shuddering, and I released my cock to cup her head in both hands. She stiffened, and I made myself wait, see what she'd do.

The muffled moan in her throat sent a trail of fire racing up my spine. "You like having me fuck your mouth like this?"

She awkwardly nodded her head.

"Good. Because I think I'm going to do it often." Holding her still, I thrust into her waiting mouth, keeping the movements shallow, watching her face flush below the blindfold, vaguely aware of her labored breaths, the musk of her arousal...and how close I was to coming in her mouth.

Pulling back at the last second, I scooped her up and carried her to the bed, turning her so that she bent over the edge. Kicking her legs apart, I asked, "Ready to be fucked?"

"Please..." It was a desperate whisper, and her body trembled, flushed with her own need to come.

Not saying anything else, I thrust in, hard and deep.

She arched her spine, my name coming from her in a ragged cry.

Her pussy was wet and snug, clenching around me as I buried myself to the balls.

Wet as rain, soft as silk.

No condom. For the first time in my life, I was fucking a woman without protection—and she felt so fucking perfect.

Control shattering, I groaned and gripped her bound wrists in one hand, her hip in the other, and began to move.

The sounds of hard, frenzied sex—a rough, *primal* music filled the air, flesh slapping against flesh, her cries, my ragged breaths.

It wasn't a surprise to feel her body tighten, on the verge of orgasm in what seemed like seconds. She was turned on throughout dinner, and binding her hands had only added to her arousal.

What was surprising was how close I was to following her.

And when she started to come, I didn't hold back. Hitching her up by the hips to deepen my angle, I rode her. Warning tingles raced down my spine, and hit my balls.

And then I was coming with her, harder than I'd ever come in my life.

SEVERAL HOURS AND A SHOWER LATER, I sipped from a bottle of sparkling water and stared out over the New York City skyline.

Jazz had left an hour earlier.

I'd wanted her to stay, had even had the question forming on my lips when she looked back at me over her shoulder when we were still in the bed.

"Thank you," she'd said, polite and...professional. Almost devoid of the warmth I'd started to associate with her.

Thank you.

She'd thanked me for a donation of sperm, and I was lying there, breathing hard and my dick warming up for round two.

No. It wasn't a good idea to ask Jazz to stay the night, even if the bed had felt a little empty once she was gone.

It had been a while.

That was the reason I was off-balance.

And everything with her felt a little different because...well, the rules were different. Before, whenever I was training a new sub, I always had this subtle tension, a knowledge that if any woman showed too much attraction, I'd have to end things. There had always been extra attention focused on prevention, especially since I'd found out about the circumstances that led to my birth.

My *father*, if you wanted to call him that, had been nothing but a sperm donor as well. But not because he'd had an agreement with my mother the way I had with Jazz.

No, *my* dad was a rich piece of shit who couldn't

keep it in his pants. I'd only met him once, not long after discovering my health condition—*renal agenesis*. Even though the specialists had told me it likely wasn't hereditary, I'd wanted to know for sure. Or hell, maybe I'd just used it as an excuse.

Regardless, I tracked down my father to meet him. To his credit, he'd seemed sincerely sorry for not knowing anything about me to his credit. Of course, he had a fuckton of other kids, many of which had been born to women he'd only known a night or two, so it wasn't like he didn't know how all that could work out.

I took another sip of water, and wished it was something stronger.

Ever since I'd learned about my father—and all the half-siblings I had—I'd been obsessive about protection during sex. I'd also been careful to break things off any time a woman started to show any sign she might feel something more than sexual attraction.

So why the hell was Jazz's polite *thank you* bothering the fuck out of me?

TEN
JAZZ

Caught up in the contract I was reading, I shifted on my office chair. Wincing as my tender backside protested, I checked the time and was relieved to see how late it had gotten.

I wanted to get home and pull on a pair of soft pajamas.

"You look like you just smashed your finger in the drawer."

Looking up to see Cam in the doorway, I swallowed a curse. Feigning confusion, I asked, "What?"

She cocked a brow and leaned her shoulder against the doorframe. "You're hurting. What's wrong?"

"Nothing." When she kept staring, I protested again. "I'm fine. Just a little sore."

Even *that* wouldn't have been an issue if Trent hadn't decided he wanted to push the boundaries of our...relationship. I'd told him the BDSM thing stopped at the bedroom door. But once he told me what he'd wanted me to do, then whispered in my ear what he'd been thinking about if I did it, I couldn't stop.

And so what if I went to work without any panties?

That was tame compared to what he'd done before spreading me out on his bed last night and tying me down. He'd spanked me, using enough force that the blows had stung—and I'd loved every second of it. I'd loved it so much that when he shoved a pillow under my hips, then mounted me, I was on the verge of climax. His hard entry had pushed me right over—and he'd spanked me again, punishment for coming without permission.

My ass was sore.

And I couldn't wait to do it all over again. I couldn't believe how erotically charged everything was with Trent —even when he wasn't here with me, I felt him. In the way, my skirt irritated the sensitive skin of my butt, in the way air currents whispered up along my bare legs to caress the naked flesh between my thighs. *Everything*.

"Okay." Cam shut the door and strode over to the scooped seat, settling on the padded cushion and curling up with her feet tucked under her butt. "You're blushing now, and I'm not leaving until you spill. What's going on?"

Hesitating, I wondered what she'd say, then decided, what the hell. I was still confused over all of this. What was a best friend for if not to listen?

"I'm...involved with somebody," I said slowly.

"You're seeing somebody?" she asked, a grin lighting her face. "Oh, now, you must spill. Who is he? Do I know him?"

"I didn't say *seeing*. We're not dating." Nibbling on my lower lip, I tried to find the best way to explain, then realized the only way to do it was with the truth, plain and simple. "He's my neighbor. He's only in New York for a couple of months. And..."

The words lodged in my throat. Grabbing my thermal water bottle, I took a long drink, the icy cold a relief to the heat that was now scorching my face.

"We're having sex," I said bluntly.

"Oh." Cam blinked, clearly caught off-guard. "Well, sometimes it starts that way."

"No." I shook my head. "Sex is all this is, all it's going to be. We're not going to hook up and get together. Neither of us wants that."

Cam straightened in the seat, swinging her legs around, so her feet rested on the floor. She leaned forward, elbows on her knees, studied me closely, then shook her head. "You're not wearing that look because you're only having sex with a guy, Jazz. There's more to it. I can tell. I know you."

Closing my eyes, I let my head fall back against the padded chair. Thinking of the heat I felt with Trent and the deal we'd made, made my heart race. But I didn't *want* to be involved. He didn't want that, either.

"I want a baby, Cam," I said softly.

When she didn't say anything, I lifted my head and opened my eyes. My best friend had a worried look on her face, but there was a glimmer of understanding in her eyes.

"I want a baby," I said again. "But I'm not having much luck in the relationship area. I don't want to settle for somebody who doesn't make me happy just so I can have a chance at motherhood."

"So...this neighbor of yours...does he know you're

using him for his...bodily fluids?" Cam was blushing now, her cheeks as hotly scarlet as mine.

"Of course." Now that I'd opened up about it, it was easier, I realized. "I told him what I wanted, that he'd never be responsible for anything if I got pregnant. And he agreed. He agreed to get tested, we signed a contract and everything."

"And he gets...what?" Cam still looked confused. "Sex?"

I hesitated too long. Even to my ears, my flippant response sounded flat. "What...he's a guy, isn't that enough?"

"What are you giving him, Jazz?" Cam demanded.

Well, hell. Shooting a look at the door, I focused back on her. "Keep your voice down. And before I tell you, you have to promise me you won't tell *anybody*."

"Spill, Jazz. *Now*."

"He's a Dom," I said, exasperated.

Cam frowned. Then she blinked. Then she opened her mouth. Closed it. Blinked again. Finally, she asked, in a faint voice, "He's a...what?"

I'd just managed to successfully shock my best friend—and Cam wasn't all that easily surprised. "A *Dom*. As in *Dominant*, from BDSM."

She shook her head and tapped the ball of her hand against her temple. "I'm not hearing you right."

"Are you not understanding?" I said, my tone taking on a teasing note while a nervous laugh built in my chest. "He's kinky, okay?"

"And how does *that* involve you with this deal you made?" she demanded, sounding strangled.

"Well..." I swallowed and lifted a shoulder. "He's not

from here, and he needed—*wanted* a sub while he's in town. So he's...teaching me."

"Fuckballs." Cam shook her head and lurched up out of the chair to pace to the nearest window. Our office space wasn't anything super-fancy, but we did have windows—mine facing out over Broadway, while Cam had the back view—that featured the buildings behind us, and the little private garden maintained by our building manager and available for private events. Bracing her hands on the window, she stared outside, thinking so furiously, I could practically see the steam coming out of her ears.

"Stop worrying about me."

Cam turned and gaped at me. "Stop *worrying*? My quiet, level-headed best friend suddenly goes off the deep end and hooks up with a master kinkhead in exchange for some sperm, and you want me to *stop worrying*?"

Sighing, I flipped the contract I'd been reading face-down and rose. I didn't go to her, though. Instead, I leaned against the desk. My tender butt didn't appreciate it, but I hid my discomfort and forged on. "He's kinky in bed. That doesn't mean anything other than *he's kinky in bed*. As for me wanting a baby...Cam, you've known this for a while."

"There are sperm banks," she said with a scowl.

"I know. And they sound horrible. Clinical. Cold. I wanted to know something about the man who helps me conceive a child, so I can at least have *something* to tell that child when they get older. Is that so wrong?"

Cam turned back to me, her face softening. "Of course, it's not. But...Jazz..." She stopped, clearly still not sure of how she felt. "You're only thirty-five. We don't put single women on the shelf these days and write off any chances of them having a family, you know."

"It's my choice."

She closed her eyes.

"It's my choice," I said again. I walked to her, took her hands in mine and squeezed. "I've never been all that good at relationships—except for you, stubborn weirdo that you are."

She managed a smile then, the old joke between us a familiar one.

"None of the guys I've met in the past few years have done anything for me," I said. Brushing a stray lock of hair back, I pulled her close, hugged her. "And I'm tired of wondering if I'm ever going to have a chance at what I want."

"A baby," she said softly.

"Yeah." With a half-shrug, I said, "If there were more guys out there like Danny, maybe I'd try a little longer, see if I couldn't find that fairy tale sort of ending like you have. But I keep getting toads."

"This neighbor...is he a toad?"

No. Trent was definitely not that. But he wasn't my prince, either.

"He's not a toad, but he's never going to be Mr. Right. I don't think a Mr. Right exists for me...and I'm fine with that."

I WAS STILL BROODING over that comment several days later.

Each time I'd been with Trent until now, it had been

at his place. It was easier that way, for me, at least. I could control when I came, when I left, and maintain the structure of this strange, not-relationship relationship.

But a few hours earlier, just after I woke, he showed up at my door, knocking.

I opened the door to find him standing there, arms laden with take-out.

Breakfast and all of it was still hot.

Belly stuffed full of delicious French toast and bacon, I found myself on the couch with him, watching movies for half the afternoon.

After a superhero flick which we both loved, a comedy he loved and I'd never seen, he found another movie—one I only heard of in passing.

Not long into it, I found myself breathing hard while my nipples went tight, and the flesh between my thighs grew wet.

And Trent was watching. *Me*, not the provocative movie he'd put on—*me*.

I have no idea how we went from lounging on the couch to him sprawled over me with his head between my thighs and my hands in his hair, but the man did things with his tongue and mouth and fingers that should be illegal.

Two climaxes later, he kissed his way up my body and flipped me onto my knees before coming into me, deep and hard.

"I want your mouth on my cock next," he said in my ear.

I moaned, pushing back against him.

"I'm going to fuck your pretty mouth until I explode,

and you'll love it, won't you, Jazz?" he asked, gripping my hip and holding me still for his possession.

"Yes."

He spanked me. "Yes, what?"

"Yes, master." The words were a broken whisper that rose into a wail as he slammed into me so hard it should have hurt. Should have, but it didn't, and soon, I was coming, clamping down on him hard as my body convulsed and jerked in orgasm.

He came, too, the hot wash of his semen flooding me.

I didn't have time to catch my breath before he pulled out of me and flipped me, dragging me up until I was propped up between the back of the couch and the arm. He fisted his cock in his hand, still hard, wet from his orgasm and me, and braced his free hand on the back of the couch.

"Open your mouth, pet. I already told you what I want."

I opened for him, watching him with dazed eyes as he fed me one slow inch after the other. He shuddered and came to a stop, already knowing my limit. Hand moving to my hair, he began to move, slow, shallow movements at first, giving me time to adjust.

My heart was pounding, and I was nowhere close to catching my breath.

But I wanted to see him shaken. I wanted that hard, cool exterior to fall apart to see if any of this affected him.

No. You don't want anything more than the physical.

I kicked the thought away, but it resurfaced.

I wanted more...so much more.

And when Trent shuddered above me, eyes closing,

something inside me, something greedy and deeply female, went hot with that small victory.

I WAS ALMOST asleep when I felt him leave the bed.

He was quiet, but feeling him pull away woke me quickly, and I sat up as he came around the bed to sit next to me.

"Did I wake you?" he asked.

"I wasn't quite asleep yet," I said, not really lying, but not telling the whole truth.

He pushed something into my hand. "You seemed to enjoy the last time I had you do something outside of bed. I thought perhaps we'd do it again."

My mouth went dry, and I looked down at what I held. "I...um...oh."

He leaned in and bit my lower lip. "Is that a yes?"

Heat, unlike anything I'd ever known spread through me as I met his eyes. Slowly, I nodded.

ELEVEN

TRENT

THE MUSIC IN MY HEAD WAS COMING OUT ALL wrong.

It wasn't bad music.

It was pretty fucking amazing, and I needed to show it to Stephen. It was some of my best work. But it wasn't the work I was being paid to do, which was a problem.

The music pouring free was richly, hotly seductive, a primal soundtrack for the thoughts and fantasies coming non-stop ever since I'd left Jazz alone with the little toy I'd bought for her.

The butt plug wasn't a large one. I was tempted to stay and show her how to use it—then fuck her again, but I'd left, sticking to our unspoken agreement that we wouldn't spend nights together.

That unspoken agreement was starting to annoy the hell out of me because I wanted more time with her.

I didn't like dishonesty, even from myself, and truthfully...

I wanted more time with Jazz.

I liked her.

It wasn't just the sex.

I liked *her*.

The music flowing from me suddenly stopped, a harsh discordant note making me wince before I stilled my hands and glared at the baby grand as if it was responsible for my sour mood.

With a scowl, I collected the sheets of music I'd done for the project and went through them, trying to focus once more on the music I was being paid to interoperate.

I pushed on for another hour and managed to finish a piece I'd been working on for days—the one I'd wanted to have done the previous week.

It was better than nothing.

And it was all I'd be good for until I had my hands on Jazz.

Looking at the time, I blew out a breath.

She wouldn't be home from work for a good six hours.

Six hours before I could push up the vivid pink skirt she'd been wearing when I caught a glimpse of her in the lobby this morning. Six hours before I could push down her panties and see the base of the plug, I'd told her to wear today.

Six hours before I could push into her pussy and feel her clench tight around me.

"Fuck this shit," I muttered.

If she wasn't opposed to going without panties, or wearing an anal plug to work, then maybe she wouldn't have a problem with me showing up at her office.

I RECOGNIZED the cute blonde who appeared as I stepped into Jazz's office.

She looked me up, then down, the piercing intellect in her eyes a warning to tread carefully. "Hi...I'm Cam. Can I help you?"

"Yes, I'm looking for Jasmine." I was out of my mind for doing this. I'd forgotten. Jazz worked with her best friend. And I'd just walked right into the lion's den.

"Oh, so you must be—"

"Trent!"

The sound of Jazz's voice cutting across the broad, open floorplan was a staggering relief. Her friend Cam, on the other hand, looked irritated.

"Saved by the bell," Cam said. Then she patted my arm. "Don't worry. We'll come back to the inquisition."

The comment had me staring after her. But then Jazz was in front of me, her cheeks flushed and her eyes bright.

"I...ah, what brings you here?"

A thousand things came to mind, most dirty and inappropriate for an audience. I went with the safe option and held up the cups of coffee. "I was in the area and decided to see if you needed a caffeine hit."

She bit her lip, then released the abused flesh.

It took a lot of restraint not to echo the action.

Angling her head to the side, she said, "Come into my office."

I smiled.

She blushed even hotter.

I behaved as we crossed the wooden floors, nodding

to the few who attempted eye contact, ignoring those who pretended not to notice.

Once inside her office, after she'd closed the door and leaned against it, I faced her. "You don't get many visitors."

"Outside of those who have something to do with business?" She twisted her lips and tugged them to the side. "About next to...zero."

I leaned in and bit her lower lip like I'd wanted a few seconds earlier.

She shivered.

"Want me to leave?"

"No." Her breath came out in a shudder. "The nice thing about running the place—I can take a break when I want."

Straightening, I looked around. The office space wasn't huge, but it wasn't small. Commanding a row of windows that looked out on Broadway in a nice section of SoHo, I imagined the place cost a pretty penny. I'd already known Jazz and her partner Cam were successful, but this emphasized just *how* successful.

"So...we have privacy?" She nodded. I smiled and watched as her breathing hitched. She nodded, eyes going hazy with heat. "Bend forward over the desk."

Her cheeks flushed but she did as ordered. "Like this, master?"

The glint in her eyes made me want to smile, even as it made me want to spank her. That she submitted to me at all was a gift, and she subconsciously knew that already. Some subs relied heavily on their chosen Doms, while others did it for the sheer kink.

I was still trying to understand why Jazz had chosen

to give in, especially when it came to crossing that line she'd drawn—outside the bedroom—but it was a choice she'd made.

Crossing to her, I admired the view, then moved close enough to press against her, lowering my head to kiss the nape of her neck, left bare by the way she'd scooped her hair up for the day.

She shivered.

"You like that."

"Yes," she said in a raspy whisper.

I kissed her again, then nipped at the flesh between neck and shoulder, listening to the soft cry before she managed to smother it.

Stepping back, I caught the hem of her skirt, a rich, vivid pink that made her soft skin glow. It had a flirty style, swaying around her knees, making it easy to push up. The panties underneath were a lacy scrap of fabric, almost the same shade of pink. Tugging them to the side, I sank into the seat and stared at the base of the plug I'd bought.

"How does it feel?"

She squirmed. "Strange. It hurt a little at first, but not now."

"Spread your legs."

She hesitated, her head rising. She was checking the door.

"You'll just have to bite your lip when you want to scream," I told her. At least for now.

With a shuddering sigh, she spread her legs.

She tried to close them a split second later as I pushed two fingers into her cunt and twisted them.

A broken, muffled sound escaped her, and she rose onto her toes, her back arching in reaction.

I covered her mouth and pulled her against me. "No, Jazz. You can't scream, unless you want them to know I'm finger-fucking you in here. Should we let them know?"

I didn't personally care, but I didn't like the idea that she might have to deal with repercussions from her employees.

Furiously, she shook her head, and I eased the pressure of my hand over her mouth. "I should have brought a gag. Would you like me to gag you the next time I fuck you?"

She didn't move.

I kissed her cheek and screwed my fingers into her pussy. "Not certain?"

That earned me a hesitant nod. "Okay...we can play with that later. For now..." I kicked her legs farther apart and nudged her back over the desk. "You're tighter now....feel how tight you squeeze my fingers now?"

She moaned in response and pushed back on me as I withdrew my fingers, clamping down when I thrust them back in.

Her entire body tensed, her muscles quivering.

"So close...you're so close, Jazz." Her pussy tightened, luscious and wet, and my dick pounded with the need to be inside her. But not yet. She shuddered as I slowly spread my fingers wide inside her cunt, then twisted them. "Don't come yet. Not...yet."

"Trent..."

Her ragged gasp was hoarse, raw with desperation.

"Not yet," I said again. She pushed hard against me, her ass a plump, tempting curve.

Too tempting.

Pulling back, I jerked at my zipper, and the button on my trousers. She whimpered again, lifting one hand around to reach for me. I caught her by the wrist. "No. I haven't given you permission to touch me."

"Please, sir. Let me...*oh*..."

I barely managed to get my hand over her mouth in time to smother the sharp cry, my other hand gripping her hip as I slammed into her.

"Bad girl." I bit her earlobe. "You're supposed to be quiet."

"I'm sorry, master. Please..." The words were quiet, her moans feverish.

I spanked her hard and felt her clench so tight around me that I thought I'd die from the pleasure of it. My cock swelled, jerked inside her, and she whimpered again.

I covered her mouth once more and whispered against her ear, "Do I have to keep doing this?"

She nodded, shuddering against me.

"Good." I bit her earlobe once more, then spanked her. "I like it."

She bounced onto her toes as I drove into her again, her pussy made so much tighter by the plug. I couldn't wait to stretch her until she was ready to take my cock in her ass. Every second of that preparation would be torturous perfection.

She tensed, her pussy contracting around me while her body grew hotter.

"Don't come." I licked her neck. She jolted as I spanked her, then moaned as I released her mouth and urged her forward until she was bent over her desk.

"Cover your mouth. I want to fuck you good and deep now, pet."

"Yes, sir." She moved to obey, and once I saw that she had her mouth covered, I took her hips, hauled her to the edge of her desk, and thrust. Hard. The impact had my hips slapping against her, the sound of ragged breaths, all of it rising until the music of our lust drowned out everything else. I stared at the flared base of the plug between her cheeks and felt my climax racing closer.

"Come, baby," I told her. "Come for me."

She shuddered, her pussy convulsing and milking me almost immediately, a sign of just how hard she'd been fighting to wait for my consent.

The knowledge filled me with savage pleasure, intense and hot, unlike anything I'd ever known.

Then, it hit me. I might be in a little bit of trouble.

TWELVE

TRENT

AFTER MAKING ONE LAST ADJUSTMENT TO THE FINAL song, I played it through again. Eyes closed, I let the melody wrap around me, the notes of the song twining together to form a story of sorts.

The first month in New York had flown by, and I would be turning in the first draft for review later in the afternoon. They'd no doubt have a request for changes, but it felt good to have accomplished something. Stephen had been right that this wasn't exactly the kind of job I normally enjoyed. I preferred to create the music entirely myself, and while I'd done good work with the score, I'd built on the creation of another musician.

But it was solid material, and the pay was nothing to sneeze at.

Plus...there was Jazz.

If I hadn't come to New York, I wouldn't have met her, and that would have been a damn tragedy. Not just for the sexual pleasure. She actually inspired me. I couldn't remember the last time, music had come to me so effortlessly.

The silence engulfed me, and I realized I'd stopped playing.

Blowing out a breath, I shoved a hand through my hair. Concentration shot, I didn't fight it when my thoughts centered on Jazz.

Fuck, I was addicted to her.

It had been nearly a week since I'd last seen her.

She wasn't ghosting me or anything. She'd let me know last Sunday she probably wouldn't have much time until the coming weekend—Cam had accepted a last-minute project, which meant working long hours to get it done.

We had a weekend planned ahead of us—for once a weekend that wasn't the two of us fucking our brains out. The fact that I was looking forward to it was something I didn't let myself think about too hard, although I knew I should.

But we were adults, unattached, and we liked each other. So what if we spent some time at a movie, or out to eat—things that weren't included in our baby-making deal?

Roughly a month from now, I'd head back to California, whether or not Jazz was pregnant, and that would be the end of it.

The end of this crazy thing with Jazz.

No more movie marathons, no more cooking her breakfast and watching her sit at the island while trying to coax her sleepy brain to wake up. No more seeing that playful light in her eyes—right before she submitted to me with a cry, the word *master* a broken moan on her lips and sexual surrender turning her body hot and molten.

The sound of my phone ringing caught me off guard, and I swore, shoving back from the piano.

Recognizing the number for the building's concierge desk, I answered.

"Good afternoon, Mr. Dixson."

"Hey, Howard." I believed that was his name. "How are you?"

"I'm well, sir. And you?"

"Good, thanks." Walking over to the windows lining one wall, I stared outside.

"Wonderful. Sir, you have a visitor—Ms. Avery Gilmore."

"What?" I frowned, wondering how she'd tracked me down. "Okay, send her on up."

What in the hell was Avery doing here?

I hadn't seen her in...I did the mental math, then scowled as I realized it had been over a year. I'd known Avery for more than a decade, ever since I took my first step into the world of BDSM. She'd introduced me to a whole new world I'd never even imagined. We hadn't been together for years, but we were still friends. And she was, until recently, the only woman I couldn't say no to.

What was she doing here?

I was still trying to figure it out when the doorbell rang.

Avery beamed at me from over the threshold, and when she stepped forward to hug me, I automatically opened my arms to accept. "Avery, hey."

Her scent was familiar, as were the lush curves, the soft curls, and the smile she gave me after stepping back.

There had been a time when just the sight of her was enough to bring me to aching readiness. A hundred memories were stirred by the scent of her, and how she'd looked stretched out on a bed, with her round, curvy ass flushed red from a spanking.

Not now.

"Hi, Trent."

"Avery." For the first time in years, I felt...awkward. Although Jazz wasn't home, I had to fight the urge to peek out the door toward her apartment.

What the fuck?

Guilt.

What in the fuck did I have to feel guilty for? Jazz and I weren't in a relationship outside of my agreement to help try to impregnate her—and her agreement to be my sub.

We'd never even discussed exclusivity. That was for a monogamous romantic relationship. We definitely didn't have that.

"Trent?"

Forcing a smile, I shook my head. "Sorry. Brain's still in work mode."

"I figured." Lips curving in a fond smile, she kissed my cheek. "You're so talented. I don't know how you slip into this...creative state and do what you do."

"That's a nice way of saying I lose track of everything and everybody while I'm working on projects," I said with a smile. I stepped back and gestured for Avery to come in. "What brings you to New York?"

She sauntered in, her head swinging back and forth as she took in the apartment where I'd been living for the past month. It wasn't until she reached the sitting area of the open floor plan and sat on the edge of the couch that she answered.

"You do, baby." She crossed her legs and gave me a slow smile filled with sensual promise.

I stood by the door, feeling stupidly awkward. Turning away from her, I took a deep breath and slowly closed the door.

"Yeah?" Facing her again, I started for the sitting area. I took the fat armchair across from her rather than the couch, hoping she wouldn't notice my intentions to steer clear of her. "And why is that?"

"I thought maybe you could use a friend." She offered a playful, warm smile. "I'm hearing from some mutuals you've been in a funk lately."

I had a feeling it would be something like that. The scene we both belonged to wasn't necessarily *small,* but it was small enough, and I'd spent a lot of time with Avery. Next to Stephan, my relationship with her was the only one that had lasted more than a few weeks.

"A funk, huh?"

Her eyes softened a fond smile on her face. "You're not denying it. We all go through...periods."

"I just hit a rut with my music, Avery." With a one-shoulder shrug, I glanced toward the piano, thought of the project I was working on and of the new music, something of my own I was slowly putting together. "I'm working through it."

She didn't look convinced.

"I'm fine, Avery." More than fine, really. Staring absently at the far end of the couch where Avery sat, my thoughts drifted to the afternoon Jazz and I had shared, the movie marathon we'd enjoyed—I'd sat in that spot right there, Jazz cuddled against me, and it was one of the best afternoons of my life.

"So you haven't been suffering from some...ennui?"

"Ennui? You think my life lacks excitement?" Laughing, I relaxed back in the chair and stretched my legs. "Maybe I did, for a while. But I worked through it, and I'm good now. It's sweet of you to worry, but I'm fine. How did you even know where I was?"

Her eyes crinkled at the corners. At forty, she was still gorgeous. When she smiled, she was stunning.

But that smile didn't hit me like it once had.

"I sort of tricked it out of Stephen." She rolled her eyes. "I wasn't sure what floor you were on, but the concierge was kind enough to call up."

"Yeah?" I grinned at her, well aware of how much of a flirt she was. "How much did you butter him up?"

"I barely even smiled," she said in a lofty tone. She settled more comfortably on the couch, looking around with open curiosity. "This is a lovely apartment. You did nicely getting this job, honey."

She wasn't lying. "How long are you here for?"

"Only a few days. I just wanted to check on you, see if I could cheer you up." She lifted a brow, "You don't seem *too* down."

"Like I said, I'm fine. Where're you staying?"

She winked. "With you, silly. I'm sure you won't find me an imposition?"

Fuck. "Of course not." I most certainly did, but I couldn't tell her that.

"Oh, lovely! Can you show me around?" She clapped her hands, then stood, walking over to the wall of windows beyond the baby grand piano. "This *view*..."

Once she wasn't looking at me, I sighed and shoved a hand through my hair.

Fuck, fuck, fuck.

The timing of this was...*fuck.*

As Avery continued to talk about the view, asking questions and then moving on before I could answer, I shoved to my feet.

"You want something to drink, Avery?" I asked. "I'm going to grab some water."

"That sounds lovely, Trent." She still had her gaze locked on the view outside the window.

Pulling my phone from my pocket, I headed into the kitchen. The *timing*. Frustration twisted through me, and on the heels of it, guilt. All the plans I'd made for the upcoming weekend, and just like that, everything fell apart.

I couldn't tell Avery I already had plans.

Fuck. I pinched the bridge of my nose as the reality settled in.

I was starting to feel something for Jazz, and I had no right. No right at *all*.

I had to cancel my plans with Jazz—and somehow, I had to stop feeling these...*feelings* for her.

The painful ache in my chest spread and grew heavier.

Fuck it all, and fuck me, too. I'd gone and done the worst thing I could have possibly done and started wanting something more from Jazz.

Things between us had moved beyond the physical. Yes, she was fucking *hot* in bed. But it was more than that. At least for me.

THIRTEEN
JAZZ

THE PHOTOGRAPHY EXHIBIT AT THE SMALL GALLERY not far from where I worked, didn't hold my attention as much as I'd hoped.

Typically, I would have been enraptured. I loved photography, and on the rare vacations I took—when Cam all but pushed me out of the office and locked the doors—I went to scenic places that fed the creative part of my soul that didn't get out to play often.

Yet here I was, walking around a gallery where the portraits and landscapes were staggeringly beautiful. And I was...disinterested.

When the gallery owner approached me for the *fifth* time, I decided to head for the exit. Yes, the photographs were gorgeous—and many were for sale—but I wasn't putting two grand down on any of them.

Out in the warm sunshine, I started in the direction of the subway.

I wasn't planning to go home. If I did that, I'd just think about Trent and our canceled weekend.

"Stop brooding," I muttered. It's one weekend. We still had almost four weeks together.

It wasn't as easy as that to push my sour mood aside.

I wanted to tell myself I was in a shitty mood because less *copulation* meant fewer chances for *conception*. But I knew better.

I...*liked* being with Trent.

The times when we weren't together and when I wasn't working, I was acutely aware of how empty my life had become. How empty it had always been, pretty much until I met Cam.

But Cam was going to be a mom soon.

She wouldn't stop being my friend, but the relationship between us had already changed several times over. First when she met Danny, then when she realized they were in love, and when she got pregnant. Neither of them made me feel like a third wheel, but I wasn't part of that unit. I never would be, not the kind of unit with Cam and me.

Being with Trent had filled a void inside me I hadn't even been aware of.

Yet what we had was only temporary.

Feeling a knot settle in my throat, I headed into a familiar restaurant and accepted a table near the open windows, the spring air a welcome breeze. When the server asked if I'd like anything to drink, I asked for a martini.

I needed a drink—and sex wasn't happening today, probably not tomorrow, either. So why the hell not?

"Jazz?"

At the sound of my name, I looked up and found a

good-looking man, shaggy brown hair framing a vaguely familiar face.

"Ah..." Shaking my head to indicate I didn't recognize him, I leaned back in my chair.

Then he smiled, and I knew.

"Oh, wow. Roger." Without thinking, I rose and hugged him.

He hugged me back and was still smiling when I pulled away, that familiar boyish grin almost the same as when we'd dated in high school.

"I thought that was you." His dark brown hair tumbled into his face, and he brushed back absently, then glanced at the other chair. "Are you expecting anyone?"

"No." I waved at the seat, more than happy to occupy myself with something other than my heavy thoughts. Maybe I'd luck out and *not* brood over Trent for a while. "Please. Join me. I'm just out killing time, enjoying the weather."

Roger grinned. "Same. I couldn't believe my luck when I saw you a few minutes ago. You look as beautiful as ever."

My cheeks heated, but I accepted the compliment with a smile. "It's been a while, hasn't it?"

"It has." He cocked his head to the side, studying me. "I don't remember seeing you at our fifteen-year reunion."

"I didn't go—not to any of them." With a self-conscious shrug, I added, "High school wasn't the worst time of my life, but it wasn't the easiest, either. Not with my mom and all."

His eyes softened. "I remember. Is she still about the same?"

"No." Swallowing past the knot in my throat, I started to speak, but the server returned my martini on the tray and two glasses of water. Waiting until she'd taken Roger's order for a beer, I sipped my martini. Once we were relatively alone, I met his eyes. "She was in a car accident a few years ago. Didn't make it."

"Shit. Jazz, I'm sorry."

"No, it's okay." Managing a smile, I said, "A part of her already died when my father left us behind. But enough about that. How have you been?"

Over the next hour, we talked about friends from high school and memories from our short dating relationship. I hadn't thought about Roger in years, but it was…easy, sitting there, chatting with him, and laughing about things I'd forgotten.

The dinner rush was starting by the time the server asked if we wanted a single or split tab.

"I'll take care of it," Roger said, giving me that familiar smile when I started to object. "Please, Jazz, let me. I was expecting a dull afternoon, and you made it so much better."

"Okay."

A few minutes later, as we walked down the sidewalk, Roger said, "You know, I've thought about you off and on over the years. A lot."

"Oh?" My cheeks heated as I looked over at him and saw the interest in his eyes.

"Yes."

A crowd came up out of the nearby subway entrance, and he stepped closer, using his body to shield mine. He stumbled when someone bumped into him, catching my arms as the movement jostled us closer.

"Sorry," he said, a one-sided smile tugging at his lips.
"Not a problem."

He slid his hands down my arms, caught my hands, and squeezed gently. Nerves pinched in my belly, but he didn't try to take my hand when he pulled away.

"Anyway...as I was saying. Yeah, I've thought about you quite a bit, Jazz, if I'm being honest."

From the corner of my eye, I glanced at him.

"Bumping into you today..." He sighed. "Well, now I'm wondering if it's a sign."

"A sign?" I slowed at the intersection ahead and turned to look at him.

"Yeah." He lifted a shoulder. "You've always been so practical, and I know destiny or fate is not your thing...but. Hell, I'm getting nervous. I don't suppose you'd be interested in...maybe giving things with us another go?"

SOAKING in my tub later that night, I replayed the afternoon in my head.

Roger hadn't called. I'd given him my number, not sure if he'd use it, nor if I wanted him to.

But my mind kept going back to Cam. She kept telling me there were nice guys out there, and I'd never really given any man I met a fair shot.

Thinking she might be right, I'd given Roger my number.

We had gotten along reasonably well in school, and today had been...easy. Fun.

I'd even been smiling as I exited the elevator.

Right up until I walked past Trent's door.

And I couldn't let Trent be the reason I turned down a nice guy if he called and asked me out.

Trent wasn't around forever. He only had another month here. And the thing between us was about me getting pregnant.

Whether or not that happened, Trent was leaving.

I realized that being with Trent had changed something in me. Maybe I *could* find a way to share my life with someone? If Roger called, didn't it at least make *sense* to give the relationship thing a try?

FOURTEEN
JAZZ

My phone buzzed as I walked into my building.

I offered a half-wave to the doorman and pulled out my phone. When I saw the message Roger sent, I found myself smiling.

He was a nice enough guy. No, he didn't make my heart race or anything, but that wasn't the only thing in the world that mattered, right?

Trying to convince myself, I stepped onto the elevator. I noticed a pretty—no, *gorgeous* woman all but trip into the car with me, laden with more shopping bags than I'd ever seen in my life.

Rich brown hair pulled into a high, tight ponytail swung around as she wobbled, trying to catch her balance. Without thinking, I grabbed her arm and steadied her. "Whoa," I said, hitting the button to stop the doors from closing.

She gave me a wide, friendly smile. "Thank you. I haven't been shopping out here in ages, and I kind of went a little overboard."

"So I see." Now that she was steady, I let the elevator button go and hit the one for my floor. "Where are you going?"

She told me, and I blinked, puzzled because I hadn't seen her before, and as far as I knew, nobody on my level had moved.

Then her comment clicked. *Haven't been shopping out here in ages.*

"Are you visiting?" I asked as the elevator whisked us up.

"Yes." A friendly smile curled her lips, but she watched the digitized panel over the door, the numbers whirling as we climbed higher. "My feet are *killing* me. Why on earth do we torture ourselves with shoes like these?"

Glancing down at the hot pink, high-heeled sandals that matched her flirty skirt, I suggested, "Mental instability?"

Her husky laugh brightened her face and her eyes. She was absolutely beautiful.

I bit back the urge to ask who she was visiting.

She pushed off the wall as the doors opened, juggling her bags. With a hand on the door, I waved her out. "Go on."

A bag fell, and I bent to pick it up, jerking my head out of range as she spun around, one more bag falling.

"Shit!"

"I'll get it," I said, grabbing the other one. The paper handle had torn away from the body of the sack, and I gathered the sides of it, lifting it that way. "Which way are you?"

She beamed at me. "You're so sweet."

I almost shoved the bags back at her when she stopped in front of Trent's door.

Trent.

She was here to see Trent.

The bottom of my stomach fell out.

My heart felt hollow.

She glanced at me with a smile trying to juggle the bags to reach her purse. "My boyfriend's in this one. He's in town working on a project, and I flew out here to surprise him."

"How lovely," I said, surprised to hear how...*normal* my voice sounded.

Boyfriend.

Trent was her boyfriend.

She dipped inside, putting her bags down on the table next to the door. I was staring numbly into the apartment as she turned to get the other bags, happily chatting away and thanking me for being so nice.

I didn't say anything. I had no idea what *to* say.

"Avery?"

I froze at Trent's voice, my face suddenly flaming hot.

"Hold on a minute, honey," she said, calling out over her shoulder.

I stepped out of his range of sight, not ready to see him.

But I forgot about the enormous decorative mirror inside the foyer. As Trent came closer to Avery, he filled that mirror. He had on pants, but no shirt.

A phone rang from somewhere deep inside the apartment, and he turned away.

"Gimme a minute," he said. "Stephen was supposed to call."

"I've got it all," she said, taking the bags from me

Avery. Her name was Avery, and she was Trent's girlfriend.

Still staring at the mirror as he walked away, I clenched my now empty hands into fists.

"It was nice meeting you," I said, turning and hurrying to my apartment before she drew Trent's attention to my presence.

I unlocked my door, slipped inside, and pressed my back to the solid surface, slowly sliding down until my butt hit the floor.

"What in the hell is wrong with me?" I whispered.

He was involved with somebody.

He'd lied.

I was angry. That's what was wrong.

But that wasn't it—and I knew it.

I wasn't angry—I was *hurt*. Anger might come later, and I'd welcome it because it would be better than this deep, wrenching betrayal that had struck me the second he'd turned around, and I'd seen the vivid red marks on his back in the mirror.

Marks that looked like the scratches a lover might give in bed.

FIFTEEN
TRENT

"What are you up to in here?"

The sound of Avery's voice, low and husky, had me closing my eyes for a brief second. Hot oil popped, and I focused back on the food I was fixing. "Cooking."

"Oh." It was almost too soft to hear. "I guess we aren't going out."

"I already told you about the situation with clubs here, Avery." Grabbing another carrot, I started to chop. "Things on the east coast aren't as laid back as in California. Since I've only got a little more time here, I'm not interested in the hassle of a background check and shit that comes with joining a private club."

"Awww..."

I didn't look. If I did, I'd see her playful pout. It hadn't ever annoyed me before, but I was annoyed now, and I hadn't even looked at her. "I've also got a major headache. If I don't eat something soon, it'll get worse."

"Okay. I didn't realize you weren't feeling great," she said, tone apologetic.

I glanced at her and managed a smile.

She'd pulled on the slinky black dress, connected in the front and back only by chains on the side. It fell a few inches below her butt, leaving long, curvy legs bare.

She looked beautiful and sexy, and I had absolutely no desire to touch her.

Focusing back on the food, I pushed the sautéing vegetables around.

"Maybe after we eat, I could give you a massage."

She came up behind me and slid her arms around my waist, but I caught one wrist with my free hand. "Cooking, Avery. Hot oil hurts like hell if it splatters on you."

She stiffened and jerked back. "Sorry."

The tight tone told me I'd pissed her off, possibly hurt her.

Setting my jaw, I forced myself to take a deep breath.

"I'm going to go watch TV," she said before I'd managed to get a grip on my short temper.

I didn't respond.

Not even when she lingered by the door.

Once she was out of the kitchen, I grabbed the scotch I'd poured earlier and tossed it back.

While we ate, we were going to have a talk. We should have done it yesterday when she arrived, but I sure as hell wasn't putting it off any longer.

AVERY DIDN'T COME into the kitchen to join me.

I never did hear the TV come on but hadn't been in the mood to check, nor had I felt like looking for her when she didn't respond after I first called her name.

By the time I'd finished my food and cleaned up, then put her plate in the fridge, it had been almost an hour since she'd walked away in a sulk. Hopefully, enough time for her to cool off, but if not, too bad. We were having that talk.

The late evening sun shone in the partially opened slats covering the window in the master bedroom, allowing more than enough light to see that she wasn't in there. A thin beam of light fell through the partially opened bathroom door, and I caught a familiar scent as I moved closer.

"Trent?"

Nudging the door open, I met her eyes.

Steam drifted up from the steaming hot bath, the water tinted a soft peach by one of the bath bombs she loved so much. That was the scent I'd detected. Leaning against the door frame, I kept my eyes on her face, well aware that she had adjusted her position, so her excellent breasts barely broke the deep water.

"Want to join me?" she asked.

"Perfect peach bubbles don't work for me as well as for you, Avery."

"We can always shower it off." Her lips curved, still stained with the wine-red lipstick she'd had on earlier. "We've done that before."

I shook my head and backed away. "You've got a plate in the fridge if you're hungry."

"Trent!"

I stilled but didn't look back at her. "Yeah?"

"I..." She sighed, the soft exhalation full of sadness. "Nothing. I'll be out soon."

"Take your time, Avery."

THIRTY MINUTES LATER, with a horror movie streaming, I heard her come out of my bedroom.

She paused at the end of the couch. "Gross. Why do you like these movies so much?"

"Classic battle between good and evil," I replied, although the movie did bore me to tears. But I wasn't above using the movie to send a subtle message.

Avery came to me and straddled me.

Okay, maybe I had been *too* subtle.

Placing my hands on her waist to keep her from pressing closer, I said, "Avery, no."

She covered my hands with hers and tried to nudge them higher.

"*Avery, no.*" She mocked my flat tone, her eyes boring into mine in a very *non*-submissive way, the edge in her voice showing lingering anger. "I fly all the way to make sure you're okay, and all I'm getting is *Avery, no*?"

"It was nice of you to come out here," I said, not letting my frustration color my voice. "If you'd like, I can cover the cost of the ticket. But you made that decision. I didn't ask you."

Her cheeks went hotly red with embarrassment. "I can pay for my own fucking ticket. I just want to know why you're ignoring me!"

She was all but naked and wearing a slinky red silk nightgown that only went an inch below her ass. It made *ignoring* her difficult. My body remembered hers, and as she pressed closer, my dick reacted.

"Ohhhh..." Her lids drooped, eyes going luminesce as

she leaned down and pressed her lips to mine. "I knew you still wanted me."

"I don't," I snapped.

It came out a lot harder than I'd intended.

Avery jerked back as if I'd slapped her.

Her lower lip trembled before she could stop it, and she clambered off my lap, smacking my hand away when I tried to steady her.

"Well, at least now I know you're ignoring me," she said, voice cracking. She crossed her arms over her chest and hunched her shoulders in. "Why didn't you just *tell* me that yesterday? What did I do? Am I too old for you now? Is that the problem?"

"Shit, Avery. No. It's not your age." Shoving to my feet, I paced away. "You're still one of the most beautiful women I've ever met."

She sniffed and the sound was watery. I knew she wasn't mollified. Nor was she acting—I'd hurt her. That had never been my intention.

"Then what's wrong with me?" she demanded.

"It's not you." Sighing, I turned and looked at her, feeling like a bastard. "It's *not* you. It's..." I hesitated, not even sure how to say it. I'd never fallen for a woman before, and it was...weird, trying to find the words. "I...met somebody."

She blinked.

When she didn't say anything, didn't ask anything, I continued. "I don't know exactly what's going on with me and her, but it doesn't feel right being with somebody else."

"Does she know...about you?" Avery cocked a brow, her voice steadier now.

"Yeah." Annoyed, I braced my hands on my hips and met the challenging look in her eyes with one of my own. "She knows. Even if she didn't, that would be my problem, my concern, not yours. But she does know, and it's not an issue."

"So she's in the life," Avery said coolly. When I didn't respond, she smirked. "I didn't think so. Trent, you *know* you'll never be happy with a woman who isn't also your submissive."

She walked over to me, hips swinging seductively, her nipples hard and stabbing in the lush red silk that covered them.

Placing a hand on my chest, she looked up at me. "You crave the pleasures you can only find with a woman like me."

Wrapping my hand around her wrist, I tugged, then lowered it back to her side. "I know what I need, Avery. I know what I want."

She didn't take the hint and leaned into me again, arms curving around my shoulders and her breasts flat against my chest, nipples stabbing into me.

"I know what you want…what you like. I love to give it to you. Let me show you." She kissed my neck. "Bend me over, Trent. Fuck me, make it hurt. Punish me."

The last words were spoken against my lips.

I curled my hands around her waist, then pushed her back, moving out of reach simultaneously. "No. It's over, Avery."

Even when this…thing between Jazz and me ended, I could never be satisfied with Avery again. I'd spent too much time with a woman I had feelings for—feelings that went deeper than friendship. Nothing else would be quite the same again.

"Trent—"

"Enough!" I held my hand up when she tried to come to me again. "I'm not doing this, Avery. And if you can't get that through your head, you need to leave!"

Her mouth fell open, eyes wide and shocked. "I...are you kicking me *out*?"

"No." Staring at her, angry and frustrated, I said, "I'm trying to make you understand something, but you're not listening. However, if you're going to keep pushing, if you won't respect the choice I've made, then you'll have to leave—and that's *your* call. Not mine."

Tears flooded her eyes.

She blinked rapidly to clear them, but a few escaped.

"Fuck you, Trent." She turned on her heel and strode away, her movements angry, her breaths ragged.

Swearing, I blew out a breath and spun to brace my hands on the mantle over the gas fireplace. The hurt I'd seen in her eyes gutted me. Avery meant a lot to me, always had.

But she was a friend now, nothing more. If she couldn't understand that...

I made the right call.

I knew that, but I still felt like a miserable mean son of a bitch.

SIXTEEN
JAZZ

WALKING PAST TRENT'S DOOR, I FORCED MYSELF NOT to look at it.

It had been two days since I'd seen the gorgeous brunette—Avery. His girlfriend.

I'd holed up in my apartment all weekend, ignoring texts and calls—including two from him. Last night, I'd finally answered a call from Cam because she'd threatened an invasion if I didn't respond.

Other than that, I blocked out the world.

I would've loved to keep doing that, but that was the bitch about being an adult. You had to do the adulting shit whether you wanted to or not, and today, I had adulting shit to do.

First and foremost on the list was an appointment with my OB/GYN. I knew there wasn't much of a chance I was pregnant, but I'd gone for my yearly not long after my birthday and told the doctor that I'd been thinking about maybe having a child.

She'd asked questions about my family history, then

examined me, drew some blood, and had her assistant schedule a follow-up. I'd already rescheduled twice.

The last thing I wanted was to see her now—or any of the happily pregnant women who usually filled a typical OB/GYN's office, especially since I was pretty sure I wasn't pregnant yet.

Yet, I told myself, holding onto that thought as I stepped onto the elevator.

Of course, if I *wasn't* pregnant, I would need a new plan since Trent had a girlfriend he'd conveniently forgotten to mention.

Asshole.

Just thinking of him made my throat tighten. Shifting my focus to the projects slated for the coming week, I pulled out my phone to read whatever new threats and jokes Cam had sent, trying to get me to talk to her.

I would do that.

But not until after the appointment because I wanted a martini—or five—to help ease some of the hurt before I talked to Cam.

"HELLO, Ms. Moors. You don't need to sign in."

I blinked at the receptionist, confused. "I always have to sign in."

With a friendly smile, she shook her head. "Not today. Come around to the door, and I'll let you back. Dr. Nguyen is waiting for you."

My gut went cold, but I forced myself to put the pen down and smile at the receptionist before doing as she'd asked.

I'd been dreading sitting in the waiting room full of pregnant women, but maybe I should have been dreading something else.

A cold sweat broke out at my nape as the receptionist met me at the door, already there before I so much as rounded the wall where it angled into a sharp L, breaking off into the back part of the office.

"Is everything okay?" I asked her.

"Dr. Nguyen wants to go over your bloodwork." She still smiled.

But the look in her eyes before she looked away had my throat tightening up. Something was wrong.

When she led me to an office instead of an exam room, I had to fight the urge to turn away and leave, tossing out whatever empty lie came to mind.

Dr. Nguyen rose as I came inside.

I stiffened. I could leave, walk out of the office, get in the elevator, go to work. Whatever it was the doctor wanted to tell me, if I didn't *hear* it, I could pretend everything was fine.

"Jazz. Please, come inside," the petite, vibrant doctor said, a gentle smile in her eyes as she came around, hands extended.

Instinctively, I offered mine.

The receptionist closed the door behind me, trapping me inside, cutting off my desperate, ridiculous thoughts of running away.

With a weak laugh, I let the obstetrician escort me to a chair. "Did she know I was thinking about bolting for the door?"

Dr. Nguyen didn't pretend not to understand my meaning. With a rueful, sympathetic smile, she said,

"We've all been there, Jazz. Whether it's for the reason you're here or some other matter—who doesn't have a knee-jerk instinct to back away when they sense they're about to face something difficult?"

"So it is bad news," I said. Tears fell. I didn't wipe them away.

"It's...not terrible. But I do have some difficult news to discuss." Instead of returning to her seat behind the desk, she took the one next to mine.

"What's the difference between difficult and terrible?" I asked as her hand closed over mine.

"Well, I can't confirm it without a few more blood tests. But I'm making this speculation based on my knowledge of your mother's medical history."

"My mother's?" Confused, I shook my head.

"I had to check her records and make sure you were listed, but your mom went into menopause at an earlier age. She was only a couple years older than you when she started hormone replacement therapy."

"Yeah, I know. I remember..." I stopped, shaking my head. That was an old, uncomfortable, miserable history I didn't want to think about. "But I can't be going into menopause. I don't have any symptoms of that. I'm still having periods."

"Irregular periods." She squeezed my hand again and patted it. "And for the past year, we've been monitoring you because you've had trouble sleeping, more trouble concentrating, decreased libido. Last year, when we checked your bloodwork, your estrogen levels were on the lower end. It's possible there's nothing wrong, but I'm concerned you might have a condition that can make conception difficult."

"Difficult." I swallowed, trying to process everything she'd said. "Wait—my libido—"

As blood rushed to stain my cheeks red, she arched her brows. "Okay, we'll move decreased libido off the symptom list."

Looking down, I blinked back even more tears. Damn Trent and his too beautiful girlfriend. Fuck him. Fuck her. Fuck them both.

Dr. Nguyen covered my hand in hers and squeezed. "Jazz."

When I looked up, she offered a reassuring smile. "I may be wrong. That's why I wanted you to come in, so we can set up the testing and find out for sure."

"Okay." I clung to her hand like I was drowning, and she was the only way to keep afloat. "What's this condition called?"

"Primary ovarian insufficiency." She offered me a box of tissues, then leaned back in her chair when I tugged my hand free. "Or POI, for short. Basically, it's when the body tries to go into early menopause. The ovaries stop releasing eggs, or only release them sporadically."

I nodded to indicate I understood.

With a squeeze of her hand on mine, she continued. "Having POI doesn't mean you can't *get* pregnant. Equally important, you're in a financial situation that could allow you to take steps that would make conception easier."

"Okay." I swiped at the tears with the tissues, but more just fell. They wouldn't stop falling. "I...are you talking about artificial insemination? How do we find out for sure if I have this?"

"We need to do a few more tests, spaced out at

specific intervals to get a better picture," she replied. "We need to know what your estrogen levels are throughout your regular cycle and your FSH hormone. Do you understand the function of that hormone?"

"Not really." I managed to smile. "Biology was a long time ago."

"FSH is short for follicle-stimulating hormone—it controls your menstrual cycle and stimulates the growth of the eggs in your ovaries. So pretty important stuff."

"And if my estrogen and FSH are low...?"

"Then we take the next steps if you decide you want to get pregnant. The best option is *in vitro* fertilization, which is expensive, but it's an option."

She continued to talk for several minutes, and I nodded, trying to understand, trying to take it in.

The odd silence finally got through my numbness, and I looked up to find her watching me.

"Are you okay?" she asked softly.

"No." With a watery laugh, I got up and walked over to the window. "No, I'm not."

"Would you like me to call somebody for you?"

I shook my head, not trusting myself to talk without bursting into tears. *Why?* I thought. *Why can't I ever have just one thing I want? Just one?*

"Jazz—"

"I need to go," I said abruptly. "Whatever we need to do, tests, blood work...they call me for that, right? Good."

I didn't give her time to answer, just turned and hurried out.

I had to get out of there.

Once outside, I flagged down a taxi and gave the driver my home address. Maybe he saw something on my face because he didn't treat me to the typical death-defying speed race typical of so many New York cabbies.

As he drove, I sent Cam a message.

Won't be in. Went to doctor. Sore throat. Don't call, hurts to talk.

Yes, it was lies wrapped in truth, but I couldn't handle talking. Not even to my best friend.

The short drive to my building was over blessedly quick, and I blanked my mind on the elevator ride up to my floor, focusing on the simple task of breathing so I wouldn't think about what the doctor had said.

Breathe. Breathe. Just breathe. Almost there—

"You gotta be kidding me," I said, voice cracking as I stepped out of the elevator to find Trent sitting in front of my door.

He rose at the sound of my voice and stepped toward me.

I jerked back, about to dash into the elevator, but the doors had already closed behind me.

"Jazz?"

I glared at him. "Where's your girlfriend?"

SEVENTEEN
TRENT

It hadn't occurred to me that Jazz wasn't home. It was Monday. Of course, she was at work. Shoving away from the door, I fell back against the opposite wall.

Fuck.

Now what?

The obvious answer was to go back to my apartment, try to call her, and send another text.

Instead, I slid down to the floor and drew up my legs, frustrated and mad.

I'd spent half the night pacing the floor. By the time I'd realized how little time we had left before I returned to LA, it had been so late that I'd look like an ass calling her.

Thumbs pressed against my closed eyes to stem off the rapidly-building headache, I considered my short list of options.

What would I even say? *Hey, we're running out of*

time, and I don't know if you're pregnant, but I've got feelings for you. What do you want to do?

She'd been pretty damn clear on not wanting a relationship—with anybody.

Then who the hell was that guy?

It was obvious he was interested in her.

Maybe she doesn't want a relationship with you. You're leaving, remember?

The elevator chimed as the doors opened.

It took a second to process the sound, but then I felt my heart racing at the sight of the woman walking toward me.

She didn't notice me right away. When she did, she stopped, eyes widening slightly.

"Jazz." I shoved a hand through my hair. "Hey, I wanted to...ah, okay, look, this is awkward."

She didn't move, didn't so much as blink.

"Where's your girlfriend?"

"My girlfriend?"

"Your girlfriend, Avery," Jazz said, voice hollow, eyes dull. "Yes, I met her."

"She's not my girlfriend." Fuck, Avery had *talked* to Jazz? When the hell had that happened? "She's...she *was* my sub. Years ago. We've been friends—*just* friends—for years."

Jazz lowered her eyes, staring at the floor.

"We didn't sleep together. We didn't fuck—I mean, shit. I haven't had a sexual relationship with Avery for years. I didn't know she was coming in this weekend. I was..."

She drew in a breath that made her shoulders rise

sharply, then fall. The dejected air about her hit me square in the chest.

"Jazz?"

She looked at me then, and the glitter of tears in her eyes hit me like a blow to the chest.

Moving to her, I cupped her cheek. "What's wrong?"

"Nothing." She looked away from me, stepping back, so I wasn't touching her. "It's not your concern, okay? Whatever...this is, it's ending, right? We're not even friends, so it's not like you—" Her voice hitched, then broke off in the middle of a sob.

Without thinking about it, I pulled her into my arms. She didn't resist, her arms banding tight around me as she buried her face against my chest. Her keys jingled, one of them jabbing me in the back, but I blocked it out, the slight pain nothing compared to whatever was devastating Jazz.

"I—I'm—suh-sorry—"

"Hush," I whispered against her temple, lifting one hand to cradle the back of her head. "Whatever it is, just let it out."

My gut told me this had nothing to do with Avery.

She clung even tighter, shudders racking her hard. I pressed my face against her shoulder, aching to do something to fix whatever had hurt her.

Hearing the chime from the elevator, I swept her into my arms, somehow managing to get the keys.

Heading for her apartment, I got inside as voices behind us filled the hall with bright, animated chatter and laughter.

Kicking the door shut, I carried her over to the couch and sat.

Jazz curled against me, still clinging to me, each sob cutting into me like shards of broken glass.

THE CRYING jag seemed to last a lifetime. The helplessness left me frustrated, but I didn't press her to talk. Whatever this was, it cut too deeply, and I had no right to expect that she bare whatever was wounding her.

I kept track of the time as the shadows cast by the sun changed, the angle moving as noon crept closer, then passed.

The shadows were starting to deepen when Jazz nudged at my chest.

"I have to use the bathroom," she said, her voice raspy, head bent.

Letting her go, I said nothing until she was on her feet. But then I caught her wrist. "Should I stay?"

She darted a look at me with red-rimmed eyes and nodded. "Please. I don't want to be alone right now."

After she left, I rose and started to pace my mind racing. I tried to figure out what could have upset her like this.

Water came on in the bathroom just as I realized what might have upset her. I knew one thing that might cause her to look so heartbroken.

A knot settled in my throat as I moved to the hallway. Hearing the faucet, I knocked on the door.

Jazz didn't answer, so I pushed on the door.

It opened to reveal her standing in front of the sink, the water spilling out of the faucet while she stared at her reflection, that devastated look on her face starker under the bathroom's bright, unforgiving lights.

Moving closer, I turned off the water, then pulled her against me.

"What's wrong?"

She was quiet for so long. I didn't know if she would answer.

Finally, her lashes lifted, and she met my gaze in the mirror's reflection.

"I had an appointment with my OB/GYN this morning."

Fuck.

Her eyes closed as tears broke free, sliding down her cheeks. "I'm probably not going to be able to conceive without medical intervention."

Then, she turned into me, sliding her arms around me to hold tight.

"Maybe this is fate's way of telling me I should just let it go."

"Hush." I kissed her temple, her cheek.

"It could be," she said, lifting her head to meet my eyes. "Some women aren't supposed to be mothers—or shouldn't be. My mom wasn't very good at it, especially after my dad left. This could be—"

I kissed her.

I had no doubt Jazz would make a good mother, but instead of trying to figure out a way to tell her that, I just kissed her.

She didn't react for a few seconds, but she pressed closer, shoving her hands into my hair and clinging to me. The sudden desperate need I tasted on her lips set my own aflame, turning it into a raging inferno.

I spun us around and pushed her against the wall.

She arched closer, her belly rubbing against my cock, her heat reaching me even through layers of clothes.

Grabbing her skirt, I pulled it up, cupping her ass.

She gasped as I bit her neck, sinking my teeth into the sensitive curve where it gave way to her shoulder. "Trent..."

Pushing my hand between her thighs, I stroked her through her panties, and found her already wet.

"Jazz?"

She nodded jerkily, hearing the question in my voice. Then, as if to assure me, she stroked my cock through my jeans before tugging at the button to free it.

I yanked at her panties until they tore while she fumbled with my jeans, shoving past my boxers to free my cock.

Boosting her up, I met her eyes.

Her lips parted on a broken breath as she wrapped her hand around me, then guiding my penis to the swollen, slick folds between her thighs.

"Hurry," she whispered, the word a demand and a plea all at once.

I didn't think about her submitting, about drawing the sexual hunger out until it was a fine, taut line between us.

I thrust in, deep, watching her eyes as I filled her, listening to her broken, ragged cry when I started to withdraw.

She arched closer, trying to deepen the contact and urge me to go faster.

That was the only thing I denied her.

As much as I wanted her, as much I needed her, I wasn't going to rush and let her control this.

We were running out of time.

We both knew it.

I could see it in her eyes, and knew she saw it in mine.

So I rode her slowly, making sure she felt every slow, deliberate thrust, each teasing withdrawal.

But as she tightened around me, her orgasm coming closer, it got harder to hold back.

And when she started to spasm around me, my control shattered.

"Jazz..." Growling against her lips as she started to milk my cock, I moved harder, faster, determined to imprint every second of this on my mind and hers.

My orgasm hit while she was chasing her second, and she cried out in protest when I withdrew.

"We're not done," I promised. Then, for the second time that day, I scooped her up into my arms and carried her into her bedroom.

Putting her into the middle of the bed, I spread her thighs and drove into her again, harder this time.

She exploded, her nails clawing up my back, her hoarse voice shattering again as she cried out my name.

Pushing her thighs up and hooking them over my elbows, I fucked her harder, rougher, refusing to think about the hours creeping away from us.

How in the hell was I supposed to walk away?

How in the hell could I ask her if she wanted me to stay?

M. S. PARKER

"WHEN DO YOU LEAVE?" she asked, her back pressed to my front, her hand stroking the arm I had wrapped around her waist.

"Tomorrow," I told her, wondering if she'd ask me to stay longer. If she did, I'd find a way.

But she just sighed and kept petting my arm.

"I'm sorry," I said a long time later. "I know how much you want a baby."

She didn't answer.

"Do you maybe want to try..."

Before I could figure out the right way to ask if she'd like me to hang around so she could maybe try one of the medical interventions, she shook her head.

"You've already held up your end of the bargain," she said. "I need to figure out if I want to keep trying—even if it means more complicated stuff, or give up."

Kissing her shoulder, I said, "You aren't the giving up type, Jazz."

"No." She swallowed, the sound painfully loud in her quiet, night-dark bedroom. "But sometimes, it's too painful to keep trying...to keep hoping."

Long moments passed.

I wanted to tell her to...try. Hell, to encourage her to try. But I didn't have that right, did I?

"I'm glad I met you, though, Trent. Even if things didn't work out the way I wanted. Even though you're leaving. I'm glad I met you."

She brought my hand to her lips and kissed it.

I couldn't answer then.

Because all of that had felt like good-bye.

EIGHTEEN
JAZZ

"You look like hell."

I barely glanced at Cam, my gaze locked on the computer code on my screen. I'd been in the office for more than three hours and hadn't made even the most minuscule bit of progress. "I'm working."

"No. You're *trying* to work, but you're stuck, and you only get stuck when you have something on your mind. Now spill." She came into my office and carefully lowered her hugely pregnant self into the armchair Danny located for my office. She had a similar one in her own office. Those two armchairs had become the only comfortable places she could sit, thanks to her belly.

I felt like shit because looking at my best friend right now *hurt*.

"Jazz?"

The uneasy note in her voice cut through me, and I closed the program on my computer so I could look at her. I had to deal with this. Otherwise, I'd end up risking a friendship that meant everything.

"I can't get pregnant," I said, voice quivering.

Cam closed her eyes. One hand came up to cup her belly, almost protectively, and I fought the urge to flinch.

"Is that why you have difficulty looking at me right now?" she whispered.

Fuck.

"I'm having a hard time looking at *anybody* right now," I said. "I'm sorry."

She opened her eyes and met mine. "What's wrong? Why can't you..."

She didn't finish, and I was glad because hearing it made it too real. "The doctor still has to run tests to confirm, but she thinks I have something called primary ovarian insufficiency. Basically, my ovaries seem to think it's time to shut down. Permanently."

I managed to smile and shrug like it wasn't a big deal.

Then the tears threatened to come, and I covered my face with my hands.

"I want to hug you, but I don't want to make it worse," Cam said, her ordinarily confident voice filled with uncertainty that hurt me.

I wanted to kick myself.

"You can't make it worse," I said, realizing it was the truth. Lowering my hands, I got up and went to her before she could try to haul herself out of the chair. Going to my knees next to her, I hugged her. "I'm sorry. This isn't your fault. You know I love you more than anybody."

She hugged me as hard as she could.

The kid in her belly kicked.

I surprised myself by laughing. "She's already demanding attention from her godmother."

"She's always demanding attention." Cam took my hand and pressed it to the curve of her belly.

I smiled as the baby kicked again before lowering my hand and resting my head on Cam's knee. "Trent left. He's gone back to California."

She stroked my hair, not saying anything.

"I think I fell for him, Cam. Hard."

"I kind of figured that was the case." She tugged my hair gently. "Did you tell him?"

"Was there a point?" Closing my eyes against the lingering pain, I sighed. "He has a life there. We only met because he had a job out here that lasted two months. Job's over, so he left."

"And does he know you had feelings for him?"

"No." My cheeks heated, thinking about how I'd exposed myself, bared myself to him that last night.

I'm glad I met you, though, Trent. Even if things didn't work out the way I wanted. Even though you're leaving. I'm glad I met you.

No, it wasn't some shining declaration of love, but I'd tried to let him know I had feelings. If he felt the same, wouldn't he have said something?

He hadn't.

He'd left.

I'd gotten one text from him since, a stunning picture of the sun setting over the Pacific Ocean and a few words that made my heart ache.

I missed California sunsets, but I'm glad I went to NYC. Meeting you was one of the best experiences of my life. If you ever need anything, let me know.

I needed *him*, but neither of us had gone into our agreement looking for a relationship. Even if my feelings had changed, it didn't mean it was fair to expect anything from him.

"Ugh."

Looking at Cam, I narrowed my eyes. "What?"

She sighed and waved a hand at me. "You're practically bleeding broken heart emojis here, Jazz. It's obvious you feel something serious here. Why not tell him? Maybe he feels something, too."

"Aren't you the one who fussed at me about trying to give nice guys a chance?"

"Nice guys never made you smile like Trent did." She hitched a shoulder. "I just want you happy."

She held out a hand, and I helped her haul herself out of the chair.

"Anyway." She offered a piece of paper. "That guy Roger called earlier and left a message."

Frowning, I took it and read it.

"Why is he calling the office instead of your cell?"

I grimaced and looked away. "I've already had three or four annoying calls today, so I put it on *do not disturb*. He probably called after I turned that on."

It was a lie. He'd been the second call of the day. I hadn't wanted to talk to him or the owner of a popular gaming blog who called before him.

"Thanks for bringing this." I waved the note absently and went back behind my desk.

"This Roger guy..." Cam cocked her head. "Do you like him?"

"Yeah. I guess."

Even I heard the lack of heat in my answer.

Cam just stared at me.

"He's a nice guy," I said. "You keep telling me..."

"I know," she cut me off. I wish I hadn't said anything." She shook her head. "Jazz, more than anything, I just want you happy."

She left then, leaving me holding the note and the certain knowledge that Roger wasn't the guy who could do that for me.

I CALLED ROGER ANYWAY, a couple of hours later, after I managed to get some work done on my current project finally.

"Jazz." His voice was warm as if we'd stayed in contact all this time. "I'm so glad to hear from you."

"Hi." I eyed the time on my computer, already wanting to end the call. "Sorry I didn't answer when you called earlier. I was in the middle of a project. I tend to get tunnel vision when I'm working."

"I understand. I get that way when I'm putting together a presentation." He paused.

I had the feeling I was supposed to ask something, but I didn't know what. "Did you need something earlier?" I asked when the silence continued. "When you called, I mean?"

A few more seconds of silence passed, and he cleared his throat. "I was mostly calling just to talk. I was on my lunch break, but I figured it wouldn't be a problem for you when I called since you own the company."

Scowling, I lowered the phone to glare at it. Was that a dig? It sounded like one, even if his voice was still all warm and friendly like.

"I'm not the sole owner. I've got a partner. And

several employees who've been with us since our first year have small shares," I told him, keeping my voice neutral.

"Of course, of course. I mostly called to see if you wanted to join me for lunch again this week—since you've got an agreeable boss." He chuckled as he added the last bit.

The chuckle rubbed me wrong, like that reference to me owning the company. I started to decline the invitation, but movement outside my open office door caught my attention.

It was Danny, bent over Cam where she leaned against a desk, his head lowered so she could talk to him quietly. He had a hand on her belly, stroking lightly.

They painted a beautiful picture, one filled with love and connection. My throat tightened.

I wouldn't be able to have that with Trent, no matter what. He'd made it clear from the beginning that whatever happened between us would end because his life was in California.

That didn't mean I couldn't find something real with another man.

Maybe even Roger.

"Sure," I said. "What day were you thinking?"

"YOU LOOK STUNNING."

"Thanks." I felt out of place in the narrow black skirt with its attached suspenders and a colorful top that bared an inch or two of my midriff. I'd had a podcast interview and a photo shoot with a couple of popular gamers in the area and Cam, as always, had helped with my wardrobe pics. The fun, sexy outfit had been great for the interview and photo op, but I felt out of place in this five-star restaurant. I decided to take a page from Cam's book and brazen my way through, returning Roger's smile with a confident one I'd cultivated after years of working in a primarily male-dominated field.

"You mentioned you had an interview and photo deal earlier," Roger said, his eyes darting briefly to my abdomen before quickly moving back up.

"Yes." I didn't expand on that as the server approached, smiling at both of us as she put water down and asked about drinks. Roger requested a Tom Collins. I declined and waited until the server was out of earshot before addressing his comment. "The majority of our interviews are with podcasters or people with large followings on either Facebook or TikTok. That's why I mentioned I'd be good with almost anything that had a business casual vibe."

I let it go at that and reached for the menu, not bothering to see his expression at my not-too-subtle jab.

"Did I upset you?" he asked quietly.

Glancing at him after I'd carefully blanked my expression, I said, honestly, "No."

He hadn't. He'd irritated me, but that wasn't *upsetting*.

Cam and I had been in our line of work too long to be easily upset.

But I didn't feel like sharing that with him, and he didn't know me well enough to see the truth I didn't expand on.

"Oh, good." He relaxed, taking my words at face

value and picking up his menu. "Have you been here before? I can offer some suggestions if you haven't."

"No. I'm fine." Skimming the offerings, I debated what would be quick and easy to eat and what wouldn't sit like a lead weight in my stomach if I decided to end this early.

"Are you sure? I bring clients here all the time, so I'm pretty familiar with almost everything here."

"I'm good, Roger." Hearing the edge creep into my voice, I shut up before I could let more of my temper show. "I already know what I want, but thanks."

As I lowered my menu, I caught sight of our server and inclined my head.

When she nodded, I had to resist breathing a sigh of relief.

This lunch was already turning out to be a debacle, and I couldn't wait for it to be over.

It dragged on, although, according to my watch, it had only been forty-five minutes since I'd sat down when the server returned with our tickets—separated as I'd requested.

I signed mine, included a tip that would cover Roger's, too, if he was a cheapskate, then rose, giving him the first genuine smile I'd felt all day.

"I've got to be getting back."

"In such a rush! I thought setting your hours was a benefit of being your own boss." He hurriedly scribbled on his tab and rose to join me.

As we walked out together, I reminded myself I was probably being unfair.

I didn't care.

He was annoying me more and more with every second that passed.

"That might apply to self-employed people, but business owners who employ others have to respect the time of their employees if they want to retain those employees," I said once we were outside. I made a show of checking the time. "I have to be going if I want to catch this train. Otherwise, I'll be holding up my employees—I think I have an afternoon meeting."

"Yes, of course—oh, wait!" He pulled his phone out and checked, then smiled. "Excellent...I wanted to make sure everything was in line before I asked. I've got tickets to a show this Friday, four of them. I thought you and your friend, and her husband, might like to join us."

"My friend?"

"Cameron?" His brow furrowed as he studied.

"Cam." Already forming the refusal, I went silent as he turned the phone around and showed me a message via a Facebook app.

It was from Danny.

"When did you two become friends?"

He grinned, clearly pleased with himself. "Not long after you and I started talking again. I figured if I was going to have any chance with you, I should make sure I got along well with your friends, especially your best friend. Danny said you and Cam loved this particular play."

I was going to kill Danny.

"Yeah. We do." I offered a tight smile.

"Then it's a date!"

NINETEEN
TRENT

My alarm went off while I was going through pictures on my camera roll.

After dismissing the alarm, I went back to pictures of Jazz. It had been one of the first I'd taken, a rainy afternoon we'd spent at her place, watching a movie. The rest of the world, my job, and LA were irrelevant thoughts, too inconsequential to intrude on our time together.

A text from Stephen popped up. I dismissed it and continued staring at Jazz.

Ten minutes later, another text popped up.

Swearing at the interruption, I shot Stephen a response.

You're a fucking mother hen. I'm up. Leave me alone.

Putting the *do not disturb* feature on, I dropped the phone onto the bed next to me and closed my eyes. In a couple of hours, Stephen would be picking me up for the meeting we had with the playwright and producer to go over the score I'd written.

Usually, I'd be thrilled. The job hadn't been the most thrilling thing I'd ever done, but there had been challenges, and I'd worked hard to stick true to the original music while putting my own stamp on it.

I wasn't excited, though.

I kept thinking about Jazz.

Missing her was like this giant empty void inside me, and I didn't know how to live with it, handle it.

Eying the time, I ditched the immediate option. Getting drunk before nine in the morning wasn't much of an answer, even if it would dull my thoughts.

Tired and miserable with missing Jazz, I flung my arm over my eyes.

I'd get up and get ready. Soon.

Just not...yet.

"YOU LOOK LIKE SHIT."

Since I'd seen my reflection a couple of minutes ago, I couldn't argue. I flipped off Stephen instead after settling in the backseat next to him.

While the driver closed the door, I rested my head on the padded seat, a bone-deep weariness settling through me.

"Are you okay?"

Hearing the concern in Stephen's voice, I made myself answer. "I'm just tired, man."

"I've seen you tired before. I've never seen you walking around half-dead."

"I'm *fine*," I said, not bothering to hide the edge in my

voice. If I ever told anyone about Jazz, it would be Stephen. But I wasn't ready to talk about her. Not even to my best friend.

"Okay." Stephen lapsed into silence, not saying anything else on the forty-five-minute drive.

But when the car came to a slow stop in front of a privately-owned music studio, I looked at the driver. "Can you give us a minute?"

"Of course." He climbed out and closed the door, giving us a few minutes of privacy.

I wasn't ready to talk about her. But I needed some space, so I had to tell Stephen something.

"I met somebody," I said into the waiting quiet. Looking at the back of the seat in front of me, I pictured Jazz's face. "I wasn't looking for it, and I know she wasn't. Nothing will come of it, either. But I just need some time to deal with it, okay?"

Without waiting for an answer, I climbed out of the car.

Stephen joined me, but he caught my arm when I started for the doors.

"Take whatever time you need, man. Just...let me know if you need to talk."

I gave a short nod, then tugged free. "Let's get this done, okay?"

THE NEXT HOUR passed in a blur of music, questions, and strained smiles that made my cheeks ache, and nods that left my head pounding.

M. S. PARKER

The check in my hand was larger than I'd expected, and when I turned it over to Stephen for him to handle, he'd been momentarily speechless.

If I'd been able to summon up any genuine enthusiasm, I might have been the same.

But my mind kept drifting back to the day I'd played for Jazz and everything that followed.

"This is a *very* generous bonus," Stephen said, dropping a heavy hand on my shoulder and squeezing.

"Yes, thank you," I said, parroting what seemed to be an acceptable phrase.

"You are a musical *genius*." Lincoln Mayes clapped his hands together and rubbed them, looking more like a cartoon villain than anything else, especially with the gleeful smile on his face. "I can't wait to—well, never mind. We'll talk about that later on."

"Talk about what?" Stephen asked.

"Nothing we can mention right now." Frank Gotti gave his friend a narrow look. "Ignore Lincoln. He has a big mouth. We might be giving you a call soon, though."

Moving to the second-floor studio window, I looked outside, eyes moving to the iconic sign up in the hills, lingering on the *H*, while my mind drifted even further away.

What was Jazz doing now?

Did she miss me even half as much as I missed her?

"WE'RE GOING OUT."

Instead of dropping me at my place, Stephen

dismissed the driver and followed me into my condo. In the kitchen, there were empty beer bottles lining one counter.

After checking my nearly empty fridge he glanced over his shoulder at me. "Collecting glass?"

"Waiting for recycling day." I sat on the couch and put my feet on the coffee table, unlocking my phone.

"That was yesterday."

"Was it? Oh." I scowled, then shrugged. "Okay, I'm waiting for the next recycling day."

Stephen leaned over the back of the couch and snagged my phone. "We're going out," he said again. "You need to celebrate. And you need to stop pouting like this. It's not like you, man."

"I'm not *pouting*." Shoving upright, I shot him a glare.

Stephen gave me a sympathetic look. "Then what's going on?"

"I..." Sucking in a breath, a hundred angry words trapped in my throat, I tried to find the right answer. What *was* going on?

Jazz hadn't called, hadn't responded to the one text I'd sent her—the one where I'd laid myself out bare—except to say she was glad I'd made it home safe.

Glad I'd made it home?

What the fuck kind of response was that?

Throat tight, I glared at Stephen. "I don't fucking know."

"Alright. When you do, we can talk. But for now? I'm dragging you out of here, putting food in your belly, and taking you to the club." He paused, then said, "Got it?"

I almost told him to get lost.

But then I realized if I didn't go out with him, I'd just spend another night alone. Thinking about Jazz and all the miles between us. Thinking of the things I'd left unsaid, wondering if I shouldn't have tried to say more.

Throat knotting up on me, I nodded, "Fine. Whatever."

"Good." Relief showed up in Stephen's eyes. "Now go take a fucking shower, and shave, damn it. You look like you've been living under a bridge for a week."

THE RESTAURANT HADN'T BEEN bad.

Stephen was amusing enough that I'd relaxed and enjoyed myself by the end of dinner, and when we climbed into the car, I could even smile.

"Hell, it's about damn time I see you smiling."

Looking up, I found Stephen eying me, the concern once more apparent in his eyes.

"I'm fine," I told him. It was a lie, sure. But for the first time since I'd left Jazz, I felt like maybe I could be okay. Sooner or later.

"You did a good job on the score."

"I know." Looking outside at the rush of life that was a Los Angeles night, I tried not to compare it to New York City. Both were busy, thriving cities. Yeah, I'd missed the endless, almost balmy summer of LA nights, but I missed Jazz in New York City more than anything I missed here in California.

"You haven't mentioned Avery."

Groaning, I pinched the bridge of my nose. "You talked to her?"

"She might have left a message or two. Dozen." Clearing his throat, he said, "I'm guessing she figured out where you were by going through my phone or some shit like that."

"I guess." Dropping my hands, I looked out the window as he pulled onto the freeway entrance ramp. "I ended up kicking her out of my place, Stephen. The two of us had been friends for a long time. I thought if I told her I was serious about somebody else, she'd understand. But she didn't."

"I'm sorry." Clearing his throat, he said, "For all of that—for not realizing she'd come snooping through my things to figure out how to find you, and whatever she did to make things rough while she was out there."

"It's not your fault," I told him. It wasn't. I couldn't blame anyone else for how Avery had acted. I couldn't blame myself, either. "She's back in town?"

"Yeah, as far as I know." Blowing out a breath, he added, "But let's not worry about it, okay? Today was a big deal. We need to be celebrating."

I didn't want to celebrate. I wanted to be back in New York, holding Jazz in my lap, her hair sliding through my fingers as we debated what to order in for dinner before picking out a movie to watch.

How fucking domesticated.

I looked up to see Stephen shooting me a narrow look, speculation in his gaze.

"Watch the damn road," I said.

The need to talk to somebody—even my best friend who'd hassle me to hell and back—was strong. But I wasn't sure I was ready to discuss things with Jazz. I didn't know if I'd ever be.

So I closed my eyes and emptied my mind, listening to the low throaty hum of the car as we sped along the freeway.

TWENTY

JAZZ

"You'd think a couple of VIPs like you ladies would get better service."

I heard him, but it wasn't until Cam nudged me under the cocktail table with her foot that I realized Roger had been talking to me—*about* me. And Cam.

Looking up, I saw him offer a humorous smile.

I tried and failed to return it. Was he trying to be funny? If so, he'd missed the mark. It could have been my miserable mood, though, so I opted for a weak smile.

"We're going to go grab drinks while we wait," Danny said, grabbing Roger's arm and dragging him off without giving the other man a chance to argue.

"That was...rude," Cam said.

"It was, wasn't it?"

I winced at my tone, wishing immediately I'd kept my mouth shut because I just sounded...*wrong*. Tone flat, voice husky—not because I'd done some crying last night. Nope. Not a single tear shed. A few hundred, sure. But not a *single* tear.

Cam turned to me, swinging her legs around and using the chair and table to balance as her big belly was getting more and more unwieldy every day.

"What's going on?" she asked quietly, covering my hand with hers.

Swallowing the knot in my throat, I looked away. "Not right now. They'll be back soon."

"Nope." She wagged her phone at me. "Danny texted to let me know the line's *loooonnnggg*—and I told him to take his time and make sure Roger stays with him. You need a drink—and I need a break from that asshole."

"He's not an asshole," I said defensively.

"Honey, he's a Class A asshole—top of the line, and please tell me you're going to dump him." With a gentle squeeze of her hand, she added, "But he's not why you're miserable."

No. Roger had nothing to do with my current state of mind—even if he *was* showing some signs of sneering arrogance here and there, an attitude he hadn't had in high school. I'd thought I imagined it, but if Cam was seeing...

"Jazz. *Talk*."

The ever-present knot in my throat worsened, and I took a deep breath, and swallowed to try and ease it. But it just got bigger, and the more I tried not to think about Trent, the worse it got.

" I already told you he's gone." Clearing my throat, I added, "Trent, I mean. The job he was working on is over, and he flew back to California."

Cam's eyes softened with understanding. "You fell for him after all, didn't you?"

"Who the hell was I kidding?" After tugging my

hand free from hers, I braced my elbows on the table. "Yes, I fell for him. All this time, I looked down on my mom for how she fell apart after my dad left and look at me now, moaning over a guy I've only known a couple of months."

"Hey."

I didn't look up.

Cam poked me in the arm. Hard.

Scowling, I dropped my hands.

She glared at me. "I only knew Danny a couple of *weeks* before I knew he was the one. Don't go acting like it's a federal crime to hurt over the person you love. It's *not*."

"I don't love him," I protested.

Cam arched a brow.

"I don't." But this time, it rang hollow, even to my ears. "I *can't* love him."

That was better.

"Why not?" Cam gave me a cool look, the question so utterly logical, that it left me floundering for the right response.

"Well...he lives on the west coast. My life is here—with *you*. We run a business together!" I pointed out.

Cam leaned forward. No. She *tried* to, then grumbled as her belly got in the way. Deciding to poke me again, she said, "This is going to be a shock to you, but in this day and age, people can actually *work from home*. They use this funny device called a *computer*."

"Smartass."

"Tell me something." She shifted in the chair, winced a bit, and pressed a hand to her belly. Several seconds passed before the pro kicker in her belly settled down but then she focused on me. "Does he feel the same way about you?"

"I..." Frowning, I realized I didn't know.

I'd never *told* him how I felt. It was supposed to be short-term, right?

"I guess you didn't ask, huh?" Cam sighed and moved around in her chair, grimacing as she tried to get comfortable. "Honey, you can either *try* to reach out and talk to him, see if he feels anything...or you need to let it go. Figure out which one will have the best chance of making you happy and do it. This thing with you living here, him living there...all of that you can talk about but find out what's going to make you happy—and *do* something about it because right now, you are miserable."

"I *know* that, thanks."

"Then decide what you want." Cam's eyes flicked past me. "They're on their way back. FYI? I really hope Roger isn't what you want. I don't like the asshole."

Her winning smile fixed firmly in place as she shifted back around in the chair, Cam accepted the ice water from her boyfriend while Roger offered me a glass of wine.

"Hope we didn't miss anything fun," Roger said, his smile warm.

"No." I took the wine and downed half of it. "Just girl talk."

Man, I wanted this night over.

HAVING a pregnant best friend can come in handy.

Not long after we'd finished dinner—no dessert—

Cam pushed up from her chair and gripped my shoulder. "Guys, I'm worn out. Hope you don't mind if we call it quits early, Roger."

"Ah, no." He shoved his credit card into his wallet as he rose, but before he could get to my side, I was already escorting Cam out of the crowded restaurant.

"Thanks," I said in a low voice as a server with a heavy tray passed by behind us, separating us from Danny and Roger. "I owe Danny about a hundred pounds of his favorite cookies from that bakery."

She snorted. "Definitely—and pay up soon so I can eat half of them."

"Only half?"

The familiar teasing managed to lighten my mood by the time we were outside, but it faded as Danny flagged down a cab. He pressed a kiss to Cam's forehead before meeting my eyes, his dark with an unspoken question.

"I want to get Cam home," he said. "She might act like she can party until midnight, but that baby is hardcore and likes to keep her up half the night."

"Go on." They lived in the opposite direction of my apartment. "I'm good. I'll call in the morning."

Cam hugged me while Danny and Roger made small talk.

"Call me later if you need to talk," she said. "Danny's not joking about this little monster keeping me up half the night."

She rubbed her belly with a gentle hand, eyes aglow with love.

Monster? Not even close. The tug of envy wasn't as sharp as it might have been even a couple of days ago, but I knew that didn't mean much. My love for my best friend was stronger than any jealousy I could ever feel for the family she was making. But I was too pragmatic to think I was over the hurt of realizing I'd never have one of my own—not like the one Cam was building.

"Thanks, but I think I'll bury myself in Haagen-Dazs, and watch a couple of sappy movies."

Once they were in the cab, I turned to look at Roger.

"I've got a car service on the way," he said, holding up his phone.

Crap.

"That's great," I lied.

I was glad to see the gleaming black town car pull up only a couple of minutes later. After giving my address, I folded my hands in my lap and crossed my legs, angling my body more toward the door than Roger.

He didn't seem to pick up on the body language.

"Cam and Danny are pretty happy together," he said.

"Yes."

"How long have you known her?"

Okay, so monosyllables were too subtle. Pinching the bridge of my nose to stem a growing headache, I replied with a vague answer. "Years."

"You can tell. You two have that kind of vibe going."

As he continued to talk about a couple of guys from high school he was still in contact with, I closed my eyes.

"...to work with, though. Don't think I could handle that. Hey, you want to stop and have a drink? Raul, can you let us out here?"

The car came to a stop almost on the tail of Roger's last word, and I stiffened, eyes opening to see the brilliant pink neon of a familiar restaurant a few short blocks from my apartment.

The pounding at the base of my skull had increased by the time Roger opened the door and offered his hand. Feeling the driver's eyes on me, I climbed out but didn't accept Roger's offer of assistance.

"I'm pretty tired, Roger. I think I'd rather just go home," I told him.

"Just one drink? I've missed talking with you, Jazz. So much." He took my hand and squeezed. "Letting you slip away has been one of the biggest regrets of my life."

The car pulled away while he was talking.

Shit.

Yeah, I needed to end this thing *tonight*. With a tight smile, I said, "I guess one drink. We should probably talk, anyway."

Telling him he was wasting his time with the corny lines would take about as long as it took to finish half a drink, I figured.

Once inside, I waved to the back of the restaurant. "I'll meet you in the bar, okay? I just need to use the restroom."

One drink with Roger. And then I'd go home—alone—and dig out the ice cream, trying to forget all about the dreadful double date.

TWENTY-ONE
TRENT

"I'VE BEEN WONDERING IF YOU'RE SICK OR something," Stephen said after the server left, our drinks on the small table between us refreshed without asking.

I picked up the scotch, waiting to see where my friend was going with this.

"I've got a new theory, though." Stephen picked up his drink, took a sip, then gestured to the stage. "I think you might be dead."

"Dead." Faintly amused, I smiled into my glass. "Where did that theory come from?"

"From the fact that you haven't so much as looked at the stage, and they have the most amazing shibari artist I've seen in...well, maybe ever." He narrowed his eyes. "And yep, you still haven't looked. Maybe you *are* dead."

"If I am, remember you don't get my Steinway." Sipping the scotch, I looked over at the stage. Nope. Not even a stir of interest. After a few seconds, I looked back at Stephen.

A change in the shadows had us both looking up.

A slim woman, her curves wrapped in a dress made up of nothing more than silver chains and leather straps, looked at me, then dipped her head before going to her knees and coming to me.

"Liesl." Stephen glanced at me, mouth curving in a wicked smile. "Well, if she can't help you..."

I didn't recognize her, but I'd been out of the city for several months.

Her red hair was scooped into a high, tight ponytail, leaving her lovely features unframed.

She knelt in front of me, lifting her eyes to meet mine. "Hello."

"Hi." It suddenly hit me that it could be awkward as hell to talk to somebody in one of these places if you weren't in the mood to play. Feeling Stephen watching me and aware Liesl was *definitely* watching me, I decided to get it over with. "I'm not in the mood to play tonight. With anybody."

She took it with a smile, head cocking to the side slightly as she asked, "Tonight only?"

"Actually...no."

The words surprised the fucking hell out of me—and Stephen, too, if his stunned, "*What the hell?*" was any indicator.

That did have a bit of an impact on the pretty, confident sub still kneeling in front of me, and I smiled, leaning closer to touch her cheek gently.

"It's nothing personal. I've just...met somebody."

"Oh." She touched the back of my hand with gentle fingers, a soft smile returning to her face. "Lucky woman."

She held out her hand, and it wasn't so awkward

anymore as I helped her up. I was even able to appreciate her excellent ass when she turned and walked away.

"You're really serious, aren't you? About this woman you met?" Stephen asked, his tone incredulous.

I tossed back half the scotch in my glass before looking at him. "Yeah. I am."

"I don't believe it." He put his drink down and rubbed his hands over his face as if trying to wash away a bad dream. "You don't *do* this...*meeting* people shit. You avoid relationships like the plague."

"Yeah, well, joke's on me." Looking down into the remaining booze in my glass, I swirled it around. "I've spent so much of my life just existing, Stephen. Having a good career, landing some decent gigs from time to time and never worrying too much about money, having the club here, and you for a friend? I thought it was enough."

I finally talked.

I told him about Jazz, leaving out the baby-making part of the agreement. That was personal.

But I told him about how she'd made me feel. How I was missing her.

I felt hollow inside like somebody had cut me open and scooped out everything that made me who I was before stitching me back together and expecting me to be okay.

I wasn't okay. I couldn't even successfully get a friend to believe I was okay, much less myself.

"So, what are you going to do?"

Stephen's quiet question had me looking up.

"What's there *to* do?" I asked. "It's over. I put a two-month time limit on everything, and she made it clear she didn't want any sort of relationship."

"Yeah, well, you obviously didn't plan on falling for her," Stephen pointed out. "But you did. How do you know she didn't go and do the same thing?"

I grabbed my glass with a frown only to discover it was empty.

"We're not ordering another," Stephen said. "So consider this...do you really want to spend the rest of your life regretting that you were too chicken shit to ask this woman if she felt anything for you?"

He held up a hand when I went to reply.

"Don't answer now." He pulled his wallet out, and swiped a card on the digital device. "You can answer tomorrow when I call you, bright and early. And I *will* call because I want to know if you're going to listen to reason and fly back to New York and talk to her."

"You're a very persistent asshole, you know that?"

He smiled. "Maybe. But I'm not the one hiding from reality."

TWENTY-TWO
JAZZ

Discomfort woke me. My head hurt, my body ached, and my tongue had a fuzzy coating on it that made me crave a gallon of water, even as my gut roiled, a warning that anything I ate or drank might not stay down.

Groaning, I rolled onto my side and grabbed a pillow. I was so miserable that I wanted to bury myself under the covers and sleep for a week.

A muffled grunt made me freeze. That hadn't been *me*. The only other person it could have been, left New York City and was in California.

A long, deep sighing breath came to my ears, and I squeezed my eyes closed. It definitely wasn't Trent.

Slowly, I eased upright and looked around.

Okay...don't freak out.

Blinking rapidly to let my eyes adjust to the room's dim interior, I looked around. The small, cramped space was unfamiliar territory, but when I gave the man next to me a look, I recognized him.

Roger.

My skin prickled, my nausea increasing as I put two and two together. Goosebumps broke out across my flesh as I lurched off the bed and into the nearby open door, my feet cold against the chilly bathroom floor. Clamping a hand over my mouth, I fought back the urge to puke, forcing myself to breathe through my nose until the nausea eased.

Was he awake? I didn't know. I was afraid to look back out there, too, because if I saw him awake, I'd have to talk to him.

We had slept together. How had *that* happened? I was sore between my thighs, and my head hurt. Sex and a couple of drinks could explain both, although yesterday, I wouldn't have thought it possible that I'd be drunk enough to sleep with the man still snoring in the bed a few feet away.

Panic tried to overtake my mind once more, and I took another deep breath, counted to ten. Two more repetitions and I eased away from the wall and peeked around the door frame. He was still sleeping.

I braced myself against the wall and took another breath to prepare myself. The sight of a small trash can by the sink caught my eye just before I would have slipped out of the bathroom. Easing forward, I looked inside, and saw a ripped foil packed, a rubber—used.

Okay, well, that was good, right? We'd used protection, at least.

That small relief gave me the boost I needed to slide from the bathroom so I could find my clothes. I'd slept with Roger. We'd had all of one date, and I wasn't even into him, but I'd slept with him.

Gathering my clothes, I moved to the farthest wall of

the cramped studio apartment and dressed in the dark. My purse and shoes were easy to find, both of them tossed aside right inside the apartment. Grabbing them, along with my jacket, I ducked into the hallway and eased the door shut behind me. Silently, I pleaded, *"Don't wake up, don't wake up, don't wake up..."*

Once I was out on the street, I could breathe easier, but I didn't fully relax until the taxi driver I'd flagged down dropped me off in front of my building.

What had I done?

The sarcastic inner bitch told me, *Well, instead of listening to me, you went out with Roger, got drunk, and decided to jump into bed with him.*

I strode past the early morning staff handling the door and went straight for the elevator. It didn't look like the walk of shame if I kept my chin up, right?

You might not let on to anybody watching you, but they aren't the problem. You are.

"Go to hell," I muttered.

"I beg your pardon?"

Cheeks flushing, I looked over to see another tenant standing a few feet away, clad in a bright pink tracksuit. She had a white, fluffy dog with enormous eyes in her arms.

"Nothing, Ms. Hatfield," I said. "Just talking to myself."

She made a disapproving sound and shook her head as the doors slid open, and we went into the elevator.

I made it to my place without pausing to look at the apartment where Trent had stayed.

That was good because my control was shredding under the weight I carried.

Unlocking my door, I collapsed against it and slid to the floor.

"How in the hell did I end up in bed with *Roger*?"

My head was spinning, and I wasn't sure if it was from the booze the night before or plain old shock from waking up in the wrong bed. I went to press my hands to my face but froze.

I could smell him on me. Lurching upright, I half-stumbled, half-ran to the bathroom, undressing as I went.

I had to get rid of that scent.

Bile churned in my belly, threatening to climb up my throat and spill out in a noxious explosion, but I battled it back. If I started puking, I might not stop.

My hands shook as I climbed into the shower and turned the water on. I made the temperature as hot as I could handle it. Despite the heat, I still felt cold inside.

What had *happened*? My mind spun back to the last clear memory at the bar.

I had gone to the bathroom as soon as we came to the bar. Then I'd gone back out there to sit and talk with Roger for a few minutes.

I'd planned on getting a glass of wine, but he'd already ordered drinks, and he was smiling as I took a seat.

The smile had brought back nice memories, so I'd relaxed a little, sipping the drink as he asked about my job.

Then...nothing.

I didn't remember finishing the drink or how many more I'd had after that. My head was hammering, though. I must have gotten wasted. Had I made a move on Roger?

Still shivering, I lifted my face to the spray of hot

water. It sluiced down over me, washing away Roger's scent, my sweat, and the tears that had started to fall without me noticing.

Throat tight against a wave that promised even more, I sagged against the wall and wrapped my arms around my middle, holding on tight.

That wave of tears came, and I couldn't fight it. I wasn't even sure if I wanted to.

I cried. I cried for a long, long time and wished Trent was here to hold me.

TWENTY-THREE
TRENT

I was up well before nine and already on the phone when Stephen tried to call the first time. Ignoring the familiar *click*, I listened to the crap music playing while I sat on hold with the airline.

I'd made up my mind. I was going to talk to Jazz. Stephen had been right to call me out the way he had. I couldn't think about going the next month wondering if Jazz cared about me, much less the rest of my life.

I was gritting my teeth and suffering through endless waits and awful music as the customer service rep tried to find a flight that would get me to New York by tomorrow.

Stephen's pragmatic voice echoed in my ears when I fell face down on the bed last night. It was the first thing I thought of when I woke at six, my body still semi-accustomed to New York time despite being back in LA for days.

Do you really want to spend the rest of your life regretting the fact that you were too chicken shit to ask this woman if she felt anything for you?

I already knew she felt something.

I'd seen it in her eyes, in the rich, blue-ish purple that could hold so much emotion.

The last time we'd made love.

Made love.

What a strange concept.

I was thirty-three years old, and until Jazz, I hadn't really made love to a woman before. I'd had sex—wild, hot sex, yeah. And the best sex, the hottest sex, had been with Jazz.

We both felt something. But I had no idea if Jazz wanted to do anything about it.

The only thing I knew was that Stephen was right—I *was* chickenshit. The thought of going to see her and risking rejection left me feeling cold all over.

The dismal music broke off.

"Mr. Dixson?"

"Yes?"

"Thank you for still holding. My manager is still looking at possible options. Can you continue to hold?"

I clenched my teeth and tried not to snarl. "Yes."

Going to my piano, I put the phone on speaker and started to play. A frantic, angry melody escaped while I stared outside, eyes on the ever-changing waters of the Pacific.

Another five minutes passed, and the customer service rep came on the line to tell me she was transferring my call to her supervisor.

"For fuck's sake," I muttered as I was placed on hold *again*.

A notification popped up—Stephen. Texting.

Since you're either awake and ignoring me or still asleep, I'm heading over. I've got news.

"Yeah, I need this like I need a hole in my head," I muttered, and I pushed back from the piano. Phone in hand, I headed for the kitchen.

The coffee I'd brewed earlier was cold, so I poured it in a cup and stuck it in the microwave. The appliance's digital *ping* sounded at almost the exact moment the front door opened.

"Hope you're up, Trent!" Stephen called out. "I'm waking you up if not—I don't care how hungover you are."

"I'm in the kitchen, asshole." Coffee in hand, I leaned against the counter and took a sip, waiting for my friend to join me.

He glanced at the phone. "Who are you calling?"

"The airlines." I rolled my eyes, "I'm trying to get a flight out to New York today. It's not going well."

Stephen came over and picked up my phone.

I was too tired to wonder why until he ended the call.

"What the fuck, man!" Shoving off the counter, I glared at him.

He pushed the phone into my free hand before going to the coffeemaker. "There's none left," he said.

"Too fucking bad! Why'd you disconnect the call?"

He grinned at me. "Didn't you see my text? I've got news."

He dragged out a chair at the island I used for meal prep and eating. After taking a seat, he laid down a messenger bag, the same one he'd used for years.

I eyed it, then slowly lifted my gaze to his.

That bag only appeared when he was out on business and had contracts or other important business shit.

Curiosity piqued, I sat across from him and waited.

He pulled out a blue folder and pushed it over to me.

"Guess what musical was just optioned for a major motion picture deal?"

"No way."

Putting my coffee on the island's granite countertop, I grabbed the folder and flipped it open. Dots spun in front of my eyes for a few seconds, blood roaring in my ears. Clearing my throat twice, I finally managed to speak. "Is this for real?"

"Real as it gets, man." Stephen clapped his hands together. "Apparently, this deal has been in the works for a while, but only the playwright and his inner circle knew about it. Everything was finalized this morning, and I got a call immediately after from Alfonse Macri himself. He insists that you handle the music score for the movie, which he wants to have several new, original pieces."

Placing the folder and contract on the granite, I closed my eyes and ground the heels of my hands against them.

"When do we get started?" I asked, eyes still closed.

"Today."

I dropped my hands and gaped at Stephen. "What?"

"Well, work won't officially start today, but the director insists on meeting you. Macri was adamant that you handle the music if you agreed, and the director and executive producer who greenlighted the project are cool with it. But they want to meet you before anything gets started."

Dropping my gaze to the phone, I thought of the

flight. Thought of Jazz and her beautiful eyes and how she melted against me.

"Trent?"

Dragging my gaze from the phone, I met Stephen's eyes.

"I was trying to book a flight out to see Jazz. Today."

Stephen winced. "She's not going anywhere, man. This opportunity, though, will. They aren't going to wait while you worry about your love life."

"Aren't you the one who was telling me I needed to ask her if she felt anything for me?" I glared at him.

Stephen shrugged. "Yeah. But that doesn't mean you have to fly out *today*."

I lowered my eyes to the phone while a war raged inside.

"Fine," I said after what felt like forever. "Where are we supposed to meet up?"

"Hollywood Hills." He gave me a critical once-over. "But you have to shower first. And shave. You look like you're a step away from living in a bottle."

"Fuck you, man," I said tiredly.

On my way out of the kitchen, my phone rang. Stephen picked it up from where I'd left it on the table. "Looks like the CS rep from the airline."

I shook my head. "Answer it and tell them I'm not interested or just ignore it."

If I got on the phone, I might change my mind and take whatever flight they offered, the need to see Jazz a visceral ache.

Soon, I told myself. *Soon, I'll go back and talk to Jazz.*

TWENTY-FOUR
JAZZ

The Lyft driver found a spot in front of the employee entrance, and I only had to dart a few feet to get under the protective awning, but even a second in the pouring rain left me soaked, flattening my hair and the clothes I'd selected with deliberate intent, hoping to distract from my pale features and the circles under my eyes.

I'd looked like crap when I saw my reflection upon rising this morning. After an hour of work, I'd looked fine, and the dress I'd selected moved me from fine to sexily competent.

Now I probably fit in the category of a drowned wet rat.

Once inside, I locked myself in the bathroom and tried to fix the worst of the damage. Fortunately, my umbrella protected my face, so my makeup wasn't running in streaks down my face. I brushed, then sectioned my hair into parts before weaving it into a loose braid.

My clothes, however, there was nothing I could do but change.

Since I kept a spare set on hand, I changed into jeans and a geeky t-shirt with a sad T-Rex lamenting his inability to do push-ups. I dumped my wet clothes into my gym bag and took them with me into the central part of the office.

I was far from the only person looking a little bedraggled, seeing several commiserating smiles from my employees who glanced at my casual clothes.

Cam was in her office on the phone and tried to wave me in, but I pretended not to notice, hurrying past her open door to reach mine.

The plan was to sit, get on the phone, and look busy —*too* busy for us to talk until my spinning head settled.

She derailed my plan by calling out my name before making it around my desk.

"How can somebody with a belly like a watermelon move that fast?" I shot her a dark look as I dropped down into my seat.

"Bitch," Cam said mildly. She came around the desk and managed to hop onto its edge with the same grace she'd shown pre-watermelon belly. "The way you came running in here makes me think you wanted to avoid me."

"I'm not avoiding you," I said, giving her my best innocent look."

"Liar." She crossed her legs at the ankles and studied me.

I had to fight not to look away from her. Cam hid it well, but she was deeply intuitive, and she knew me better than anybody else in the world.

"I was going to ask how things went with Roger, but looking at you now, I think it'd be a waste of time. You're definitely not basking in the glow of crazy monkey sex."

Something sour rose in my throat.

Shoving back from the desk, I walked over to the mini-fridge and grabbed a can of ginger ale. Even downing half the can didn't wash the bad taste from my mouth, though, and I could feel Cam's razor-sharp focus.

"Jazz?"

The concern in her voice almost broke me. I had to clear my throat before speaking around the huge knot swelling there. "Give me a minute."

Instead of answering, she came over and took my hand, leading me to the couch tucked between two windows. I didn't resist. My legs were feeling kind of shaky, and the longer I thought about what happened Friday night, the shakier I felt—and not just my legs.

"I slept with him."

Cam blinked, her surprise obvious. "Okay...that wasn't what I expected to hear. Not considering how you look now—or how you were Friday night." She brushed back my hair and tucked it behind my ear. "If I'm going to be honest, I'd say you had plans to cut him loose that night. You just weren't into him. Am I wrong?"

"No." I took another drink from the soft drink, then put it down. "There just wasn't anything there. Plus, I'm still hung up on Trent. But he wanted to stop for a drink —it was that Italian bistro a few blocks from my building."

Cam nodded. "Okay."

"I had to go to the bathroom first, and when I went out to join Roger, he already had drinks." Shaking my head, I told her, "They must have been strong. I don't remember much of anything after two or three sips."

Cam took my hand and squeezed. "What?"

"I ended up plastered." With a half-hearted shrug, I said, "I'm not exactly a lightweight, but I'm not a heavy drinker, either. After those first couple of sips, everything is black until I woke up in his apartment. We were both in bed, naked. I put two and two together."

A cold sweat broke out over my skin, and I shivered.

"Sweetie, I think you're missing a couple of numbers."

"What?" Confused, I shook my head.

Cam leaned—or rather—swayed close, bracing a hand between us so her belly didn't throw her off balance. With her free hand, she touched my cheek.

"Listen to what you just told me. You went into a bathroom, let some guy you don't know all that well order drinks. Then you wake up hours later naked and in bed with him." She paused, anger and sympathy both warring in her eyes. "What does that sound like?"

The bottom of my belly dropped out as my mind connected all the dots.

No.

My mind had already figured out that equation—I'd just been hiding from the knowledge.

Why else had I felt so sick, so...*wrong* every time I thought about waking up at his place?

"He roofied me," I said, voice flat.

"I can't say for certain one way or the other." Cam had an opinion, and it burned in her eyes. "But if you were in my shoes, what would you think?"

Lurching off the couch, I paced the floor, mind spinning as I tried to pierce the veil of black that separated me from the memory of the time with Roger after that drink.

"Shit. Shit. *Shit*."

I spun around and faced Cam from across the room. "What should I do?"

Cam lifted her hands and shrugged. "I don't know if there's anything you *can* do. I remember from a class I took in college—some drugs are so fast-acting, metabolized so quickly, and are out of your system in eight hours. Others are slower. It's been over forty-eight hours, regardless, so if you want to do *anything*, we need to get you to the ER so you can get checked."

I felt sick. Having to talk about this to *anybody* made me want to puke. Every TV show I'd ever watched about sexual assault flashed through my mind.

"I don't want to go to the ER." Crossing my arms over my chest, I shook my head. "Isn't there someplace else?"

Cam considered, then pulled out her phone. "Hold on."

Moving to the window, I leaned forward and pressed my brow to the cool glass. Closing my eyes, I blocked out Cam's quiet conversation.

Why hadn't I seen it sooner?

"Okay, Jazz. I've got something arranged. Let's go."

Turning, I met Cam's eyes. "Go where?"

"One of the clinics we support also offers assistance to rape victims. I'm friends with several of the doctors there. One of them will get you in." Her face softened as she came to me, offering a hand. "It's completely confidential. But you and I both know you'll worry sick if you don't at least try to get answers."

DR. AIDA DOUCETTE came in quietly, shutting the door behind her.

Cam was sprawled in the chair by the window, and I was on the wheeled stool, fighting the urge to fidget.

Dr. Doucette didn't look uncomfortable because she had to hitch herself up onto the table to sit since the other two seats were taken.

I frowned and started to stand. "I can—"

"You're fine, Jazz." Her voice was like molasses, thick and rich, sounding of the deep south and full of kind concern. "I've got my best nurse handling the tests. It will be forty-eight hours before all the tests come back, but I need to warn you. Some drugs are out of the system so quickly, unless you came by bright and early the morning after, we're not going to find any sign of them in your system."

"I know." I gave a jerky nod and blinked until the burning in my eyes faded. "I just...I needed to try, at least. I mean, maybe it's nothing—"

"I think we both know that's not the case."

I couldn't hold the tears back this time.

Swiping at them, I nodded. "I woke up feeling so...*wrong*," I whispered.

"It's possible some of your memories are just waiting until you're ready. The mind has a way of protecting you." Her face softened, and the compassion in her eyes nearly broke me.

"I feel so *stupid*."

"That's natural," Dr. Doucette said. "And I want to tell you that you're wrong. You're not stupid. And you're not to blame for what somebody *did* to you. This was somebody you had a history with, too, so you had every reason to think you'd be safe with him." She sighed, the sound bearing the weight of too much knowledge. "In a perfect world, we'd never have to worry about whether or not we were safe with those we spend time with, would we? But that's not our world."

"YOU DON'T HAVE to do this."

Cam poked me in the arm. "Hush. Yes, I do. Now hurry up and tell me what you want because I'm *starving*."

She pushed the take-out menu at me again, and I sighed, giving in. After a cursory look, I told her what to order before cuddling back into the couch to resume staring out the window at the pouring rain.

Once she finished calling in our order, I said, "It's going to flood if it keeps this up."

"Yeah." Cam eased her body down next to me and kicked off her shoes. "Fortunately, you've got a well-stocked fridge, so we'll be fine. Danny will be in dire straits, though. We've got about ten frozen pizzas and beer. Maybe a few bags of pretzels and some canned soup."

"Danny could live on pizza and beer."

"I could, too. Until…" Cam sighed and looked down at her belly, a soft smile curving her lips. "It's okay, cutie. I love you more than all the pizza and all the beer."

"That's love right there." The words came out a little hoarse.

Cam levered herself up from her corner of the couch and came to sit next to me. The tears threatened again as she leaned into me.

"It's okay to cry, Jazzie," she said. "I'd be crying and kicking and throwing things."

"I'm too tired for that." *Literally* too tired.

Cam straightened and looked at me, her hand folding over mine. "Then sleep. If that's what you need, you sleep. There's no right or wrong way to feel right now, honey."

She grabbed the remote and turned on the TV.

I half-laughed, half-sobbed when she went to one of my streaming apps and found a popular painter's series. "The guaranteed method to help us both relax and snooze. Of course, *I* won't sleep until I eat, but you can."

"You're a menace." I smiled as I said it.

"You know you love me." She pulled at the decorative throw I always kept on the couch and draped it over us. "Now, let's see if we can learn how to paint happy little trees."

TWENTY-FIVE
TRENT

The phone rang for the third time in ten minutes. The first two times, I hadn't bothered to see who was calling. This time, annoyed to be jerked out of the groove while working, I grabbed it and barely glanced at the screen, ready to snarl at the caller.

Then I lost my breath at the impact of seeing Jazz's number.

"Jazz," I answered, finally, right before it would have gone to voicemail.

"No. Try again."

The woman's voice, throaty and vaguely familiar, but most definitely *not* Jazz's, had me scowling. Turning away from my piano, I walked to the window and stared out of the beach. "Hi, Cam. Why are you calling me from Jazz's phone?"

"Because I don't have your number on mine, and I need to talk to you," she answered, her tone breezy and light as if we talked every day of the week. "Listen...hold on, I need to check...okay, we're good. I think there's something you should know, but before I get into that...tell me. Do you have feelings for Jazz?"

Heat suddenly blistered my cheeks. "Excuse me?"

"You heard me. It's a simple enough question. Why is it so difficult for you to answer? I mean, considering how kinky you like to get, answering a question about a recently-ended relationship should be child's play."

"I'm...I'm...well, I can give an answer," I said, although the words came out strangled, proving Cam's point. "Is there a reason you're poking around in my private business?"

"Because it's not *just* your business. It involves Jazz, too. Since she's my best friend and I love her to death, her being happy means everything to me. And if you have feelings for her, I need to know so I can make a decision about something." Cam hesitated, then, voice going soft and quietly somber, she added, "Something sort of serious. But if you don't care—"

"I do," I said, cutting her off. The way her voice dropped and roughened, my concern blatant had a knot forming in my gut. "What's going on?"

"Something might have happened over the weekend." Cam sucked in a breath, then, in a rush, said, "We were all out on a double date Friday. Jazz met up with somebody she briefly dated in high school, and it could maybe be kinda my fault—I'm always on her to give the guys asking her out a chance. Her mom and dad...well, she's not big on trusting people and this is going to make all that worse."

She paused for air.

I jumped in. "What *happened*?"

"He might have slipped her a roofie."

A second passed. Another. I was in my studio, and the soundproofing was so solid, that not even the cars speeding down the highway penetrated the silence.

The sound of my hard breaths seemed unnaturally loud.

Blood roared in my ears, thundering like a freight train.

A primal, red-hot rage pounded in my head, and I had to fight not to throw my phone. "Did he hurt her?"

"Physically?" Cam sighed. "No. But there's nothing but a blank spot between the time she had the drink he probably spiked with a date-rape drug and when she woke up at his place. She's kind of a mess right now. Trent, I don't know if you're aware, but she fell for you. I know that's not the sort of relationship either of you planned, but she was *happy* with you—the kind of happy she hasn't ever been. Then you were gone, and I pushed her into saying yes to this asshole, and he..." Her voice cracked. "I'm going to kill him, but that's another topic altogether. If you care about her, you should be here."

Her words hit me like a fist—several fists. One was a blow straight to my heart, already bruised from walking away, leaving the only woman I'd ever cared for. The other was straight to my gut, knocking the breath out of me as I tried to process what Cam was saying.

Jazz had feelings for me.

And all that fucking *paled* under the news Cam had given me.

Some bastard had drugged and raped her.

"Trent?"

"I'm here." My voice sounded raw and gritty like I'd sucked in a bucket of sand.

"Can you come?"

"Fuck." I shoved a hand through my hair and spun away from the window to look at the piano, the notes I had spread on the table near the far wall, the project board hanging above it. "I was just contracted to do a movie soundtrack. I'm literally supposed to be meeting my agent and the movie director in a couple of hours."

"I see." Cam drew in a breath and blew it out. "Well, okay, then. I'll take care of her. Bye, Trent."

"Cam, wait. It's not that I don't *want* to be there. But I signed a fucking contract. I...fuck."

"You gotta do what you gotta do, Trent," she said, voice soft, sympathetic even. "I'll take care of Jazz. The two of us have been holding each other up for a long time now. Good-bye."

"I CAN'T FUCKIN' believe it." The words exploded from Joe Hook, Jr for what had to be the third time since we had been seated in a semi-private nook in a new Beverly Hills restaurant Joe had sworn was worth dying for.

So far, I wasn't impressed by anything, from him to the wine list to the appetizers that had been brought out, but then, my mind was almost three thousand miles away. They could serve me deep-fried sawdust, and I probably wouldn't notice.

"You boys are way too calm about this. Don't you know what a problem this is?" Joe leaned forward, his elbow bumping into the glass of bourbon—filled almost to the brim he'd poured from the bottle he had brought to the table.

Some of it splashed out, and he swore, grabbing a napkin and blotting at it as if the liquor had jumped out of the glass to attack his white linen shirt.

"Fucking service around here," he muttered. "Open a month, and it's already going downhill."

"Maybe if you didn't fill it to the brim or bash things with your elbows," I muttered.

Under the table, Stephen kicked me.

Hook narrowed his eyes and leaned back.

I returned his stare.

"Guess we're all on edge about the news that we can't start as early as hoped."

Considering I'd just signed on the fucking dotted line, I hadn't expected to start working for several weeks —or longer. I'd much rather be on a plane flying to New York City.

I didn't point that out, though. I gave a humorless smile. "What are you going to do?"

"Fuckin' A." Hook grabbed his bourbon and tossed half of it back. Making a face, he hit his chest with a closed fist. "Yeah, that's the stuff."

The server reappeared at that moment and served our entrees. Hook, fortunately, decided not to be an ass, and we were left alone in under two minutes.

"Okay." Hook gave me a sidelong glance, talking around a mouth full of food. "Here's what I think we should do. Sure, our leading lady is holding shit up— nobody has a work ethic these days. But we've got others ready to go, and I think we should get started on rehearsals. We can have somebody do Divinity's lines, and that way, Trent, you can get a better feel for the movie from the get-go."

"If that's how you want to go, I'll give it a try." Staring into my glass, swirling it, so the amber liquid sloshed around, I wondered how Jazz was. Had Cam stayed with her? Was she alone? Fuck, my head was a mess.

"Great to see how enthusiastic you are, Dixson," Hook said, the words thick with sarcasm.

Stephen kicked me as I started to respond. Probably a good thing because I was about to enthusiastically tell Joe Hook, Jr to kiss my ass.

The phone laying on the table between Hook and me lit up, ringing loud and shrill. Joe grabbed it. Without looking at us, he said, "I gotta take this."

While he was on the phone, Stephen stood up and grabbed my arm. "We'll give you a few minutes, Joe."

Stephen couldn't have been more obvious with his irritation if he'd pulled me along behind him by my ear. He let go once we were in the men's restroom but shut the door and leaned against it, preventing escape—or interruption by others.

"What the hell crawled up your ass and died?" His eyes were hard and flat, but there was concern. "This is your big shot, what you've worked for, and it seems to me like you're *trying* to blow it."

"I'm not trying. But that guy is a douche—a class-act douche," I said. Turning away from my friend, I paced the ivory and smoke tiles, Jazz's face flashing through my mind.

"Yeah, he's an asshole, but you've worked with bigger assholes, Trent. It's part of the job. So what gives?"

I stopped at the far wall, bracing my hands against it,

and lowered my head. I'd been playing that call from Cam through in my mind, over and over, all day. The more I thought about it, the angrier I got at myself. What was I *thinking*, staying here while Jazz was alone in New York City?

"Trent, talk to me," Stephen said quietly.

Pushing away from the wall, I turned and faced Stephen. "Jazz's best friend called me earlier."

Something flickered in Stephen's eyes. "Yeah? Is she okay?"

"I don't know." Looking away, I stared at the row of stalls, the doors glossy and black. "This stays between us. No matter what, okay?"

"Yeah, man. Sure."

"Jazz and Cam were out a few days ago, a double date. The guy with Jazz was some high school friend." The ugly rage began to brew inside, and I paused, counting to ten. "It looks like he slipped her some drugs, took her back to his place."

Stephen said nothing.

Looking back at him, I said, "Cam wanted me to fly back to New York, and I told her I couldn't. Because of a fucking musical score. I finally found a woman who makes me want things, and when she needed me, I said *no*."

"You didn't really say *no*, though, did you?"

Frowning, I shook my head. "As good as."

"Bullshit." He came over to me and gripped my shoulder. "Go home. Call a Lyft or whatever, pack, and get to the airport. Take the earliest flight you can and get to New York. Take care of your lady, man."

"And what about Mr. Charm out there?"

Stephen smirked. "I'll handle him. Besides, he's the one who pointed out we can't do much until the leading lady is ready. There's no reason for you to be on hand throughout line rehearsals. You got a few days, easy. And you can work on the preliminary stuff anywhere. So *go*."

I hesitated.

"*Go.*"

TWENTY-SIX
JAZZ

Eyes on the screen and earbuds in place with music blaring to block out distractions, I worked on the press release, giving it one more go-over before sending it to our PR company.

We'd only started farming out that job the previous year, although Cam and I still did most of the writing when it came to press releases. Cam had offered to handle this one for me, but the mundane task was exactly what I needed—simple but requiring focus and attention to detail.

A *lot* of attention to detail.

Halfway through my third time, a vibration on my table had me looking up.

CeCe, our receptionist, gave me an apologetic smile as I tugged out my earbuds.

"Sorry, Jazz. You have a call on line two. It's a nurse from your doctor's office. They weren't able to get through on your phone."

Frowning, I looked at my phone, then sighed as I realized I'd never turned the *do not disturb* feature off from last night. I'd gone to bed early and set the app for a manual turn-off instead of auto.

"Thanks, CeCe."

She smiled. "No problem. Want me to close the door on my way out?"

Muting the music on my phone, I nodded. Once she was gone, I sucked in a desperate breath, my lungs already squeezing shut on me.

There was only one doctor's office that would be calling right now. It made perfect sense that my hand shook a little when I picked up the phone, just as it was normal that my throat felt tight, right?

"This is Jazz."

"Hello, Jazz. This is Dr. Doucette."

"Oh...I...well, I thought it would be a nurse calling." I pushed my hair back, then crossed my free arm over my belly. I felt like I was about to come apart inside.

"I'm sorry. Several of your employees might recognize my name since I've been in the office before to thank you and Cam for your donations to the clinic. I wanted to protect your privacy."

"Oh. Well, thank you."

"I'm calling about your test results." She paused, then asked softly, "Is this a good time to talk?"

I had the insane urge to yell *no*, toss the phone down and run out of the office. The saying *ignorance is bliss* had to come from somewhere.

"Yes."

"Alright. Well, the first thing—your bloodwork and all the tests for any possible STI—sexually transmitted infection—came back clear. I know you mentioned seeing a condom, but it's still good news that these tests came back clean. We'll need to do follow-ups as discussed, and you need to continue the medication regimen—unless you think you want to find a way to have the man who assaulted you tested. If he's clean, chances are you'll be fine."

"I'll take the meds for now," I said in a weak voice. Just *thinking* about seeing Roger made me want to hurl.

"Alright. Just keep in mind, we'll have to rescreen."

"Yes." I licked my lips and found them painfully dry. "I know. About the...other stuff?"

"Yes, the drug screens." She sighed, a world of weary resignation in the sound. "I'm afraid it's as I'd suspected. Both bloodwork and the results from the urinalysis were clear. I'm afraid just too much time passed before we could take the labs."

"I'm sorry."

"Now, none of that," she said, voice firm. "You are *not* to blame for any of this."

"If I'd come in sooner..."

"Honey, some drugs are metabolized so fast, if you sleep even just a few hours, we can miss it. None of this is on you. The blame lies with *him*."

"*If* he drugged me," I muttered. How was I supposed to cope with *not knowing*? My mind tried to spiral away —that question circling through my thoughts, again and again. *Focus! Listen to the doctor!*

It helped, the soothing rhythm of her voice anchoring me to the here and now. It wouldn't last. In the back of my mind, a storm was growing, and had been growing ever since waking in Roger's bed. But I was scared of that storm, and the emotions, afraid to let myself feel all that misery and hurt and betrayal.

So I listened to Dr. Doucette.

"Whether you were drugged or simply inebriated doesn't change the fact that he assaulted you. If you were so out of it that you couldn't recall the night's events the following morning, you weren't in any condition to consent. And he likely knows it. I'm sorry we can't give you the closure that comes with definitive answers, but there is *nothing* you did wrong."

Tears burned my eyes, and her compassion made the knot in my throat even worse. "Thank you, Dr. Doucette. I'll work on telling myself that." With a tired, watery laugh, I said, "Logically, I get it. But logic and what I feel inside..."

"They don't always see eye to eye, do they? Listen, I can't tell you how to proceed from here, but talking to somebody, whether a group or a private counselor, *does* help. If you decide that's what you want, call me, and I'll recommend someone."

After another minute or two of quiet conversation, I hung up. Once I no longer had the doctor's voice as a distraction, I sucked in air and spun away from my desk, leaning forward as the pain inside threatened to double me over.

My skin felt clammy and cold chills started wracking me.

I never heard Cam come in, but she was there, leaning against my desk while I leaned against her, her arm around my shoulders as I fought to hold it together.

"You can cry," she said. "You don't always have to be so strong, Jazz."

"I can't cry here. I can't let the staff see me falling apart, Cam. It might scare them, and I can't give them answers that wouldn't make them ask more questions." Shaking my head, I focused on the things I could touch, feel, see, smell, and hear. The scratchy-soft material of Cam's hip-length summer sweater. The hard swell of her pregnant belly. Her hand stroking my hair. The faint scent of the lavender lotion she loved. Chatter out in the main area of the office. The *Lush Lotus* pink polish on my toenails.

Bit by bit, I dragged my emotions under control.

"Was it Dr. Doucette on the phone?"

I nodded, the dull headache pulsing behind my eyes, sending a sharp spike of pain through my skull at the movement.

"Want to talk? Or should I let it go?"

"They didn't find anything." I hugged her, then eased away. Rising to my feet, I moved to the window and stared outside. "Too much time had passed. If I'd had the sense to go Saturday..."

"Don't play that game, Jazz." She walked toward me and bumped her shoulder against mine. "Whether he slipped you a roofie or just intentionally got you plastered, the results are the same—and the results are conclusive proof of his asshole-ishness."

"Asshole-ishness. Is that a word?"

"Yep." She rested her head on my shoulder. "Why don't you go home? Take the afternoon off."

"I need to finish the press release."

"I'll do it. Or you can leave after you finish. Or we can delay it another day. Go home, Jazz. Take some time to cry, then figure out what you want to do."

"There's only one thing I *can* do—put this behind me."

"Well..." Cam drew the word.

The tone in her voice made me give a wary look. "What?"

"We could corner that bastard at his work and kick his balls up into his brain stem."

Her bloodthirsty smile made me laugh, and I hugged her. "I'll sleep on that option."

DESPITE THE OVERWHELMING urge to cry at the office, I was numb by the time I got to my building.

I'd *been* numb for days, my emotions strangely blunted even as the raging storm in my head grew louder and stronger. The numbness was a shield but not a strong one.

Sometime soon, it would break, and the onslaught of pain, panic and betrayal would drop down.

Like a tidal wave, it was going to sweep me under. I'd be helpless against it, powerless.

Lost.

Alone.

Hurrying past everyone in the lobby, I got on the elevator and jabbed the button for the doors to close. I breathed a sigh of relief when nobody joined me, slumping against the wall and clinging to the handrail as the car swept me up to my floor.

Arms folded over my middle, I stepped off. But before I could take a step, I saw him.

Trent.

He was sitting on the floor outside my door, almost exactly as he'd been the last time, we'd seen each other before he left.

The ache in my chest swelled and threatened to explode.

"Trent," I whispered.

He was already on his feet, coming to me.

Then I was in his arms, my face buried against his chest as the tears I'd been fighting finally fell. I could feel his heart pounding against my cheek, feel the strength of his arms around me, holding on so tight.

Finally, *finally*, I felt grounded again and connected to the world in a way I hadn't since waking up Saturday morning to find myself in bed with a man who was all but a stranger.

Shudders wracked me. Trent pressed his lips to my temple and kissed me softly. "It's okay, baby. I'm here. I got you."

Burrowing in closer, I clung to him. He hadn't said anything, and I didn't ask, but somehow, I knew he was aware of what had happened. Maybe I should be embarrassed or ashamed, but in that moment, I was just *relieved* to have him there. Relieved that I wasn't alone.

"Don't let go," I said, burrowing in even closer. "Don't let go."

"I won't."

TWENTY-SEVEN
TRENT

Once I had Jazz inside her apartment, I scooped her up into my arms and carried her to the couch.

She cried, the sobs shaking her body, and I would have given anything to fix what was hurting her. I couldn't. All I could do was hold her while she cried through the pain.

Pressing my lips to her temple, I murmured to her without thinking about the words. When she twisted in my arms, I let go.

Was she afraid now? Afraid to be touched after somebody had likely violated her?

But she twisted into me, throwing one leg over mine, so she straddled me. Her hands cupped my face and tugged until I met her eyes.

"Make me forget," she whispered, pressing her mouth to mine. "Make it all go away for a little while."

I was gripping her hips. I didn't remember doing it, but the curves of her body, the heat, everything about her seduced me.

But...

"Are you sure?"

"Yes." As if to emphasize that single word, she shoved her hands into my hair and pulled hard, dragging my head to hers so she could press her mouth to mine.

The kiss she gave me was demanding, fervent with hunger and a blind need to lose herself.

It was the sort of kiss I'd never had from a woman—the demand in it one I'd never expected to find myself responding to.

Pushing up her skirt, I closed my hands over her hips, the sparse layer of her panties an unwanted barrier. Sliding my fingers under the lacy edges along her legs, I whispered, "We should take these off."

She kissed a line down my neck. "I don't want to stop touching you to do it."

The butterfly caresses as she brushed her mouth along my neck were so light, so gentle. How could such a soft touch be so damn arousing?

Shoving my hand into her hair, I fisted and tugged. Her eyes burned with an inner fire as she met my gaze.

"Make me forget," she said again. Then she kissed me, her lips hungry on mine—but only for a moment. She slid from my lap to kneel on the floor in front of me, her fingers nimble on the buttons of my shirt as she freed each from their moorings, one by one.

I released her hair and caught hold of the couch cushions beneath me, heart hammering against my ribs.

She pressed a kiss to my chest with every button she freed, painting a trail down my body that blazed hotter with every touch. She stopped when she reached my waistband, her path now blocked by my belt and jeans.

She looked at me from under her lashes, the silent question there clear as day.

"I'm yours," I said softly. If she'd asked, I would have told her just how completely she owned me.

But she just smiled and undid the belt buckle, drawing out each task until I was gritting my teeth against the urge to tell her to hurry.

When she'd finally freed my cock, I groaned, reaching down to wrap my hand around the base, fisting myself in an effort to ease the ball-busting ache.

A shuddering breath escaped Jazz.

Looking at her, I saw her lashes drop, her tongue sweeping across the lower curve of her lips.

"What are you going to do now?" I asked, the words gritty.

"What can I do?" she asked.

"Whatever you want."

The purple-blue of her irises darkened, and she leaned forward, her hand coming up to wrap around my cock, fingers lacing with mine. The wet, slick caress of her mouth had me arching up, the pleasure sending a lick of heat down my spine.

She retreated, and I tried to follow, only for her to slide down again, the wet, delicious heat of her mouth sheer bliss.

Mindlessly, I tangled my free hand in her hair, hips pushing upward to urge her deeper.

She responded by scraping her teeth along the sensitive underside of my cock when she withdrew. Her eyes blazed at me, held me, challenged me.

Freeing my hand from hers, I shifted, now gripping both sides of her head.

"Yours," I said again. "But you can't expect me to be quiet and still when you're driving me crazy."

A light glinted in her eyes. Then she moved back down, pausing as the head of my cock hit the back of her throat—then she swallowed, the silken heat tightening a fraction before she slid back up.

Her hands stroked along my tense thighs, her nails raking over the denim as she dragged them down. I groaned when she broke away from me but stood at her silent urging when she tugged on the waistband of my jeans.

She pulled and tugged until she had the denim and my boxers down but stopped once she had them just below my hips, her hands coming up to grip my hips, her eyes holding mine as she licked my dick to the top before circling her tongue around the tip.

Growling, I gripped my cock at the base with one hand and tangled the other in her hair. She smiled, the fervent, blind desperation no longer haunting her eyes.

"You want to make me crazy," I said.

"You've been doing that to me almost from the beginning." She scraped her teeth gently over my cock before giving me another teasing smile.

"Open," I said. "For fuck's sake...please, Jazz."

She licked the tip again, opening to take me inside, but at a pace so slow, I thought I'd lose it.

Groaning, I shifted my other hand to her head as well, staring down at the picture she made, on her knees in front of me, my cock slick as she pulled back, then swayed forward, each movement tantalizing, erotic. I tugged on her hair when she went to pull back but stopped, reminding myself I was letting her lead here.

She saw something in my eyes, awareness, understanding, and reacted by covering the hands I still had cupped over her head, pressing harder.

I got the message and gave in to the insanity growing between us, thrusting into the hot, wet cave of her mouth, muttering to her, feeling her body heat rise, feeling her shake.

It was bliss, having her mouth on me, her hands clutching at my hips as if she wanted to hold on tight.

But before I could come, I stopped, gripping Jazz under the arms and pulling her up. She was breathless, her mouth gleaming and swollen. Catching the hem of her fitted blouse, I stripped it off, then dipped my head to kiss the swells of her breasts rising over the pretty lace bra.

"Fuck, I want you," I muttered. "I've gone crazy not having you with me."

Her hands gripped my biceps, nails digging in. "Same. I want you inside me, Trent. Now."

She pushed against my chest, the edge of the couch an inch or two behind me. I sank onto it, fisting my cock and stroking as I watched her.

Jazz came to straddle me.

I shook my head. "Panties off, or I'll rip them."

She slipped her hands under her skirt and shimmied her hips, a scrap of lace falling to the floor as she came to me.

She swung one leg over my hips. I groaned as she rubbed against me, the sweet, slick heat of her a decadent caress against my cock.

"Put me inside you," I whispered as she rubbed my mouth against mine.

She did, and we groaned as she sank down, her pussy clamping tight around me.

My cock jerked.

Her body stiffened, and her spine arched forward to make her breasts strain against the confines of her pretty lace bra.

Unable to resist the offering, I dipped my head, licked the curve of one, and felt her harsh exhale. She shoved her hands into my hair. "More."

"My pleasure." Working the lace and silk cups down until her breasts were free, I took one nipple into my mouth, scraping my teeth over it gently.

"Trent!" Her strangled cry echoed through the empty apartment and bounced off the walls before coming back to me in a sweet refrain.

Hands going to her hips, I lifted her, then dragged her back down.

Her pussy spasmed around me, the milking sensation unbearably erotic.

My hands tightened on her hips, mouth more demanding as I sucked on her nipple.

Jazz whimpered and began to rock against me, her head falling back.

"You're so fucking beautiful," I said.

"Flattery will get you anything." She curled her arms around my neck, her knees tightening until she embraced me with her entire body.

"Don't make promises you can't keep—I just might try to collect." I bit her lower lip.

"Collect what?" she asked, the words breathy against my lips.

"Everything. You. *All* of you." I arched under her,

thrusting upward as I dragged her back down, unable to get deep enough, unable to have *enough* of her.

Her eyes widened. But when her body started to clench and the orgasm hit, her first and me seconds later.

As the sensations swept over us, thought, reason and rationale were lost.

But the lingering warning hovered in the back of my mind.

"Everything. You. All of you."

All of her—it was the only thing that would ever be enough for me now.

And I had no idea how to ask her for what I needed.

HOURS LATER, over a delivery of Italian food that included the best damn bread I'd ever eaten and tiramisu that left Jazz moaning in a way that had my dick going hard, I debated how to ask her the questions burning inside me.

She saved me the trouble.

After putting her spoon down, she picked up a glass of wine and sipped. She lowered it slightly as if she knew she'd need another drink in the seconds before asking, "You know what happened, don't you?"

"Yeah." A heavy breath burst out of me—I felt like I'd been gorging on oxygen to keep my rage in check, but that same rage made it hard for me to breathe right, so the trapped air in my lungs had everything feeling tight, imprisoned, my ribcage far more restrictive than I could ever recall. "Ah...don't get mad at her, but Cam called me."

"Cam?"

I picked up my wine and nodded before taking a drink. I'd already had one drink today and knew I shouldn't have any more than this, but for now, I was in a *fuck it all* mood—all that mattered was Jazz.

"She told me she was worried about you—*is* worried." I hesitated, then smiled. "I wanted to come anyway."

Jazz touched my cheek, brows drawn together. "Why?"

"Because I can't stop thinking about you." I took her hand and kissed the tips of her fingers. "Because you're in my every thought, under my skin. I feel you with me even when we're separated by thousands of miles. I needed to see you and tell you that."

A look of wonder filled her eyes, and she leaned forward, pressing her brow to mine.

I kissed her gently, then pulled back, cupping her chin.

She swallowed before offering a shaky smile. "I haven't been able to stop thinking about you, either."

One of the tangled knots in my chest loosened. "Yeah?"

"Yeah." With a hard sigh, she added, "I might consider not being mad at Cam."

"Do that." Hoping I wasn't about to make it worse, I asked, "Can you tell me what happened? If you don't want to talk about it, I understand. But I'm having a hard time not hunting this bastard down and killing him, based on what I know."

"I don't know much." Her eyes moved past me, taking on a far-off look before refocusing. "Let's go sit down, okay?"

A few moments later, in the living room, she sat curled against me, her drink in hand and her head on my shoulder. She started talking about running into Roger shortly before I'd left New York, then the double-date with Cam and Danny, and how that had ended in a blur of black and emptiness and her waking the following day with no idea of how she'd come to be in Roger's apartment.

"And the doctor's sure there's no way to ascertain any sign of drugs?" I asked as she came to the end, her voice soft and husky.

"Yes."

"Where was the bar?"

She lifted her head to look at me. "Why?"

I considered lying and decided against it.

"Because I bet, he's done this before. I was thinking about going by there, find out if he's a regular, and maybe ask a few questions."

Jazz narrowed her eyes. After a silent moment, she told me, "I doubt you'll get much of anything asking around. The place was packed."

"I know it's a crapshoot. But I'll try anyway. It can't hurt." Kissing her forehead, I cupped the back of her neck. "I'm so fucking sorry this happened, Jazz."

In response, she just cuddled closer, and I held her tight.

If there were any way to find answers—and make that prick pay—I would find it.

TWENTY-EIGHT
JAZZ

JERKING UPRIGHT IN BED, I GASPED FOR AIR.

Trent was lying next to me. His body solid and warm, and all I wanted to do was curl into him, wake him up, and beg him to make the nightmare disappear.

A soft, deep breath escaped him as I wiggled closer. His arm came around me, and I burrowed closer.

It didn't work.

Roger.

Shuddering, I tried again to push the broken shards of the dream out of my head.

My chest ached as if I'd been struggling to breathe and couldn't. I didn't know if it was just a panic reflex or a memory.

The dream...

Sliding out of bed, I hurried into the bathroom and closed the door. After fumbling to get the lights on, I found my robe and wrapped it around me.

I still felt cold, those broken bits of memory still clear.

Dreams usually faded more and more with every passing second after I woke but this wasn't fading.

I had a bad feeling because it had really happened, and it wasn't a dream, but memories working free.

Bile rushed up my throat. I fought it back, but the urge to puke was strong. Turning off the lights, I eased the door open.

The shadow looming on the other side made me yelp.

"Hey."

"Trent..." A harsh breath escaped me, and I groaned, half-collapsing into him when he held out his arms. Eyes burning, I buried my face against his chest. "Did I wake you?"

"The empty bed woke me." He brushed my hair back from my face. "Are you okay?"

"Nightmare." I never even considered not telling him. Shivering in reaction to the vivid images, I whispered, "I think it was more of a memory, though. From that night. I was...there. At Roger's."

Trent stiffened, and I squeezed my eyes shut.

"Tell me," he murmured, voice gentle despite the anger I knew was burning inside him.

"It's not clear." I clenched my hands, a tight, hot fist clenching in my belly. The trembling got worse, and I fumbled free of Trent's embrace so I could turn away from him and hit the lights. They flashed too bright, and I winced, instinctively shielding my face as I blinked.

"He held me down," I said, voice shaking. "I can't remember everything—I don't know if I even *want* to. But he held me down even when I told him to stop. I...he..."

Anger locked my throat, and I spun around, glaring at Trent because there was nobody else to take my anger out on. "He hurt me. I remember that. He *hurt* me, and he didn't care."

Trent came to me. I shoved him back, hands to his chest.

He went still, eyes watchful.

"Should I leave?" he asked quietly.

"No." Now tears burned my eyes. Flinging myself at him, I wrapped my arms around his neck. "I'm just...*angry*. I'm so *angry*. It's like this rage has been hiding, and now it's filling me up, and there's not enough room for it. It's spilling over, and I can't *stop* it."

"Then let me have it. I can take it." He fisted a hand in my hair and pressed his brow to mine. "Take it out on me. Let me help."

"He held me down," I said again, my voice shaking. "It's not like...it's nothing like what we do. But there's poison inside me, something bad in me. It makes me want to hurt, makes me want to lash out.."

"No." Trent kissed me, quick, hard. "There's nothing bad in you. *Nothing*."

He was wrong. There was anger, grief, sadness, and too many things that *weren't* me and I hated it.

But I couldn't figure out the words to explain any of that.

"I...Trent, I feel empty." Eyes burning, I hauled his head closer. "Kiss me. Touch me. Make me forget."

The kiss he gave me was sweet, almost gentle—and at any other time, I might have cried from the care I sensed in it. But I needed fire and passion. Pushing my fingers into his hair, I bit his lip. "Not like that, Trent. Make me burn. Please."

His eyes bore into mine, the harsh flags of color on his

cheekbones stark against the tense lines of his face. "We'll both burn."

He jerked my robe open, then caught my waist and lifted me onto the sink counter. The cold marble was a shock against my naked butt, grounding me, a contrast against the heat of his hands. His lips devoured mine until, breathless, I tore away, needing air.

He was undeterred, kissing a line down my neck until he found the sensitive spot between neck and shoulder.

"Trent!" I gasped when he bit me, then laved the small hurt with his tongue. Needing more, needing him —*all* of him, I went to wrap my legs around his waist, but he stopped me, his hands catching my thighs and holding me still.

He met my eyes, and I looked at him, then lowered my gaze, whimpering as he closed his hand around his cock, stroking up, then down, the hard length jerking in reaction to his rough touch.

"Don't close your eyes," he said softly as he moved closer, one hand still gripping my thigh, the other steadying his cock as he tucked the head against my entrance.

At that point, closing my eyes wasn't even an option. His gaze held me captive even as the heat of me, the strength of him filled me, overwhelmed me. Reaching for him, I tugged him down, pressing my lips to his.

The kiss was desperate and needy.

His cock swelled as he pushed into me, hard and fast.

Crying out into his mouth, I gripped his shoulders.

"Jazz?"

"More," I whispered to him. "Harder. Faster."

He did as I asked, and I held on tight. Soon, we were lost within each other, and the dregs of the nightmare disappeared.

For a little while, at least.

TWENTY-NINE
TRENT

THE MEMORY OF JAZZ CRYING WAS BURNED INTO THE fabric of my mind as the Lyft driver took me back to the apartment building.

I rode the subway with her to work.

Once she was inside, I'd called for the Lyft, too impatient to get on with the idea I'd had yesterday. Jazz had given me the name of the restaurant where Roger had roofied her, and I wasn't going anywhere or doing anything until I talked to the people who managed the place.

The restaurant wasn't open yet, so I settled in at the coffee shop across the street. Ordering an espresso and a muffin nearly half the size of my head, I sat down to wait it out.

I was running high on rage and probably didn't need to add caffeine and sugar to the mix, but what the hell.

Passing the time by making notes on my phone as I read the script for the movie project, I destroyed the monstrous muffin and worked my way through another espresso. After that, I added some water to balance out the sugar and caffeine.

The open sign flicked on just as I was debating another espresso. After hitting the restroom in the coffee shop, I headed to the restaurant.

Doing a slow mental countdown from a hundred, I went inside and hoped the smile I gave the hostess didn't look as feral as I felt.

"Any chance the bartender working today was on duty Saturday night?"

The hostess smiled at me, a friendly curve of lips painted poppy red against a warm, deep brown skin. "It's your lucky day—well, week. Normally, he would have been off Saturday, but our regular weekend bartender got sick. Tony and Nikka are covering. I assume you want to talk to him?"

"Yes."

She glanced past me, then stepped out from behind the stand, indicating for me to follow.

"Hey, Tony! You got a guy wanting to talk to you," she said once we reached the bar, an area separated from the main room by a massive aquarium that ran from floor to ceiling, filled with brightly colored fish. Another aquarium, this one smaller but no less colorful, made up the bar's backdrop, the bottles of liquor against it lined up with neat, military precision.

I took a seat in front of Tony and asked for a beer, figuring it couldn't hurt to spend money while I tried to get what I wanted.

"How can I help you?" Tony put the bottle in front of me, his smile friendly like the hostess', but there was something more guarded about him.

A little bribe would probably help smooth things along. Glad I'd hit up the ATM before coming here. I slipped him a hundred.

"The hostess said you were working Saturday night."

"Yep." Tony's smile was polite, but he remained on guard as he discretely pocketed the bill.

"I'm trying to find some information on somebody." Pulling out my phone, I opened the photo apps and found the picture of Roger I'd downloaded from his Facebook page. "Do you remember seeing this guy?"

He held out his hand for my phone, and I turned it over.

No sooner had he looked at it than his face changed, and he returned my phone. "That prick? Yeah. I remember him from Saturday."

It was an act of willpower to keep still and stay calm.

"What about the woman with him that night?"

Tony's mouth twisted in a scowl. "He's been here before. Probably half a dozen times, almost always a different woman, and they all end up getting hammered. So, yeah, I remember him and the woman."

I suddenly noticed the security cameras in the bar. "If those cameras are recording, is there any way you'd let me see the video feed from Saturday night?"

For a long moment, Tony didn't say anything, just watched me.

Finally, he pulled out his phone. "Let me check with the bosses." He gave a half-smile.

I said nothing as he walked away, standing at the far end of the bar as he talked in a voice too low for me to hear.

It was a short conversation. In less than two minutes,

he was coming back to me, face set in tight lines as he tucked the phone away. "Give me a minute."

He returned quickly, a woman in black pants and a white shirt with him. While she went behind the counter, he nodded at me to follow. "Come on."

Leading me down a narrow hall, he talked over his shoulder. "You lucked out. If we weren't running so short this week, the video feed probably would have already been dumped. We only keep it for a couple days, so we don't fill up the hard drive. I was going to handle all of that before I clocked out at the end of the day."

He kept talking as he unlocked a door, then waved me in. He sat at a desk and pulled up a feed on a computer, then gave me a few simple instructions once he had the feed queued up on one of the monitors. "Got all that?"

"Yeah, I'll figure it out."

THE SECURITY CAMERA feed had six different camera angles, and I'd already switched so I had the bar on the monitor, but the time crawled along at a snail's pace. Finally, I texted Cam to find out when she thought Jazz and Roger might have arrived at the bar.

Cutting through maybe an hour of useless feed, I watched, jaw tight, my pulse pounding a drum beat at the base of my skull.

When I finally saw Roger at the bar, a wave of red washed over my vision. Putting the feed on regular speed, I leaned forward to watch.

Tony took a couple of minutes to get to him, and

Roger looked jumpy, casting glances in the direction of the hall that would have led to the bar's entrance and the bathrooms, where Jazz would be.

Once Roger had the drinks on the bar, he breathed easier—I could even see his shoulders drop as if he'd just exhaled a deep breath.

Leaning in closer, I watched, and waited.

Roger took a sip of his drink.

Glanced at the entrance.

Took a sip.

Glanced.

Then, as he went to put his drink down, some of it splashed out, and he hurriedly moved Jazz's drink.

Tony noticed Roger cleaning up, came by with a damp towel, wiped the surface, and gave Roger a polite smile before turning away. Roger's smug smile set my teeth on edge, so I rewound the feed to watch it again.

I'd watched the section three times before I noticed it.

As he was helpfully moving her drink to clean up, it looked like something fell into Jazz's martini.

While he tried to wipe up his mess with one hand, there was something fizzing at the bottom of hers. After a few stops and starts, I zoomed in and watched again.

Yeah, no doubt about it. He'd done *something*. He'd been clever about it, finding a way to conceal it. I probably would have missed it if I hadn't known to look for something—but there was no doubt. He *had* dosed her.

"You piece of shit." Pulling out the flash drive I'd brought along, I copied the security feed.

I took my time and double-checked to ensure I'd done it right.

M. S. PARKER

Once I left, I had a meeting scheduled with a cop at the nearest precinct. I hoped he'd find this video interesting.

I stopped by the bar and handed Tony a very generous tip.

His brows arched. "You found something?"

I gave him a smile. "Let's just say I don't think you'll see Roger here again anytime soon."

THIRTY
JAZZ

The rooftop restaurant had a spectacular view of the city. New York's twinkling lights spread out around us like jewels spilled onto a silken sheet of rich blue. Leaning against the railing with Cam, I glanced over my shoulder to see Trent and Danny were still waiting at the bar to get our drinks.

"This is my favorite place on nights like this." Cam lifted her face to the sky. "Weather's perfect, and you get this breeze..." Her face scrunched into an expression of discomfort. "Oh, *ow*."

I gave her a sympathetic look as she put a hand on the swell of her belly. "My little godchild practicing field goals again?"

"Field goals. The pommel horse. Trampoline on my bladder. She's going to be an all-around athlete." She grimaced and rubbed her hand over her belly, the material of her gauzy floral dress drifting around her ankles. "Honestly, I love this little darling already—so much, it makes me giddy sometimes. But I'm kinda done with the being pregnant part."

She looked so uncomfortable. Love for her pushed past the ache I still felt, and I put my hand over hers. "So, I guess you're not looking to be one of the moms who pops out one a year for the next decade, huh?"

Cam's eyes widened, then she burst into laughter, her hand still protectively cradling her belly as the other clapped over her mouth. It didn't do much to quiet the sounds of her delight, and *nothing* hid the merriment in her eyes.

"What's so funny?"

At the sound of Danny's voice, we both looked over.

Cam was still giggling as she accepted the strawberry lemonade from her sweetheart.

Rolling my eyes, I glanced at him and explained.

Danny's double-take had *me* breaking out into giggles. Soon, both Cam and I were laughing, leaning into each other while the two men eyed us as if we'd lost our minds.

"Are you going to stop laughing, or should I just drink this?"

Trent held up a glass of lemonade, the color a pale lavender since I'd gone with the blackberry.

"I'll take it." Still grinning at him as I accepted the drink, I wrapped my arm around Cam's shoulders. "I'm thinking this was a great idea, guys."

Trent's reply was cut off by my phone chirping out a message notification. Trent took my drink back so I could dig it out. The notification from the hostess stand popped up after I unlocked the screen.

"Come on." I kissed Cam on the cheek and pushed off the railing. "Let's eat."

THREE PLATES of appetizers sat on the table between us, Danny sipping on a beer while Trent stuck with water. I nearly froze when the server asked if I'd wanted a cocktail. Across from me, Cam spoke up, ordering a peach sweet tea for me and another strawberry lemonade for herself.

As the server walked away, I gave Cam a thankful look.

Trent took my hand under the table and squeezed. "You okay?"

"Yeah. I just..." The words wouldn't come, and I just shook my head.

"Trent told me that Roger ended up confessing to what he'd done." Cam nudged my foot with hers under the table, eyes serious, concerned. "Not just to you, but others."

"Yes." Swallowing, I picked up my nearly empty glass of lemonade and sipped, the melted ice cubes watering down the tartness of lemons and blackberries. "The detective who took my statement said they'd received almost a dozen reports in this precinct over the past five years, but there just wasn't enough information to hold the guy responsible."

"How did the cops get the evidence then?" Danny asked.

I looked at Trent and smiled. "Ask this guy."

Trent's jaw was tight. Under the table, I stroked my

thumb over the back of his hand and squeezed. It was my turn to soothe him.

After a few more seconds, he squeezed back and looked at Danny. "I went to the restaurant where they'd stopped for a drink. They let me watch the security feed."

He stopped, picked up his water, and eyed it. "Fuck, I could use a scotch right now."

Cam arched a brow. "The server is a few tables behind you. Want me to flag her down?"

"Nah." Trent took a drink of water. "I can't drink much as a rule." Blowing out a breath, he continued. "If you look carefully at the video, you can see him drop something in Jazz's drink, so I made a copy and took it to the cops. Once the detective saw it, they took Roger into custody."

Danny looked as grim as Trent, his ordinarily cheerful smile missing. "Will he make bail?"

"Yeah, but not until Monday." I selected an onion ring from the plate in front of me. "He held off saying anything last night. Didn't ask for a lawyer until he really fucked up and confessed."

"How did they get him to do that?" Cam took a tortilla chip and scooped up some guacamole.

"Smoke and mirrors." The bite of the onion ring I'd taken felt like stone in my belly. "They had interviewed several of his former dates, and a common theme was that all of them had memory lapses from their date. Then, the detective showed him the security tape and he confessed."

After Trent finished the story, I was suddenly aware that everybody at the table was watching me, and I forced a smile. "I'm okay, guys. I'm not going to break down."

"You have every right to," Danny said, compassion in his eyes, a lingering note of anger in his voice.

"I know." Blowing out a breath, I managed a shaky smile. "But I prefer to have my breakdowns in private."

Trent wrapped his arm around me and tugged me in, nuzzling my neck.

Eyes closed, I breathed in his scent, reveled in his warmth and how he made me feel so safe.

"Let's talk about something else," Cam said briskly. "Trent, what's the project you're working on?"

"HOW MANY TIMES are you going to pee?"

Cam made a face at me as she came out of the stall, our eyes meeting in the mirror. "I don't know. Ask your darling little godchild."

"Well, I could, but I doubt she'd answer." Patting her belly once, I scooted over to make more room at the counter as another woman joined us.

"No, she won't. All she'll do is bounce on my bladder harder." Cam sighed, washed her hands, and then dumped her bag on the counter.

I leaned against the wall as she found a brush, then freed her hair from the clip holding the thick mass off her neck.

"I was wrong about Trent, you know," she said, dragging the brush through her hair. "He cares about you. A lot. And the way you look at him? The way he looks at you?"

Her words made my heart ache. Averting my gaze, I

stared at the far wall where an accent mirror hung over a console table.

"Jazz?"

"I think I'm in love with him, Cam." Just saying that hurt. At the same time, the bands around my heart loosened, eased, as if keeping those words trapped inside had been squeezing the air and life from me. Smiling at my best friend, I said, "And I know he cares about me. But it won't ever work. He's got a life and a job waiting back in California. He's leaving the day after tomorrow, and that movie deal thing he's doing will take several months."

"So go with him." Cam dropped her brush, scooped her hair back, then twisted it up, securing the strands with the clip once more, the movements were all done with practiced ease. "It's not like your job can't be done remotely. And anything that needs to be done in person, I can handle. For a while, at least."

She looked down at her belly. "You hear, kiddo?"

Laughing, I said, "Babies work on their schedule, not ours. But...no. I'm not going to impose on him like that. He hasn't even asked if I'd like to come out to California."

"You could always tell him you want to see if this thing between you two could work." Cam faced me, her gaze direct and no-nonsense. "Ask him if he'd like to try. He doesn't look at you like he's ready for things to end, Jazz."

"Cam..." A hard breath exploded from my lungs, and I leaned against the wall. "It's not that simple. The way the past week has been, if I asked, Trent would say yes, whether he wanted me with him or not. I don't want that. We can stay in contact, and if things are still...well, hot, once this movie score is over, we can see what happens then."

"Or you could stop being so practical and take a chance." She leaned in and hugged me. "Come on. I'm worn out, so I'm probably going to make Danny take me home soon. After we order some dessert to go."

THIRTY-ONE
TRENT

While Cam and Jazz were in the restroom, Danny smiled at me over his beer, dark eyes alight with amusement. "Dude, you couldn't look more nervous if my mama had just walked in and found you with your hand in the cookie jar."

"Shut up." I flipped him off.

He just laughed, eyes moving past my shoulder. "They're coming back. Real smooth telling the server to take her time with the cappuccino."

"Well, I didn't want to have a heartfelt conversation with you listening in, smartass."

Danny chuckled, rising as Cam and Jazz drew even with the table. He put a hand on Cam's belly, and the two of them shared a look that left me with a strange ache in my chest. While he murmured to her, I stood and held Jazz's seat out, the pain in my chest changing, growing as she smiled at me.

"We're going to head on out," Danny said, turning to

me as the server delivered the dessert he'd ordered and my cappuccino.

"Yeah, I'm wiped." Cam kissed my cheek, then came around and bent over to hug Jazz from behind. As she straightened, she gave me a mischievous wink.

As the two of them left, I sat back down and took a sip of my cappuccino. "Are you in the mood for dessert?"

"I don't know." Jazz gave me a tired smile. "Dessert is always an option, but my mind is racing like crazy tonight."

"I can imagine." I wanted to pull her into my arms, make that strained look disappear forever. I settled on stroking my hand down her arm. "You've had a hellish week."

She leaned against me, and I wrapped my arm around her shoulders, taking in the feel of her softness, her sweet scent.

Please let her say yes, I thought, my mind focused on the envelope in my suit coat pocket.

"I've been thinking..." I nuzzled her, then kissed her temple.

"Yeah?" She straightened and looked up at me, her vivid purple-blue eyes soft, hazy. "About what?"

"You." I stroked the soft golden-brown strands of her hair back from her face. "Always you."

"If you're trying to sweeten me up, it's working."

"Oh? Well, that's good because I want to ask you something." I didn't let myself think about it another second, just pulled the envelope out and handed it over.

She looked puzzled before opening it and tugging out the folded sheet of paper inside.

Her eyes skimmed over it. Seconds ticked away.

She didn't speak.

Feeling awkward, I said, "You know I'm leaving Sunday. The idea of leaving you behind right now leaves me feeling like I've been punched in the gut. I don't *want* to be away from you but with this project..."

"This is a plane ticket," she said quietly.

"Yes." The paper was a computer print-out of a plane ticket—leaving JFK airport and landing in LAX Sunday. "It's the seat next to mine."

She blinked, eyes flicking to mine, before returning to the sheet of paper. "Why did you do this?"

"I already told you—I can't stand the thought of not being with you."

"So you just *assumed* I'd go with you?" Her eyes narrowed as she looked back at me, irritation in her gaze underlining each word.

"No." I clenched my jaw and struggled not to let the panic I'd started to feel come through as I spoke. "I'm *hoping* you will. I don't know how to do relationships, Jazz. I'm figuring this out as I go. But I didn't assume you'd go...I'm just..."

"I have a job here," she said.

"I know. I talked to Cam and asked if it would even be possible."

"What the hell?" Jazz dropped the piece of paper on the table and grabbed her tea. After gulping the rest of it down, she looked back at me. "I'm not too good at the relationship thing, either, but I think the best thing to do is ask the *person* you're involved with, not her best friend. This is *my* life, not yours, and not hers."

I started to respond, then stopped, thinking through the best way to explain. "Okay, I get that. I'm sorry. I'm not trying to control your life or anything here."

"Really?" She cocked a brow.

"No." An edge crept into my voice, and I stopped, counting to ten mentally. "After everything that happened this week, I'm going a little crazy with this need to be with you, protect you, take care of you. Maybe that's a little Neanderthal, and I'm trying my best to keep it under control. I thought maybe you'd like to get away from everything for a while, with all the shit that's happened."

Her gaze was steady, eyes unblinking as she considered, then said softly, "He broke my trust, Trent. You get that part, right? We were friends, mostly and a little more in high school. Then he did something like that—he took my choice away, and he broke my trust. I don't need anybody to make choices for me, even when they have nothing but good intentions."

A sick feeling settled in the pit of my stomach. "Jazz..."

"Don't," she said. Leaning, she kissed me gently. "I know you'd never do that. But I'm...not steady right now. I *need* to feel in control. It's going to be a while before I *am* steady. Can you understand that?"

"Yeah." Cupping the back of her neck, I pressed my brow to hers. "I never thought about taking your choices away, baby. And that's not what I was trying to do. It's just an offer. Yes, I want you with me, but if you don't want to—or can't—okay, I understand. I'll just have to fly back here as often as possible. I just...need to be with you.

As much as possible, as much as you'll let me without me driving you crazy."

She kissed me then, sweetly, gently, teasingly, her nails scraping over my scalp as she pushed them into my hair. She pulled back, the action both too soon and not soon enough because my cock was already standing at attention.

"We're going to have to sit here a while," I murmured, petting the silky skin of her nape. "You've got me hard as a damn rock."

Her smile was pure seduction.

"I think I will come with you to California," she said, pulling back and settling more comfortably into her seat.

"Really?"

"Yes." A flush rose to her cheeks, and she licked her lips, glanced away—no. Not *away*, around, making sure nobody was paying attention. "But...I need something."

"Anything."

Her grin turned rueful. "You know, you should be careful there. I could ask for the moon, the stars, an all-access pass to the movie set so I can meet the actors."

"I'll give you all of that. More."

Her tone had been teasing. But I wasn't joking. I was ready to lay the world at her feet if she'd let me. Her eyes softened as she reached up to touch my cheek. I caught her hand and pressed a kiss to the center of her palm.

"You'll turn my head saying things like that, Trent."

"Stop looking at me like that, or I'll kiss you again, and then we'll be stuck here even longer. I want to take you home, make love to you again."

Desire darkened her eyes, painted a soft blush across her cheekbones.

"Well, that's a nice opener," she said, a hitch in her breathing. She bit her lip and glanced around once more. "I want to be in control. I mean, when we..."

The words faded away, her cheeks still pink, the color deepening as she struggled to find the words. She didn't need to.

If it had been any other woman, the answer would have been a no.

But this was Jazz, so I told her what was in my heart.

"If that's what you want, alright. I'll lay the world at your feet if you let me."

A bright, friendly voice came from behind me just as I leaned in to kiss Jazz. "Dessert."

Her cheeks flushed, and Jazz glanced past me, then offered me a faint smile.

I wanted to tell the server no, pay the tab, leave, but I bit back the urge and looked at Jazz. I didn't have the chance because the server placed a brown bag with paper handles in front of me on the table. "Strawberries and cream, the lady's favorite."

"Ah..." I looked over at Jazz.

"Your friend ordered it on her way out," the server added. "And she took care of the tab, too. You're all set."

Jazz took the piece of paper from the server, read it, then shook her head. "Man, I think that nesting instinct thing is kicking in hard for Cam. She's trying to mother *everybody* lately. But...I do love strawberries and cream." As the server walked away, Jazz glanced at me. "We'll take them home...let's give 'me being in charge' a trial run."

COOL WHIPPED cream painted in a line down my chest, I clenched my teeth to keep from demanding—or begging—as Jazz closed her lips around the strawberry she'd been using to scoop up the cream.

My cock pulsed, blood roaring in my ears. When she bent down to lick up the cream, tongue flicking over my skin, I arched up, desperate to feel that soft, agile tough on my dick, right where it hurt the most.

But she straightened, selected another berry, and repeated the process—only my chest wasn't her canvas this time. My cock was.

When she finally closed her mouth around me, I shuddered and arched, jerking against the restraints she'd decided to use. But it didn't do any good. I'd walked her through how to tie me, and damn if she wasn't a quick learner.

"Fuck, Jazz..."

She scraped her teeth over me, eyes rolling up to meet mine over the length of my torso, heat and challenge and desire making them lambent. My hips jerked, hands clenched into fists.

She pulled up slowly, then back down, stopping short of taking me as deep as I wanted—as I *needed*, the need to come turning my veins molten, my skin overly sensitive, so when she scraped her nails down my thigh, it felt like a far more intimate touch.

She pulled up and took me slowly, her teasing fingers dipping between my thighs to close over my balls.

"Harder," I said with a groan, arching up.

She pulled up, smiling at me. "Say please."

"Please, damn it."

"Please, *what*?"

"Suck my fucking dick and squeeze my balls *harder*, you little minx."

She laughed, the sound velvet in her throat as she bent back over me and did as I'd rudely requested. She took me deep, gripping my sac tight simultaneously, and I lost it.

I was still breathing hard, long moments later as she straddled my waist and smiled down at me. "You weren't supposed to come yet."

"You're supposed to tell me if you want me to hold off."

"Hmmm." She pursed her lips and pretended to consider that. "Maybe. Still..."

I swore as she picked up one of the strawberries, my entire body going tight as she let it hover above my skin. But instead of stroking it over me, she took a bite of it, then dipped it in whipped cream and brought the sweet fruit to the swollen tip of her nipple.

Eyes locked on her hand now, I stared, enraptured, as she circled the hard point, over and over.

"Let me go," I demanded.

"No...that's not how this works."

"Will you let me go?" I tried. "Please?"

"No." She ate the rest of the berry, selected another, and treated her other nipple in the same delicious manner.

"You look like the best damn dessert I've ever seen," I said, my mouth watering to taste her. "Let me lick you."

"You're not very good at following orders, Trent." She licked her fingers, one by one, then reached for another berry.

"Oh." Her lower lip pushed out in a fake pout. "All gone. None left for you."

"You're the dessert I want. Let me have you." I looked at her eyes first, then slowly, deliberately, and lowered my gaze to her cream-slicked nipples, then lower. "I want to lick up all that whipped cream...everywhere."

Her breath hitched, but she still gave me a teasing smile. "I'm not ready to untie you, though."

"Then bend over me and let me do it that way. You can straddle my face, and I'll eat your pussy like that. Just come *here*."

A noise that might have been a whimper, might have been a moan escaped her, but then she was bending over me, hands braced on the headboard as she let me taste her nipples, the cream adding to the sweetness.

But I wanted more, wanted to feel her shuddering with climax. "Let me lick your pussy, Jazz. Climb up here...please, baby, let me."

She whimpered, body shaking. But she did it, and the taste of her was addictive. She shoved her fingers into my hair, rocking against me as I licked and sucked. Instinctively, I pulled against the bonds, wanting my hands on her, but the restraints didn't give. It didn't matter because she was already trembling, already on the verge of climax, and I'd barely touched her.

Her thighs tightened. Her body shuddered.

My cock pulsed, aching to be inside her.

But this, licking her as she rocked against my face and took her pleasure? It was one of the hottest things I'd ever experienced.

And when she came, then collapsed against me, the

only downside was that she still had me restrained, so I couldn't hug her against me the way I wanted.

Fuck. I was starting to need her in a permanent kind of way.

THIRTY-TWO

JAZZ

"What?"

Trent shook his head, but he was still watching me with that smile on his face, a large mug of coffee cradled in his hands.

"You're going to make me self-conscious if you keep staring at me like that," I said. When he chuckled, I crossed my eyes and stuck my tongue out. That got me another laugh.

"You're lucky I have to head into the studio today," he said, finishing up his coffee. As he slid from the stool, he checked the time. "Otherwise, I might spend all day sitting here and staring at you."

"You lead the most fascinating life, Trent."

"I know. Staring at this gorgeous woman I'm seeing." He winked at me. "She's amazing. She's got this...glow to her. I think I want to write sonnets about how beautiful she is."

A laugh snorted out of me, loud and unladylike. "You're nuts."

He came to me and cupped my face in his hands. "Yeah. About you. Are you going to be okay here by yourself all day?"

"Hmm." Resting my hands on his shoulders, I pretended to ponder the question. "Well, there's no Central Park, and the pizza here sucks, but other than that, I think I can somehow carry on."

"Bite your tongue," he said mildly. "We've got some great pizza places. And so-what if we don't have Central Park? We've got the Pacific Ocean."

The blue-green expanse stretched out endlessly outside the windows along the western wall of his kitchen, and I looked over to consider the view, lips pursed. "Okay, a couple points for that."

"A couple." He dipped his head and nipped my lower lip.

Heat flared inside, my body primed to respond to his. We'd spent the past couple of days wrapped around each other, and I was tender between my thighs, the muscles in my back, legs, and hips stretched and achy, but in the best way.

It shouldn't be possible for me to need him again so soon. I did.

But when I tried to deepen the kiss, he pulled back. "Can't...I'll get distracted, and we'll be naked in five minutes."

"Probably." Sighing, I pulled away and settled more comfortably on my stool. "Go on. Create beautiful music."

He winked. "I'll try to fit in a sonnet or two."

Once he was gone, I picked up a piece of toast from

my plate but instead of taking a bite, I grimaced and tossed it back down.

I'd been hungry when I woke up, but most of the big breakfast Trent and I had cooked either ended up on his plate or sat untouched on mine. Even the sight of the bacon made me feel a little nauseous. Getting queasier by the second, I nudged the plate away and got up from the island. Once I'd cleared the dishes, my stomach settled, although the coffee I'd tried to drink didn't settle well at all.

Neither did water, milk, or the soft drinks Trent kept on hand.

I'd already planned on running down to the small local grocery store Trent had told me about, so I made a list on my phone and added tea and ginger ale, hoping whatever was making my stomach act up was just a case of stress and nerves.

After a quick shower, I changed into a pair of leggings and a t-shirt, then settled at the desk in Trent's home office, my laptop open and a notebook in front of me.

Putting in a call to Cam, I booted up my laptop while waiting for her to answer.

"Hello, sunshine," she said, grinning at me while I adjusted the phone so I could see the screen better.

"Hey. How is everything going?"

"We haven't fallen apart here," she said airily, one hand waving loftily.

"Good to know." I rolled my eyes and pulled up my calendar on my laptop. It was synched to my phone, and I eyed several deadlines for ongoing projects. Another note —this one more personal—caught my eye and I frowned, then tucked it away until I had time to deal with it. "Where are we on the new game?"

Cam caught me up to date as I made a few notes and opened a file on my laptop to check a coding issue.

"Are you ready for the call with Unitel?" she asked, naming a local phone carrier along the east coast. They'd been asking about adding a couple of our games to the packages they offer customers, and after several back-and-forth conversations, I think we were ready to play hardball.

"Damn straight." I smiled and reached for a water bottle while she started the call.

Three hours later, I was starving, thirsty, and ready for a break.

Marking the day's necessary phone calls off my list, I went back to the calendar, that one item still nagging at the back of my mind.

It was a small red dot.

"A month," I muttered.

I'd been having issues with irregular periods off and on for years and had developed a way to keep track of them using the calendar app.

Flipping back to the past month, I eyed the two small red dots with a frown.

Minimizing the calendar, I leaned back in the seat and stared at the ceiling. I was a month late on my period. It wasn't unusual. I skipped periods from time to time, and when I was stressed, it happened more often.

My life had been a little more off-kilter lately, and that wasn't even taking Roger and his asshole self into account.

I told myself it was probably nothing.

And I kept on telling myself that as I locked up Trent's place and took the rental car to the grocery store.

IT TOOK FAR TOO much self-control to pick up a couple of things on my list and not just grab a pregnancy test and disappear into the public restrooms in the front of the store.

By the time I was back at Trent's, I was gritting my teeth and wondering why in the hell I'd bought ice cream and milk and other shit I had to put away. I left anything that wasn't perishable on the counter in their cloth sacks, anxious to take the box into the bathroom with me and see what it said.

It would be negative.

Of course, it would be.

Dr. Nguyen had been pretty open about my chances of conceiving naturally, right?

But it was better to check and make sure.

Since I knew the results, it shouldn't be a big deal to go pee on a damn stick.

And yet it took five minutes to talk myself into doing it.

CHEST TIGHT, I stared at the stick and the little blue *plus* sign.

My head was spinning.

Had I done it wrong?

These things were pretty idiot-proof, right?

I grabbed the instructions, reread them, and thought back to what I'd done.

Open box. Open foil pouch. Take off the cap. Pee on stick.

How did I mess that up?

I'd done all those steps, so that was a correct *positive*. It had to be.

With my phone clutched in my free hand, I eyed the test. What should I do? Call Trent?

I shoved that idea aside almost instantly.

There wasn't even any way to know *when* I'd gotten pregnant.

Bile rushed up to my throat at the thought of Roger. Yeah, he'd worn a rubber, but those weren't 100% foolproof.

Spinning away from the test, I tore open the bathroom door and started pacing the hall. I couldn't tell Trent. Not yet. And for all I knew, that was a false positive. Those did happen, right? I didn't know how often, and I wasn't going to WebMD myself into a panic attack.

But it wouldn't be a bad idea to double-check.

MY PHONE CHIRPED an alert almost ninety minutes later, and I picked up the third pregnancy test.

It was positive. Just like the first two had been.

I put it down and looked at the other boxes, all different brands, all promising near one-hundred percent accuracy.

Sagging against the bathroom wall, I closed my eyes and covered my face with my hands.

What was I supposed to do now?

I had been starting to think Trent and I had a chance together, that we could be *happy* together. But now...what would this do?

He'd agreed to help me get pregnant. He hadn't said anything about hanging around to help once the pregnancy was confirmed. And with Trent's lifestyle he might never want a child.

Another sickening thought snuck out from the shadows.

What if it wasn't Trent's baby?

I couldn't even guess when I'd gotten pregnant, either.

Tears burned my eyes as I gathered up the tests and wrapped them in one of the reusable cloth bags. Carrying them into the kitchen, I shoved them into the trash, adding a few more things on top, so the bag wasn't visible.

Task done, I washed my hands and walked listlessly into the living room.

When the phone rang, I answered without looking to see who it was.

"Ah...Jazz?" Cam's voice came out concerned. "You don't sound like you're living up the high life. What's wrong, honey?"

I sniffed, the sound thin and water. "I think I'm pregnant."

"What?" Cam demanded.

"I...my period's over a month late. I took a test—well, four total. And they all said I'm pregnant."

"That's *wonderful!*"

I couldn't find it in me to feel that emotion right now and hearing it from Cam made my eyes sting with tears.

"Jazz?"

"Yeah?" Dropping onto the couch, I stared at the blank screen of the TV listlessly.

"This was what you wanted," she said gently. "What's wrong?"

"How do I know the baby is Trent's?"

"Oh." Cam sighed. "I see. Well, there's only one way to be really sure. But in all likelihood, it's going to be his, honey. It was one night with Roger—and it wasn't a night you even *consented* to, so don't forget that. But you were with Trent for months."

"Okay, yeah, I guess." I didn't quite believe it but hearing it from my incredibly level-headed friend helped. It was probably what *I* would have said to a friend in a similar situation.

"Are you worried he won't want the baby?" Cam asked.

"I don't know," I admitted, the words escaping me held a world of fear.

"I'll tell you now—I think he'll be happy to help with the baby because it's a part of you...and if he helps raise the baby, then, no matter what, *he* is the father, honey. I saw how he was with you. He loves you like crazy, and I think he'd support you in any decision you make. But there's no denying you went through something traumatic, and you have to decide what the right choice is for *you*."

"You make it sound so simple."

"It sounds simple, sure." Cam's voice was gentle. "But sounding simple doesn't mean it *is* simple."

She was right.

This was not a simple solution.

THIRTY-THREE
TRENT

The music flowed around us.

Hands on the piano keys, I closed my eyes to the world, lost to the sound of piano, violin, cello, and flute. This piece hit right in the gut, exactly as I'd imagined, conveying a deep, intimate sensuality without a single lyric.

As the final notes faded from the air, I opened my eyes and looked at the musicians hired to work along with me. Each of them looked as pleased with the song as I felt.

"That's pure magic," Sylvie Mercer said, heaving out a pleased sigh as she stroked a hand down the gleaming wood of her cello. "This soundtrack is going to make you a legend, Trent."

I smiled but offered no other response. I agreed with her, but the magic in the songs had risen from a place I'd discovered for the first time with Jazz. Strange that the one thing I'd never thought I wanted, much less *needed*, seemed to be the key to opening the door to crafting the best music of my career.

I glanced up to check the time, wanting to try the piece again, but a flash of movement caught my eye.

There, standing at the monitor window that allowed observers in the control room to watch as we played, was a beautiful woman in a luxurious fur coat, her deep brown hair artfully tousled.

Avery Gilmore.

Looking away, I silently swore to myself. Then, before I could say anything that would make the next few minutes worse than they already would be, I turned off the mic and rose.

"Why don't we all take a break for lunch?" I said, looking at the musicians instead of at my former lover.

"Sounds great." Hector Suarez, the violinist, put his violin in the case, eyes on Sylvie. "Sylvie, you got any plans?"

Frank Mullins followed the other two out. I was glad when nobody asked about Avery, although who could miss her? Walking to the door separating the recording from the control room, I opened it and nodded at the engineer.

He was trying hard not to look at Avery.

"You want to grab some food, too?"

He wasn't as quick to leave, but once the door shut behind him, I locked it and blew out a hard breath before facing Avery.

The control room wasn't small. There was a lot of equipment, but it was comfortably sized, with several rolling stools and a recliner in one corner.

I sat down, hooking one ankle over the opposite knee as I studied the woman before me.

"Kind of warm out for a mink fur coat, Avery," I said, wondering what she was up to.

"I was feeling decadent," she said, moving to the open door of the recording room to peer inside. Over her shoulder, she smiled at me. "Your own private recording studio for your new project, Trent. How delicious."

"No, it's just more productive to work this way. I don't have much time, and I need to grab some food myself."

"Hungry, are you?" She turned to me, a familiar, coy smile playing about her lips.

The hint of mischief in her eyes might have turned me on once. No. There was no *might* about it. I would have already pulled her close, tried to figure out what game she wanted to play—and if I'd play along or devise a game of my own.

But that was before Jazz.

Suddenly tired, I rubbed the back of my neck.

"Avery, look, we need to talk."

Her shadow fell over me, and I looked up just in time to see her part the opening of her coat, then shrug out of it.

She pushed against my shoulders, surprising me enough that I wasn't quite prepared for the way she climbed atop me, one knee on either side of me, braced on the arms of the leather chair.

Instinctively, I planted both feet on the floor, and she shimmied closer, now straddling my lap. With a knowing smile, she rubbed against me.

"Too bad that piece isn't recorded yet," she

murmured. "It's so...sexy. But I can dance for you anyway."

I was hard—hell, we'd been lovers for years, and my body knew hers well.

But I gripped her hips as she started to rotate them.

"Do we *really* have to talk?" she asked, giving me a mock pout, her lips painted a rich shade of wine red. "I can think of a much better use for my tongue. Can't you?"

"Enough," I said, nudging her back. When she didn't take the hint, I stood and put her down, then gripped her upper arms to keep her at a distance when she would have pressed close. "We're not doing this, Avery. Okay?"

"Are you in the mood for something else, master?" She licked her lips. "I'm being bad. You should punish me. Please punish me. I'll do anything you want."

Fuck.

Staring into her eyes, I wondered if I'd ever seen a pleading look and confused it for something else. She needed...something, and it wasn't just the release from good, hard sex or having me spank her before I fucked her.

I didn't particularly like the answer I found, and I backed up another step, needing distance more than ever. "Avery, it's over."

She blinked, head cocked as if she didn't understand.

"Do you hear me?" I started to lower my hands, but she pushed into my space again.

This time, I caught her shoulders. "Stop it, Avery. We're done."

Hurt and confusion slowly filled her hazel eyes.

Lowering my hands, I stepped around her and picked

up the expensive fur she'd dropped, draping it around her shoulders. She caught at the lapels, clutching the coat to her.

"What did I do wrong, Trent?" she asked, watching me as I paced away. "Is it because I pushed too hard in New York? If that's it, I'm sorry. I should have called you first. I should—"

"Avery, this isn't about New York," I said, cutting her off. "The two of us...hell, Avery. We've been over for a long time."

The control room was suddenly too small, and I strode into the recording room, restless and frustrated with her, with myself for too many reasons to count.

"Things were—*are* good between us, Trent." The words came out husky.

I made myself look at her, jaw tight. "They *were*, Avery. But we were only ever friends—and sex partners. That's it. And now it's in the past."

"Why?" she half-shouted, letting go of the lapels of her fur to stride over and grab my shirt front in her fists. "Why are you doing this?"

"I met somebody," I said quietly. "I love her. She's the only one I want to be with."

She curled her lip in a sneer, then reached down and wrapped her fingers around my erect cock. "This says otherwise."

I caught her wrist and tugged her hand away, then stepped back. "I'm more than just my cock, Avery. I've never let him be the one making the important decisions in my life, and that's not going to start now."

"Oh, so you, one of the kinkiest Doms I know, will let a woman start making the decisions instead?" She spun away, her movements jerky as she shoved one arm, then the other into the sleeves of her coat. "I bet *that* will last a long time, honey."

An irritated response leaped to my lips, but I bit it back.

Pulling her hair free from the coat, she turned to me. Although her face was flushed and her eyes glittered with emotion, her voice was cool as she said, "You go on and have fun playing the little game of house, Trent. You'll get bored, and she won't be happy, either. When you come crawling back, I *might* be nice enough to let you touch me again."

"I'm sorry if I've hurt you, Avery," I said, tucking my hands into my pockets.

She went stiff. "*Hurt* me?"

The laugh that followed was sharp and cold, an assault on the ears. I started to reach out a hand, to offer...comfort or something, but the glitter in her eyes stopped me.

"*You* couldn't *hurt* me, Trent," she said, spitting the words out as if they tasted foul. "So don't flatter yourself."

She stormed out, leaving me alone in the quiet of the recording studio. I stood there, relief flooding me.

Pulling my phone from my pocket, I called Jazz.

"Hello?"

Just hearing her voice made the strange, tight sensation in my chest ease, and I smiled.

"Why don't you put on something extra sexy for tonight, baby?" I asked her. "I want to take you out to dinner and then to a place I think you'll love."

THIRTY-FOUR

JAZZ

The evening out was exactly what I needed.

I still hadn't figured out how to tell Trent about the positive pregnancy test, so the distraction was welcome.

A last-minute shopping trip landed me a slinky blue cocktail dress and silver heels that had Trent's eyes going hot the moment he saw me step out of the bedroom.

But he hadn't touched me other than a single stroke of his finger down my cheek.

All night, though, he'd looked at me as if he wanted to devour me. By the time he led me inside a private club, I was all but shaking with need.

I'd almost asked if we could just go home during the ride over in the private limo he'd rented for the night but had held back.

Once we were inside the club, he took my hand and led me to the edge of the dance floor.

"Look."

The brush of his lips against my ear made me shiver,

and it took a few seconds to focus past that, a few more for my mind to process what I was seeing.

By the time I did, Trent had moved to stand behind me, one hand resting on my belly. There was no way for him to miss my suddenly erratic breaths.

There were several raised platforms around the dance floor and a central stage. My gaze locked on the scene as a woman, arms bound behind her back, stood at rapt attention to the man before her.

She would have been absolutely naked if it weren't for the lush red rope twining around her form.

As I watched, the man binding her stopped in front of her and flicked one nipple, then the other.

I felt an answering pang in my nipples, then further, between my thighs, a hot, wet clenching.

"Let's go dance," Trent murmured against my ears.

"I'm not sure if I can," I said, staring at the bondage display. My cheeks were on fire, and although I felt a little self-conscious, I was so aroused by what I saw, that it washed out everything else.

"Why not?"

I craned my neck around to meet Trent's eyes, heart hammering hard against my ribs.

"Take a guess," I said tartly.

He tapped his fingers against my belly, slipping them lower, lower...

I gasped before his lips closed over mine.

When he lifted his head, the hunger in his eyes almost leveled me.

"How wet are you?" he asked, mouth still pressed to mine.

"Very."

"Good."

He took my hand and led me to the dance floor, pulling me close, my hips snug to his, the heels giving me several more inches, so I felt his cock nudging the notch between my thighs.

I whimpered and clung to his shoulders with desperate hands, my blood pumping hotter with every beat of my heart.

I wasn't sure if I'd survive the dance.

But if I died? This was one hell of a way to go.

IT WAS a good twenty minutes before he led us off the floor for a break, one I desperately needed. My legs were shaky, my nipples tight, and I felt like he'd spent the past twenty minutes doing nothing but working me closer and closer to climax—right in the middle of a dance floor.

A woman in a floor-length gown of formal black led us to a private table on the second floor.

As we sat, Trent asked for a bottle of a popular small-batch Kentucky bourbon we both liked. "Only one glass," I told her, hoping he wouldn't ask why. I wasn't ready—or capable—of clear thought just then. "I'd prefer sparkling water by the bottle if you could."

She smiled and gave a slight nod before melting off into the darkness.

"Not drinking tonight?"

I smiled. "I'm already half-drunk just from dancing with you. I think I'm better off sticking to water."

"I'm fine with that." His gaze dropped to my mouth and lingered before he glanced around the second level that surrounded the dance floor, the railing an artful display of wrought iron that let the observers watch the shows playing out on the dance floor. He nodded across to the other side of the second level, the floor curving around the dance floor like a U.

"See how the booths and lighting are designed for privacy?"

I nodded, my throat dry, my heart racing.

Leaning in, he crooked his finger at me, beckoning me to come closer.

When I did, his words were a rough rumble against my ear. "I could pull you into my lap and fuck you here—there's a way to notify the staff if I want privacy. Or I could take you down to the dance floor again. How close are you to coming, Jazz? You're so aroused, I can almost feel your pussy clenching around my cock, and I'm barely touching you."

I shuddered, instinctively tightening the muscles in my thighs and pressing my knees together against the demanding pulse that hit deep, deep, deep down inside, heating my core and spreading outward.

It didn't help. I was already so wet and swollen, the folds between my thighs slick in anticipation, so the subtle pressure of my clenched thighs, combined with me pressing my knees together was enough tactile pressure, to make me hover on the edge of climax.

Then he stroked the pad of his thumb over me, and pressed, while with his free hand, he cupped my left breast and tugged on my nipple, puckered hard and tight, stabbing into the slinky material of my cocktail gown, unfettered by a bra.

I came.

SERVING THE MAESTRO

Shaking, I grabbed onto his arm with a helpless cry as the unexpected climax slammed into me.

Trent pressed his mouth to my neck.

"Damn, Jazz. You'll barely last a second once I push inside you."

He wasn't lying.

Drained, I slumped against the luxuriantly soft seat and found him smiling.

I might have kissed him if he'd been close enough, the light in his eyes hot but combined with something...deeper. Something that spoke of intense, complex emotion. It made my heart ache to look at him and realize that maybe Cam was right.

If I trusted him with the secret that had weighed me down most of the day, he'd pull me into his arms and hold me. I wanted that comfort so much.

But just as I went to say something, the hostess reappeared.

Muscles too lax and mind too hazed to do anything, I stayed silent as she placed a tray on the table and opened the bottle of bourbon, and sparkling water.

Once she was gone, I looked at Trent. "You're dangerous to a girl's blood pressure, baby."

"Am I?"

I nodded.

He just smiled.

A FEW MINUTES LATER, my head was still spinning when I slid into the ladies' room, the restroom on the second level reserved for VIP members and their guests.

After using the facilities, I sank onto a velvet divan and closed my eyes.

"Good thing you'd already planned on not drinking," I muttered to myself. I mean, hello, pregnant and everything, right? But if that hadn't been the case and I'd had a drink, I might have a boneless mess incapable of independent thought and movement by now. I already *felt* drunk, but not the kind that came from booze.

"Trent's better than any drink, isn't he, honey?"

I jolted upright, the voice startling me.

A familiar looking pretty brunette in a snug leather bustier dress that pulled off sexy *and* classy stood a few feet away, smiling at me.

I blinked and looked around. "What?"

She came over and sat next to me without any invitation. She gave my bare knee a quick pat. "I've been drunk on him a time or two...dozen times. Maybe two thousand?" She winked. "I saw the two of you on the floor. Looked like he was rocking your world. I almost came over then and there, but decided I should be patient since I've had him all alone for so long. The threesome fun could wait."

Her words bounced together in my head, not making much sense as I tried to figure out why she looked familiar.

But those last five words? They connected, and I stiffened. "Threesome fun?"

"Hmmm." She crossed her knees, smoothing a hand down the leather of thigh-high boots that stopped two inches below the hem of her sexy-as-sin skirt. Twisting toward me, she planted a hand on the divan and gave me a long, thorough look. "You really are beautiful, Jazz. I'm glad he found such a suitable replacement."

It hit me why she looked familiar.

She was the 'girlfriend' I'd met in the elevator of my building back in New York—or so she'd claimed. I'd never actually asked Trent about their relationship because when I saw him again, it had been the day I'd gotten the news from the OB about the likelihood that I'd have trouble conceiving. I couldn't even *think* about that right now, either.

"I'm not following," I said, keeping my voice calm through sheer will alone.

She pursed her lips and cocked her head, a look of puzzlement on her lovely face. "Oh. Hmmm...well, I guess he didn't want to tell you. Trent and I were together for years. I was his...*preferred* sub, but I told him a couple months ago that I'd be moving on. He took it hard—really hard. Even moved to the other side of the country for a while. When I saw him earlier today, we talked, and...well, I *am* moving on, but he suggested one last adventure together..." She ran her eyes over me, and licked her lips. "And when I saw you two together...I'm so glad I agreed."

"Just *what* did you agree to?" I demanded, shoving to my feet and pacing a few steps away before turning to face her.

Puzzlement faded away, and she sighed. "You don't need to feel threatened by me, Jazz. I'm moving on in my life. Trent wants to keep dangling a possible relationship in front of me as a carrot, and I'm not playing his games anymore. If you want that, more power to you. But...well, we *are* friends, and I'll always have feelings for him. And I'm *never* one to turn down a threesome."

"I sure as hell am," I said. "Just *when* did this discussion happen? Because Trent never ran it by me."

Head cocked, she studied me. "If you're not up to it, just tell him. He's your Dom, but you're allowed to say no if you're not...comfortable with some things. Threesomes are definitely a more advanced level."

The smile she gave me made me want to punch her.

"That's not an answer to the question." I returned her snide smile with one of mine. I hated these power games some people of my gender liked to play, and I wasn't going to engage. "And since you're clearly baiting me, I'll just end this conversation here and now. Such a *lovely* chat."

I was almost to the door when she said, "Don't believe me? Ask Trent about the lap dance I gave him earlier today in the studio. For old times' sake."

Over my shoulder, I gave her a withering look. "For somebody who keeps saying you're moving on, you sure are hooked on this threesome thing—and now a lap dance? You *do* know what moving on means, right?"

I left before she could say anything else, but it didn't ease this strange, sick uneasiness that washed over me.

She'd given me a smug look as I walked out, filled with confidence.

Ask Trent. I knew how to tell when somebody was bluffing. It was crucial in my line of work—women in tech have to know when to call a bluff and know when to walk away.

She hadn't *been* bluffing.

THIRTY-FIVE
TRENT

"I'd like to leave, Trent." Jazz cut around me from behind, catching me off guard.

Rising, I studied her pale face, the sharp glitter in her eyes, and reached out to touch her.

She'd already turned away, picking up a lacy scrap of material that passed as her wrap and tossing it over her shoulders.

The music had picked up when she turned around to face me. She was so pale, her eyes too dark, and worry settled in my gut, but there wasn't any way to have a private conversation here.

"Alright." I tapped the small electronic tablet built into the table, closing out my tab for the night, and went over to her arm.

I was about ten seconds too late. Jazz was already halfway to the stairs across the floor and taking the first step by the time I caught up.

"Are you sick?" I asked, resting a hand at the base of her spine as we stepped outside. My driver caught sight of us almost immediately, judging by the way he flashed his lights, then pulled out from his spot halfway down the block.

Jazz was staring off in the distance. "No. I've just got a headache."

I cupped my hand over the back of her neck. "I could maybe help—"

"The car's here," she said, voice cool. Stepping away from me toward the curb, she opened the door and ducked inside, gripping the top of the door to balance on her mile-high heels instead of letting me help.

What the fuck?

I WOULDN'T HAVE BEEN SURPRISED to find I had frostbite by the time we reached my place. After a few awkward attempts to get Jazz to talk to me, I'd lapsed into silence and figured it would be better to wait until we were home anyway. She sat across from me rather than next to me and kept rubbing her temple so she might have a headache, but that wasn't the main problem.

She was pissed.

Once we were inside my place, I touched her shoulder. "Are you going to talk to me? Tell me what's going on?"

"Nothing's going on, Trent. I just have a headache, and I'm tired," she said, still not looking at me. "I'm going to sleep in the guest room."

She shrugged my hand off her shoulder and walked off.

We hadn't had eye contact for more than ten seconds

since she'd returned from the bathroom at the club, and now she was shutting me out of her bed.

Or shutting herself out of mine.

"What the hell?"

I wanted to storm after her and demand she talk to me, but the way she'd shut down had me off-balance. Should I give her some time to cool down over whatever had her angry?

What was the right way to handle it when your girlfriend was pissed?

And how the fuck did I figure that out since I'd never really *had* a girlfriend?

Swearing, I made a beeline for the bar and poured myself a healthy serving of scotch.

I tossed back half of it, enjoying the burn, refilled the glass and took the bottle with me onto the wide balcony that faced the ocean.

My place wasn't huge. Property in California—especially on the beach—came at a premium. Although I'd had some minor successes in my career, I wasn't pulling in the kind of money one would need to have some palatial spread out here. But I loved this place.

Sitting out on the balcony and watching the moon float across the sky as the waves crashed into the rocks never ceased to calm my mind.

Or rather, it hadn't.

Now, I barely took notice of the big, fat full moon hanging in the sky, so bright it blotted out what few stars managed to pierce the light pollution of a Los Angeles night.

What had happened?

She'd been fine when she slipped away to use the restroom.

More than fine—all hot, bothered, and sexily mussed.

I'd been debating whether to head on out when she got back anyway because I wanted to get my hands on her—*really* get my hands on her. As much as I liked playing at my club, I needed to have Jazz wrapped around me, and I realized I wasn't too big on the idea of sharing any deep intimacies between Jazz and me.

She'd come back fucking *pissed*, wrapped up taut, and ready to snap.

My phone rang.

I ignored it, too irritated and worried about whatever could have upset Jazz. How could I get her to talk to me?

I emptied my scotch glass and poured myself another serving.

The phone rang again.

I ignored it and leaned back, taking another sip of the rich amber liquor, eyes turned inward.

When the phone rolled over to voicemail, I breathed a sigh of relief.

Then started swearing because it started ringing again less than thirty seconds later. Slamming the glass on the rattan and glass table, I grabbed the phone from my pocket and hauled it out, ready to turn it off and throw the damn thing into the ocean.

Then I saw Avery's face on the screen.

"Stop calling, Avery," I snapped. "Leave me the fuck alone."

"Oh, honey..." Voice a husky coo, she asked, "Are you and your little whore fighting?"

Rage blinded me for a second, and I went to snarl,

but the words clicked in my head. "Why would we be fighting?"

"Oh, don't play coy, baby." She sighed on the other end of the line. "She really *is* pretty, you know. A little...soft. I doubt you'll be able to get *everything* you need from her, but maybe I'm wrong. She certainly wasn't into the threesome I suggested."

I saw red.

"You talked to Jazz."

"Oh, not for long." Avery laughed.

There was a meanness to it I'd never heard before.

"She took off running not long after I mentioned our little...get together this afternoon. She seemed a little crestfallen, Trent. You really *do* need to explain to her how things work in this world."

"Why are you doing this?" I asked softly. "I thought we were friends, but here you are trying to destroy a relationship that makes me happy. Why the fuck would you do that to somebody you say you care about?"

A strained few seconds passed, and then she laughed again, but this time, it was forced and sharp-edged.

"Don't be so dramatic, Trent. It's not like I went and lied and told her we were married or anything. If she can't take hearing about your former lovers, then she's not going to last anyway."

"Stop," I said, pinching the bridge of my nose. "I don't know what the fuck I ever did to you that would make you think it's okay to go and hurt the woman I love—to go and hurt *me* by causing trouble for us, but whatever the hell it was, I'm sorry. And whatever the hell is going on with you...I don't want—I *can't* deal with it. You're out of my life, Avery. It's over between us—completely. We're not even friends anymore."

"Trent, wait—"

Ignoring the panicked sounds of her voice, I ended the call, then deleted her contact information and blocked her number.

Rising, I started to go inside.

I had to talk to Jazz and fix this.

I ran out of nerve, though, when I found the guest door locked.

Gripping the knob in my hand and pressing my head to the smooth wood, I groaned. "Jazz..."

On the other side of the door, there was only silence.

Slowly, I let go of the knob and turned away.

"Alright," I told myself.

I'd let her sleep.

She had every right to be angry. Hell, she'd had one thing after another thrown at her for weeks now. Was I surprised she'd shut down on me?

In the morning, we could talk.

After she had some rest and hopefully calmed down, it would be easier for her to see that Avery had just manipulated her.

I'd tell her how I felt. Tell her I loved her.

I'd fix this.

I just had to wait until morning, and then I'd fix it.

But for now? I was going to have another fucking drink.

THIRTY-SIX
JAZZ

My head was killing me.

The early Sunday morning crowd at LAX, the noise, the bright lights, and endless chatter, coupled with endless announcements on the overhead, definitely were *not* helping with the headache, either.

I hadn't been lying the night before when I told Trent I had a headache—stress did that to me.

Listening to what Avery had to say about a threesome —and then the stuff about her and Trent that afternoon— had hit me like a sledgehammer to my skull.

It had taken far too long to fall asleep, and I'd woken after a few hours, then tiptoed around as I packed, scared I'd wake Trent and had to confront him.

None of that had helped my stress level, so now I was tired, and trying to tell myself my heart wasn't broken as I sat at the airport, waiting for my flight back to New York City.

My mental pep talk was an all-around failure.

My heart was totally broken, and my head hurt almost as bad.

I told myself I'd get over it as I settled in a corner seat close to my gate and sipping coffee heavily laced with cream and sugar. Part of me felt a little guilty about the caffeine hit. I'd done an internet search on caffeine and pregnancy, and while some sites made me feel like the devil incarnate for having a cup, most indicated an occasional coffee or soft drink wouldn't hurt the baby.

The baby.

I pressed a hand to my belly and closed my eyes.

That's what I needed to focus on.

My baby.

I was pregnant.

I'd gotten what I wanted in the long run, right? I wasn't going to dwell on the father because I hadn't *wanted* a father in the picture to begin with.

Any pipe dreams I might have had about Trent were just that. Dreams that wouldn't happen, and I was better off without a man in my life anyway.

Tears stung my eyes, and I blinked them back, then grabbed my phone.

It was barely seven. My flight left in a couple of hours—I'd booked the ticket last night after locking myself in the guest room, telling myself it was the only course of action. I wouldn't be like my mother, pinning my whole world on a man, then crashing when he yanked the foundation out from under me.

I didn't *need* him.

I called Cam.

"Hell, Jazz, what time is it out there? *I'm* still in bed," she said, yawning.

"Did I wake you?"

"No." She heaved out a sigh. "Danny's making me breakfast, and I'm being a lazy slug. He's babying me, and I love it."

My throat constricted. "Maybe I should call back."

"No. It's fine," she said, voice softening. "Honey, what's wrong?"

"I..." The tears threatened again.

"Jazz?"

Everything came pouring out, from the time Trent had texted me to wear something sexy to me locking myself in the guest bedroom.

"It's over, Cam. I trusted him. I thought there was something special between us, and obviously there's not. Trent slept with somebody else at his studio, or at least he was getting a lap dance from a former girlfriend."

Cam was silent for a moment. "How do you know that?"

"Because the former girlfriend told me about it when we ran into each other."

"Okay...and what did Trent say when you confronted him about all of this?" she asked.

Biting my lip, I squeezed my eyes closed. It took a few seconds to get the words through my tight throat. "I didn't."

"Say what?" she demanded. "You didn't *say* anything to him? Why the hell not?"

"Because he hurt me!" It came out louder than expected, and several people looked my way. I glared back even as I blushed, embarrassed over the outburst. Hell, my emotions were raging like crazy here. "He *lied* to me, Cam. And I fell for all of it. I always told myself I'd never be like my mom, and this happens."

"Sweetheart..." Cam's voice trailed off, several seconds passing before she tried again. "Jazz, you're nothing like your mom. She shut down and all but gave up living. You'd never do that. That doesn't mean you're not going to experience heartbreak. That kind of goes along with the loving somebody deal."

"Then I'll just do without the loving somebody deal," I muttered.

My phone clicked and I lowered it. My breath hitched as Trent's name flashed across the screen. Rejecting the call, I blocked him from my mind. I wasn't ready to think about him yet.

"Jazz, you don't even know if this woman was telling the truth," Cam said. "Don't you deserve to know that? Doesn't Trent deserve a chance to explain?"

"What's to *explain*? He tells me to look sexy, he's got a surprise for me, and we get to this club and *bam*, his girlfriend is there."

"That's *her* story," Cam argued.

"Yeah, and it would be really stupid of her to lie when he's *there*," I snapped, although, suddenly, I was a little uneasy. Had I jumped the gun?

My phone clicked again. Trent. I rejected the call.

No, I told myself. I'd made the right call, protected myself, my baby. I'd been an idiot thinking I could have the guy *and* the baby, but I was over that now.

"Look, Trent might call," I told her. "Don't tell him anything, okay? I'll talk to him once I'm home and...I'll talk to him."

End things.

"Are you going to give him a chance to tell his side of the story?"

"There's no *side*," I said shortly. "His bohemian lifestyle is not compatible with me. I'm going to be a mother, for fuck's sake. It's just not going to work out. Don't tell him where I am. I gotta go."

I hurriedly ended the call before she could press me again.

Exhaustion weighed on me, and misery was another weight. Staring at the seconds ticking by on the clock on the far wall, I willed them to go faster.

I wanted to be home, in my bed, curled up so I could cry my heart out. Once I did that, I could focus on the business of getting over Trent—and getting on with my life, me...and my baby.

THIRTY-SEVEN
TRENT

I woke with a pounding headache, a full bladder, and a taste in my mouth that was bad enough to classify as toxic waste.

As I sat up on the couch, I looked around, my brain too muddled to make sense of my sleeping arrangements. But then the fog cleared, and I groaned. A nearly empty bottle of whiskey sat on the table, next to a phone I'd come close to smashing the night before.

I was still in the shirt and trousers I'd been wearing when I'd finally crashed. Between the hangover headache, the toxic waste dump that was my mouth, and the wrinkled clothes, I felt like shit, and the day was barely starting.

At the very least, I needed to get some water in me and some painkillers for the head, then brush my teeth so I wouldn't send Jazz into hiding just from the stench of my breath.

After I took care of those basics, the two of us were

going to have a talk because I wasn't letting whatever shit Avery had fed her come between us.

I loved Jazz.

I loved her and wanted to spend the rest of my life with her.

Despite the headache, hangover and even my lingering anger toward Avery, I found myself smiling.

I *loved* Jazz.

And we were going to make this work.

I knew it in my gut.

FIVE MINUTES LATER, I had to admit my gut and I were both complete idiots.

"She's gone," I whispered to the empty room in front of me.

I'd walked through the bedroom and checked the ensuite bathroom—twice—as if I'd somehow find her hiding in the towel closet or the tub on the second trip. Then I went through the house, calling her name as panic built inside me, chased by the burgeoning realization that Jazz was *gone*.

She'd left.

She hadn't tried to have it out with me, asked my side of things—she'd just *left*.

My heart felt like it was shattering to pieces in slow time, and the world around me slowed with it as if to make sure I didn't miss a single second of the misery.

Falling back against the door frame, I stared at the empty bed, all neatly made up. There was no sign she'd ever even been here.

"How could you just leave?" I asked.

But the empty house offered no answer.

Shoving off the wall, I raced to the living room and grabbed my phone. I called, heart racing as I waited for Jazz to answer.

The call cut off abruptly, and I swore.

She was either on a call with somebody or didn't want to talk to me. Either was an option. I gave it five minutes and called again and when the same thing happened, my gut told me she was dodging my calls.

"Fuck." I pinched the bridge of my nose, then decided to try one more thing. If this didn't work out, I'd buy a ticket to New York and camp out at her door. She would be going home, most likely.

If I had to race across the country to talk to her, I'd do it.

But first, I put in a call to Cam.

I counted each ring, the ache in my chest expanding.

"Yeah?"

Cam's terse greeting had me closing my eyes in relief, even if she sounded like she wanted to reach through the phone and strangle me.

"Where is she?" I demanded. "I need to know."

"I'm not telling you. Just leave it alone, okay?"

"Damn it, Cam! Don't hang up, just give me two minutes to explain, okay?" The desperate note in my voice was impossible to miss, but I didn't give a damn if she knew I was desperate.

"Why should I?"

"Because I love her, and I know exactly what an *ex*-friend of mine told her at the club last night—it was all a fucking lie, okay?"

There was nothing but silence from her end of the line, and I squeezed my eyes shut, hoping so hard, it hurt.

"How do you know it was all a lie?" Cam asked warily. "Jazz said she didn't talk to you after she ran you into your ex, and she left before you woke up. So how do you know what—"

"Avery called me last night to gloat," I said, cutting her off. "Hell, I'd send you a screenshot of the phone call, but I deleted her number and blocked her as soon as I hung up."

"Avery...your ex?"

I shoved a hand through my hair. "She's *not* my ex. We *were* friends, and yeah, we...slept together for a while, but that's been over with for years. She came out to see me in New York when I was there, but I was already involved with Jazz and—shit, look, there's nothing between me and Avery. There hasn't been for a long time. I don't know why the fuck she decided to lie and pretend there's still something between us, why a friend would fuck me over like that—but I *love* Jazz. I don't want to spend another day without her."

A soft, sighing breath came from over the phone.

"Damn it, Cam! What do I have to do to get you to believe me?"

She chuckled, and when she spoke, her voice was decidedly lighter. "Well, you kind of already did—even if you are snarling while you swear you're in love with my friend, you *still* said you're in love with my friend." She paused, then asked, "Love, *love* her, as in no matter what and all that?"

"Crazy in love. Would do anything for her, no matter what," I said.

"Okay. Got a pen?"

STEPHEN CALLED me back as I hit the highway. It was too early on a Sunday for there to be much traffic—at least as far as Los Angeles went, and I was making good time.

"Did you get me a flight?" I demanded as soon as the call came over the car's Bluetooth.

"Yeah." He yawned sleepily. "I had to barter away almost every favor I currently have in my bag, and I might have agreed to name my firstborn after somebody, but you're on the next flight heading out of LAX to New York. Last ticket they had, and I hope you're traveling light."

"Light?" I laughed. "Hell, I ran out of the house with my phone, keys, and wallet. That's it."

"Doesn't get any lighter." He was quiet for a minute, then said, "Good luck, buddy. Hope you can work out whatever the hell happened."

"Me, too. Listen...Avery...something's going on with her. You'd be wise to cut ties with her if you're still friendly."

"You can catch me up to all of that later. She was always more into you than me anyway, so I doubt she'll even bother with me." He gave me the airline info and flight time. "You're cutting it close, but you should make it since you're not taking any luggage. Hope it works out."

The call went dead, and I blew out a breath.

"Yeah," I muttered to the quiet car. "Me, too."

I GOT through security just as they announced final boarding and ran like the demons of hell were at my heels, barely making it.

The attendant gave me a censuring look. "You almost missed it, Mr. Dixson."

"I'm sorry." She waved me on with an unimpressed look, and I rushed down the ramp and onto the plane, greeted by another airline employee, a flight attendant who clucked her tongue but offered a playful wink before waving me to my seat.

I held my breath as I boarded, heart pounding as I looked for her.

I hadn't thought it possible, but Stephen had managed to get me on the same flight as Jazz. I hadn't realized it until I'd seen the gate info while I was making my mad rush to get here, and it clicked, my memory supplying the info Cam had given me.

As I made my way to my seat, I spotted her, looking out the window, face pale and shadows under her lovely eyes.

The seat next to hers was taken. That was probably a good thing. If Jazz saw me now and raised hell, I might get booted off the plane. Harder to do that mid-flight.

Besides, I'd rather talk to her after my hands had stopped shaking.

It took a good forty-five minutes before that happened.

I downed two soft drinks as I waited for my nerves to settle and the caffeine to kick in. The headache had ebbed some, probably thanks to adrenaline and the over-the-counter painkillers I'd popped on the way out the door.

When the man next to Jazz rose, I closed my eyes. *Here goes nothing.*

After he exited the bathroom, I met him in the aisle before he could reach his seat.

"Will you exchange seats with me?"

He blinked, clearly caught off guard. "Excuse me?"

"The woman next to you—she's my girlfriend. We had a fight last night, and she left. She's going back home to New York, and I'm trying to apologize before she dumps my ass forever."

He arched a brow, looked me over, and then glanced back at her. "If she left you in California, isn't that a sign she already dumped your ass?"

"She hasn't told me to leave her alone yet, so I figure I have a microscopic opening." I tried to smile, but it fell flat, and I looked at him, not trying to hide my desperation. "Please. I love her. I never really told her how I felt, and I have to try. If she tells me to fuck off, you can have the seat back."

He gave me another long look, then nodded slowly. "If you give her grief, I'll tell the flight attendants you're stalking her ass, got it?"

"Got it." Shit, I hoped it wouldn't come to that.

We did an awkward shuffle so he could work around me and take my seat, then I went forward and sat next to Jazz.

She was still staring out the window, quiet, dejected, her shoulders slumped.

My heart cracked open a little more, the pain in her body language so clear. I wanted to shake Avery, yell at her, ask her what the fuck was wrong with her, causing Jazz pain like this.

But I couldn't do that here, and right now, I needed to focus on fixing things with Jazz.

"Jazz."

She jerked in surprise, hair flying as she whipped her head around to gape at me. "What...*you*! How?" She glared at me through red-rimmed eyes.

Knowing she'd been crying, hurting throughout the night hit hard, like a fist in the gut. I shouldn't have left her alone—fuck thinking it would be better if she had a chance to rest and *cool down*. I'd left her alone to hurt and cry. I was an ass.

"What are *you* doing here?" she demanded.

"Chasing the woman I'm in love with."

Her lips parted on a gasp.

Seeing the shock in her red-rimmed eyes, I pushed on. "Avery lied to you, Jazz. I don't know all she told you, but things between me and her have been over for years—and I was *never* romantically involved with her—ever. We had a...mutually beneficial relationship, but that's it, and it's been over for years."

Jazz looked away. I resisted the urge to tug her chin back around and get her to look at me.

"Jazz?"

Her shoulders were so rigid I couldn't fight the urge to touch her. Taking her hand, I brought it to my lips. "Please tell me this isn't the end of things...not because of lies she told."

"How do you even know?" Jazz asked, her voice husky, almost inaudible over the loud noise of the plane.

"She called me and told me," I admitted.

For the second time in under two minutes, she swung her head around to gape at me. "She...as in *Avery*? The gorgeous chick who said we were supposed to have some sort of threesome? *She* called you and *told* you? When? And...*why*?"

"To hurt me?" I shrugged, having little interest in Avery's rationale in the face of the obvious pain my former lover—and *friend*—had inflicted on the woman I loved. Why didn't matter as much as making sure it never happened again. "To piss me off. To pay me back for rejecting her in New York and again when she came by the studio yesterday. All those things."

Blue-violet eyes falling away, Jazz said, "She came by the studio?"

"You know she did." This time I did reach out, touching my fingers to her chin. Nudging until she lifted her gaze to mine, I said, "She came by, wearing a fur coat, naked under it, and tried to give me a lap dance. I turned her down."

Jazz closed her hand around my wrist. "Why didn't you tell me?"

"I don't know." Twisting out of her hold, I caught her hand and brought it to my mouth, pressing a kiss to the back. "I don't know the rules here, Jazz. I don't do relationships, and I don't know what I'm doing. I guess I figured it would hurt you, and I didn't want to do that."

Her mouth twisted in a scowl.

"If I'd known a woman, I thought was a friend would pull the shit she pulled last night, I *would* have told you. I'm sorry, Jazz."

Her gaze came back to mine. "You said you loved me. This was supposed to be a short-term thing."

"Yeah...well." With a half-hearted shrug, I said, "I already mentioned I don't do relationships, and all the rules are unknown to me. It's not like I planned on falling for you...I just...did."

"I didn't plan on falling for you, either."

Relief crashed into me. "Does that mean you'll give this a chance?"

A slow, nervous smile spread across her lips, and I leaned in, desperate to kiss her. But she stopped me.

"Wait." Licking her lips, she pressed against my shoulders. "There's something you should know before this goes any further. You might change your mind."

"Nothing can change how I feel about you," I told her. "*Nothing.*"

"Don't say that until you hear what I have to say." She bit her lip, then, with a hard exhalation, she said, "I'm pregnant."

The words just sort of rolled over me.

Jazz gave me a nervous look. "Did you hear me?"

"Yeah. I think...are you sure?"

"Unless several tests are wrong, then...yeah. I'm pregnant." She tugged her hand free from mine and put it in her lap, rubbing both palms up and down her thighs in a nervous gesture. "And I don't know who the dad is. You have to understand that. It could be you or—"

I caught her hand again, then her chin, guiding her face to mine.

"One question. Do you want the baby?"

Jazz blinked, and in a moment, her eyes filled with tears. "I'm not sure, but...I think so. I mean, I hope *you* are the dad, but even if Roger's the father..." The words faded away, and finally, she whispered, "Is that terrible? I don't even know how to feel about this. He raped me. If I ever see him again, I'll tear his face off. But...this may be my only chance to have a baby."

"It's not terrible."

Her gaze came back to mine. "But if he's the dad—"

"Don't do that to yourself, Jazz," I said, already seeing the fear and worry in her eyes. "Sperm doesn't make a guy a father. I don't know *my* father—I know his name, but *him*? No. There's more to being a parent than the genetic material. And that prick won't *ever* come near you again. If he tries, I'll rip his balls out through his nose."

Her eyes widened at that, and then a half-smile curved her lips. "Graphic, baby."

"I've got a vivid imagination." Seeing her eyes lighten eased some of the weight in my gut. I brushed her hair back. "In the end, Jazz, whatever you decide about the pregnancy, I'll back you all the way. And if you want to have the baby...and if you'll let me, *I'll* be the baby's dad. Me. Nobody else."

"You *want* that?" she whispered.

"More than anything." Pressing my brow to hers, I said, "Will you just give me half a chance to show you?"

She laid a hand on my cheek. "Baby, I think you already have."

Then she pressed her mouth to mine.

I tugged her closer, groaning as her lips parted, relief and need and love crushing me.

"Excuse me..."

I heard the words. So did Jazz.

But it wasn't until somebody forcefully cleared their throat that we parted.

The airline attendant, eyes amused but mouth stern glanced at me. "Sir, is that your seat?"

"I...ah..."

"I told him he could sit there as long as the lady was okay with it."

I glanced back and saw the guy I'd talked into swapping seats with me.

He grinned. "Guess you worked it out."

"Yeah." I shifted my focus to the airline attendant and tried a charming smile. "I'm sorry...we had a fight, and I wasn't going to let her get away without begging her to take me back."

"Hmmm." She cocked a brow and glanced at Jazz. "I guess he begs well?"

Jazz, her cheeks pink, replied, "Better than anybody I've ever met."

EPILOGUE

JAZZ
One year later

"Are you going to stop flirting with the new guy in your life and pay attention to me?"

Laughing, I put down my phone and grinned at the man sitting across the table from me. "Don't be jealous, Trent. I can't help that he's just so adorable."

Trent smirked. "He gets it from me."

"Yes, so you've said."

It was the truth, though. Early in my pregnancy, my OB had confirmed that Trent was the likely father since I was several weeks along by the time, she had me in for an initial evaluation.

Of course, no confirmation was needed once Sebastian had been born. Our baby looked like a mini version of Trent, from the eyes to the shape of his mouth.

The server came by and put a dessert down between us, offering a smile before retreating.

This was our first actual date since the baby had been born just under four months ago. Cam was babysitting, with Danny and their little girl 'helping,' which was both adorable and terrifying. Having my best friend and babysitter close by was one of the benefits of living in New York City instead of Los Angeles. Trent had said it was much easier for him to work remotely than me, so we moved back into a new apartment close to Central Park with room enough for us all, including a Steinway piano.

I reached for the dessert fork, only to see Trent had already beaten me to it.

"You're a brave man," I said. "Coming between a woman and her dessert."

He smiled and held out a hand.

But there was no fork in it.

There was a red box.

"What's..."

The rest of the question froze as he slipped from the chair to kneel next to me. Eyes on mine, he opened the box. "Jazz..."

"Oh, man," I whispered, looking around with a mix of terror and anticipation. He was *not* doing this here... "What are you *doing*?"

"I asked Cam if you'd kill me if I did this publicly. She said there was a fifty/fifty chance." He smiled. "I decided to risk it."

"Did you, now?" My heart was racing so hard, I could barely breathe, but I couldn't resist that sexy smile or the eyes that held me captive.

"I did. And I'm willing to bribe you with dessert."

I burst into laughter and slid out of my seat to kneel in front of him, right in front of the audience we'd picked up, the other diners not even pretending they weren't watching. Wrapping my arms around his neck, I kissed him, then said, "You haven't asked me yet."

"I'm working up to it," he murmured, pressing his brow to mine. "I love you. I want to spend the rest of my life with you, with our baby. If we're lucky, maybe we can even have another."

He kissed me then, soft and slow. "Say you'll marry me."

"I'll marry you, Trent."

After another kiss, he pulled back from me. To the sound of applause, he slipped the ring onto my left hand, and smiled down at it.

"Another baby, huh?" I asked as he looked back at me. "Sebastian isn't even walking yet."

"Well, it's not like they pop out overnight."

He rose and offered a hand, helping me to my feet. "Besides, we should practice. Make sure we still remember how to do it...baby-making and all."

"Oh, like we forgot." Touching his cheek, I said softly, "I might not be able to have another one. Sebastian was a little bit of a miracle."

"Both of you are." He guided me back to the seat, bent to kiss my shoulder, left bare by the halter dress I wore, then straightened and returned to his seat. "And if our family is only the three of us, I'm still the luckiest guy on earth." He winked. "But I still enjoy practicing. I'm a perfectionist, you know. Open up."

I let him feed me a bite of the chocolate and strawberry cheesecake, groaning in pleasure at the taste.

Once it was down to the last bite, I took the fork from

him, licked the tines, smiling at him as I laid the utensil down.

"I know we talked about trying to head to a club tonight, but I find I'm more interested in...practicing," I said, smiling at him. "You are, after all, a perfectionist, and there's no time like the present to get started."

Then I looked down at my hand and studied my new ring's sparkling shine. "Besides...I want to see how I'll look wearing this."

"With what?"

I winked at him. "Nothing."

He ushered me out without another word, tossing bills onto the table.

We left to a round of applause and good-natured whistles that followed us all the way to the rooftop restaurant's elevator.

After the doors closed behind us, Trent hauled me against him and covered my mouth with his.

"I love you."

I pressed close and whispered the same back.

I loved him so much...and I was never letting him go.

THE END

Printed in Great Britain
by Amazon